TIGER
GIRL

BRUIN ASYLUM NO. 8

TIGER
GIRL

GORDON
CASSERLY

Bruin Books

TIGER GIRL by Gordon Casserly

James Henry Gordon Casserly (1869-1947)

First published in 1934 by Philip Allan & Co. LTD.

Edited by Jonathan Eeds
Cover design by Michelle Policicchio

Original cover art provided by the Viet Hung Gallery, 90 Nguyen Hue Street, Ho Chi Minh City, VN.

Special thanks to Douglas A. Anderson, who played a critical advisory role in the final stages of this publication. Douglas is the Publisher for Nodens Books, www.nodensbooks.com, and contributes extensively to a number of literary publications, websites and blogs

Additional thanks to Mark Terry of Facsimile Dust Jackets LLC for supplying the first edition dust jacket image of TIGER GIRL that graces the back cover. Mark's website can be found at www.facsimiledustjackets.com

This book was crafted in the USA but is printed globally

Send inquires to bruinbooks@comcast.net

Visit Bruin Books at www.bruinbookstore.com

Printed in the USA
ISBN 978-0-9987065-2-8
Published January, 2018
Bruin Books, LLC
Eugene, Oregon, USA

THIS BOOK

IN REMEMBRANCE

OF THE

GHOSTS, SPECTRES AND DEMONS

WHO HAUNTED

THE THOUSAND YEAR OLD

FORTRESS OF ASIRGARH

IN THE CENTRAL PROVCES OF INDIA

AND, WHEN I COMMANDED IT,

DISMAYED MY SEPOYS,

TERRIFIED MY SERVANTS

AND ONCE,

TO THE BEWILDERMENT OF

THE GUARD OF THE GREAT GATE,

IMPERSONATED ME.

Contents

Gordon Casserly

Notes on the Author

Lieutenant Colonel James Henry Gordon Casserly was born in Dublin on July 25th, 1869. While growing up, his family managed a pub in the heart of the city called "Casserly Tavern". He passed his final exams at Trinity College on the 15th of November 1889. Following college, he was commissioned as a Second Lieutenant into the 4th Battalion, Royal Dublin Fusiliers. On the 10th of October 1891, he was commissioned into the Northamptonshire Regiment as a Second Lieutenant for regular service. Soon after that transfer he travelled to India with his unit. Two years later he was transferred to the Indian Army on the 5th June 1893 as a full Lieutenant. Lt. Casserly was then appointed to the 20th Regiment of Bombay Infantry on the 27th February 1897. . .

. . . The point of dryly going through Casserly's military postings was demonstrate that he was the real deal, and not some armchair adventure writer who dreamt up his plots over a sniffer of brandy. Casserly's formative years as a military officer in India had a life-long influence on his literary output. His stories have the authenticity of someone who lived them. The reader gets the sense that the writer personally enjoyed the pleasures and endured the pains of that mystical and beguiling country.

Casserly came into his own as an officer at a time when Great Britain was the most powerful nation in the world and controlled vast portions of the globe. Even so, there is rarely a hint of snobbery or racism in his writings—something that is readily evident in other books of that era, especially in those that employ exotic foreign locales for their narratives. He was certainly a man's man. He rode elephants and hunted man-eating tigers, and yet his stories remain refreshingly curious and sensitive, written with good humor and rich detail. He was a lively storyteller who tales read as fresh today as when they first saw print.

During his posting in India he spent two years as the Commandant of an outpost near Himalayas called Buxa Duar, which guards the pass into India from Bhutan. Based on his experience there he wrote one of his best-known books, *Life in an Indian Outpost*. The experience fired his imagination, for many of his adventure novels and strange stories emanate from that time. *The Elephant God*, *The Monkey God*, and *The Tiger Girl* were all inspired by his military service in the Indian jungles. The first lodge he built in Buxa Duar was trampled by a rogue elephant. He witnessed the animal's god-like power first-hand, but he was made of stout stuff and did not hesitate to build a second stronger lodge.

His earliest writing immediately caught the attention of the critics. The Belfast News printed a review of his first book, *Life in an Indian Outpost,* on 13th April 1914:

"Mr. Werner Laurie is just publishing "Life in an Indian Outpost" by Major Casserly. This is a thrilling account of the life of an Indian officer in command of a native garrison in a small post on the frontier. The outpost is called Buxa Duar, and is on the face of the Himalayas, guarding one of the Gates of India. The book gives a wonderfully vivid idea of the peculiarity and loneliness and risks of such a life. Major Casserly tells his story in a manly, straightforward, and direct way, and the book will appeal to all lovers of sport and daring."

After his assignment in India he was transferred to Hong Kong, where he witnessed the Boxer Rebellion in 1900. It was last he would see of any real military action. Major Casserly had to leave active service in 1916 due to age and health, but he remained in the Army reserves, where he was eventually promoted to the rank Lieutenant Colonel on 14th November 1919 while on the retired list. He also became an Honorary Commander of the United Arts Rifles, was a British Consul to St. Moritz, and was a life member of the Société de Géographie d'Alger. Once his public service had wound down, Casserly turned his full attention to writing. By the time he passed on April 7th, 1947, he had written eight novels, four travels books, half a dozen plays, two books on nature related to his travels, plus a number of military manuals.

Any reader picking up a Casserly book for the first time is in for an enjoyable treat. Why his enthralling books have fallen to the wayside is a complete mystery. He deserves to be read more. Reading one of his books is like having a friendly conversation with an old friend on his verandah looking out upon a garden filled with the scent of orchid and gardenia. And don't forget the sniffer on brandy.

Note to the reader: In the course of telling his story, Casserly makes reference to an old book called Occult Science in India and Among the Ancients *by Louis Jacolliot. A rather intriguing excerpt from that book is printed here in a special appendix. There is really some fascinating stuff there and it can be explored at anytime while reading*

Tiger Girl.

TIGER
GIRL

TIGER GIRL

CHAPTER I

THE STRIPED DEATH

GAY laughter and the high-pitched chatter of young voices, as along the white road linking scattered tea-gardens in the Terai Forest, the great Indian jungle at the foot of the Himalayan Mountains, came a group of Hindu girls in bright-hued garments. Glass bangles tinkled on the shapely brown arms when hands were raised to steady the bundles poised on their heads. Silver anklets gleamed above the bare feet. In their sleek, oiled black hair flowers were thrust with artistic taste. The curves of their bosoms and hips and the graceful carriage of the slim bodies would have delighted a sculptor.

Their musical voices floated back to Alan Stuart where, a few hundred yards behind them, he stopped his pony and took out a cigarette case. He glanced for a moment at the moving group, then bent down to strike a match, while the laughing girls went on between the green walls of dense undergrowth below the trees on either side of the road, all unconscious of the Striped Death lurking in the dark shadows beside their path. And a fiercer fire burned in the yellow eyes of the hidden tiger

1

watching their coming. The muscles rippled under his gaudy skin as he drew up his powerful limbs for the fatal spring.

With a light laugh the leading girl turned to address a remark to the one behind her. But the words were never uttered. A rustle in the undergrowth, an agonized shriek as a huge body leapt out of hiding, and with a fierce rush sprang at the unhappy woman, rose on its hindlegs for an instant and, with the sharp claws protruding from the great paws, half-struck, half-dragged her to the ground. The other girls screamed and fled, some forward, some back. And the tiger, with uplifted head and open mouth in which the white fangs showed, stood glaring irresolutely after them; while under him lay the crumpled body of his victim, the blood slowly spreading in the white dust.

At the shriek Stuart raised his head. The scene flashed on him—the fleeing, screaming girls, the yellow and black beast standing over the prostrate woman. Without a second's hesitation he struck his spurs into his pony, and with fierce shouts raced unarmed straight at the tiger.

The savage brute stood undecided. Was this a man, this strange creature with waving arms and menacing cries approaching so swiftly? Never before had a human being defied him. His coward's heart failed him. With a snarl he seized his still-breathing victim in his jaws, lifted her slight body without an effort and dashed into the jungle, the girl's relaxed limbs trailing on the ground and striking the stems of the trees, the thorns and sharp sticks of the bushes rending her frail garments to shreds.

And the undergrowth closed behind them and hid them from sight, as the rider pulled up over the fatal spot. The pony saw and smelt the pool of blood at its feet and shied violently across the road. The rider soothed it with ready hand, staring helplessly at the curtain of dense foliage that had dropped behind the murderer and his victim. He had hoped by his desperate charge to scare the tiger from his prey. But he had failed; and he could do nothing more now.

As he sat on his pony, which backed tremblingly still further away from the blood in the dust, all that was left to mark the tragedy save the scraps of clothing fluttering on the thorns, several of the girls whom he had passed in—his mad gallop turned and ran to him, imploring his protection in soft Bengali. The others heard and came back; and soon he was surrounded by hysterical women, weeping, clutching at him and his pony and crying out to him to save them. He could not rid himself of their clinging hands; although, knowing that there was little danger to them now, he wanted to ride hard to his destination in order to get a rifle and try to follow up the tiger on foot, mad as he knew the scheme to be. But he was forced to move on down the road at a slow pace in the midst of the terrified girls.

Two miles further on a broad, deeply-rutted track cut through the forest branched off to the right. Down this he turned; for it led to the tea-garden that was the women's goal as well as his. Presently the walls of trees and undergrowth on either hand fell back; and he entered a broad clearing in which orderly lines of trim green tea-bushes replaced the forest giants. To one side lay a village of palm-thatched huts, which sheltered the hundreds of coolies doing the work of the plantation. Ahead rose a group of ugly buildings with galvanized iron roofs dominated by a tall, stovepipe chimney—the engine-house, withering and drying-sheds and stores that made up the factory.

Not far from it was a red-tiled, white-washed bungalow raised on a high plinth, single-storied, with deep verandahs on three sides and green-shuttered windows. Behind were the servants' huts; and close by it stood almost the only tree left on the whole plantation, a giant banyan with spreading branches and broad leaves that cast a perfect shade beneath them. Under it an elephant stood with shackled legs, flapping its great ears, beating its sides with a leafy branch to drive off the flies, and incessantly shifting its weight from foot to foot.

As soon as the women saw the village they broke away and ran wailing loudly towards the huts, while spots of brilliant colour in the rows of tea-bushes rose up and revealed themselves as bright-hued garments of men and women bending to tend the plants, who all hurried towards the lamenting girls.

The white man, set free at last, urged his pony to a gallop and raced over the soft road to the bungalow. As he neared it he looked with surprise at the elephant, the sight of which made his nervous pony shy violently as they passed it. A man who had been standing by the great tethered beast turned as the rider approached and went towards him. He was a tall, fair-skinned Pathan, a man of the fierce tribes that dwell on the mountains beyond the North-West Frontier of India, with the bold eyes and hawk-like features of his race, dressed in baggy trousers, a gaily embroidered waistcoat over a white shirt, with yards of thin, gold-threaded cloth wound round and round the conical cap on his head and hanging down his back.

The rider waited neither for him nor the darker-skinned *syce* or groom who ran to meet him, but pulled his pony up short in front of the bungalow, swung himself out of the saddle and sprang up the steps of the verandah.

"Murray! Murray! Are you in?" he cried.

An elderly European appeared at the doorway of a room opening off the verandah.

"You're back late, Stuart," he cried. "I did not wait."

The horseman broke in excitedly:

"One of the coolie women has just been carried off by a maneater a couple of miles away on the main road," he cried. "I saw it happen—saw the brute strike her down and carry her off. It was infernal bad luck that I hadn't a rifle. I could have got him beautifully at two hundred yards' range as he stood over her—a perfect shot."

"What happened?" asked Murray interestedly, coming towards him.

"I rode at the beast yelling, hoping to scare him off; but he picked up the wretched woman and bolted with her into the jungle. I've come back for my rifle and my orderly, Khitab Gul, and am going back to see if I can follow up the tiger."

"It would be foolish to try that on foot. When did it

happen?" asked the older man.

"Half an hour ago at least. The other coolie women hung on to me for protection and prevented me from galloping back hard."

"Not much use going after him now, I'm afraid," said Murray doubtfully. "But Barter, the Forest Officer, is here. Came on his elephant an hour ago, awfully sick and shaking with fever; so I've dosed him with quinine and put him to bed in the spare room. Come and ask him what he thinks about it."

He walked to the door from which he had come. Lifting the *chik*—the green bamboo-strip blind that hung over it—he led the way inside. On an iron cot lay a man, his haggard face flushed, his eyes unnaturally bright with the fire of fever, at times shivering so violently that the bed shook.

"I say, Barter, this is Stuart, the Royal Engineer officer I told you about, who has come here to look for a quarry in the hills to provide stones for the new bridge over the Ganges," said Murray. "He's just seen a woman killed by a tiger on the road not far away."

The Forest Officer extended a shaking hand. Stuart took it in his own and, after expressing his sympathy for the other's illness, repeated his story.

"Another maneater?" exclaimed the sick man wearily. "This district's full of the cursed brutes. No wonder they call it Baghpota."

"What does that mean?" asked the Sapper, as Royal Engineer officers are nicknamed.

"Well, call it 'Tiger Town'! It has always been notorious for them."

"Do you think it's any use Stuart going back to look for the beast?" asked Murray.

"Not much. The woman's dead and half-eaten by now. Goodness knows how far the brute's dragged her. There's no water about here—nearer than the river, I mean?"

"Yes, there is," replied Stuart. "Not half a mile from where the kill took place there's a little pool in the jungle. I stumbled on it by accident one day out shooting."

The sick man became more animated, and raised himself with difficulty on his elbow.

"Ah, that makes a difference," he cried. "You might get him after all. Have you ever shot tiger?"

"No, I've never had the luck to come across them when I'd a rifle," answered Stuart almost mournfully. "That's what makes this all the more annoying."

"Well, I suppose you know that after a tiger has killed and eaten he wants a drink," said the Forest Officer. "If he can he drags his victim near water; and when he has gorged himself and slaked his thirst he lies up and sleeps. It's very probably on account of the proximity of the pool that the maneater took up his position at that part of the road. He's to be found by that water, I'll bet."

He sank back exhausted and thought for a minute. Then he continued:

"Now, how to get him. Maneaters are always exceedingly crafty and can distinguish between a helpless native and an armed man looking for them. They'll do the most daring things—enter a village at night and carry off a person sleeping outside his house, or sometimes even burst into a hut. But when a white man goes after them they seem to know by instinct and clear off out of the district for a time. I say, Murray, do you mind calling my *mahout*?"

When the elephant-driver, in obedience to the planter's summons, had left his shoes on the verandah and entered the room salaaming, Barter told him in Hindustani Stuart's Story. The *mahout* considered for a while, and then said:

"If the *Huzoor* (the Presence) would send me and my animal with the young sahib and we conceal ourselves under blankets, as do men hunting the wild elephant, we may approach the *shaitan* (devil) unperceived."

"*Bahut atcha!* (Very good!), Shaikh Ebrahim," exclaimed Barter. Then in English he continued to Stuart, "That's the idea. If you cover yourselves up he may take the elephant to be a wild one, and as, having fed, he'll be sluggish and disinclined to move, he may let you get right up to him."

He beat the coverlet impatiently with his fist.

"Oh, I wish I were fit enough to go with you. I hate the brutes," he said.

"It'll be all right," said the Sapper, soothingly. "Murray doesn't shoot; but I'll give my orderly my other gun and take him along. He's a useful shot."

"Is that the fine-looking Pathan I saw when I came in?" asked the sick man. "He'll have to change his gaudy clothes."

Stuart laughed. "I'll see to that," he said. "In his glad

rags he'd scare a tiger a mile off."

Ten minutes later the Royal Engineer subaltern stood on the verandah dressed in his shooting-kit, watching the *mahout* and his coolie lifting on to the elephant's back its 'pad', or thick, straw-filled mattress, and fastening it on by a surcingle rope passing around it and the animal's body. Only for shooting in open grass jungle is the *howdah*, the wooden, cage-like structure in which the sportsmen sit or stand, bound on top of the pad. In dense forest it would be at once torn off.

Alan Stuart was a man of about twenty-eight, of more than medium height, well but lightly built. His hair and eyes were dark, his features good, and his face, oval and rather long, had in repose a somewhat grave, even sad, expression. With a pointed beard and long hair, and dressed as his distant ancestor in Vandyke's famous picture, he might well have passed for a reincarnation of that most luckless of all Stuarts, Charles I. A true Highlander, the Sapper was of a serious and slightly melancholy disposition, visionary and inclined to be superstitious despite his better sense, quick to resent an insult, proud, impatient of injustice, passionately loyal, a good friend and a bitter enemy.

He was smiling slightly as he watched his orderly, now in sober khaki, directing the elephant-attendants in their work with all the arrogant conceit of the Pathan, who believes that he knows everything worth knowing, despises all coloured races, and regards himself as the white man's equal. Khitab Gul had absolutely no acquaintance with elephants. But that did not prevent him from instructing the *mahout* in what the old man had been doing all his life. Shaikh Ebrahim paid no attention to him; and presently Stuart called him:

"Bring the two guns out of my room, Khitab Gul. And the cartridges," he said in Hindustani, which was as a foreign language to the Pushtu-speaking Pathan as it was to the Highlander. But it is the *lingua franca* of India and used throughout the Indian Army, although most regiments employ also the tongue of the particular race furnishing the men in its ranks. Stuart, who was an officer of a Sapper and Miner Battalion, had brought this orderly with him from it when detailed for the special duty on which he was engaged.

Khitab Gul came out of the bungalow with a double-barrelled .470 high velocity cordite rifle and a Colonial gun, which would fire either ball or shot. The latter weapon he kept, and handed the former with its cartridges to his officer. Under his arm he had a pair of folded-up grey blankets.

The elephant was now kneeling; and Stuart and the Pathan climbed on to the pad. The *mahout* bestrode the neck and, tapping the thick skull with the *ankus*, the iron goad in his hand, cried:

"*Uth!*" (Rise up!)

Stuart had taken the precaution of grasping the edge of the pad and the surcingle rope as well, so that he was ready when the animal upheaved its huge body in sudden jerks. But the self-confident Pathan, who had disdained to listen to the *mahout's* advice, was nearly thrown off and only saved himself by clutching violently at his officer, whom he nearly dragged off as well.

The elephant coolie, watching from the ground, said laughingly:

"*Abré, Pathan-ji*, you have no animal like that in your country."

Khitab Gul was not to be beaten. Although no elephant had ever been seen in the wild mountains beyond the North-West Frontier of India where his home was, he replied contemptuously:

"My father has thirty of these clumsy beasts in his stalls to bring in the sticks to light his fire."

The *mahout* grinned amusedly, and Stuart smiled at the outrageous lie. And Khitab Gul himself laughed loudly, for the Pathan has a keen sense of humour, as the elephant bore them with plunging stride through the tea-garden towards the fatal jungle road. As they passed near the village the coolies swarmed out; and men and women rushed to throw themselves on the ground beside the road, crying, wailing, pouring dust on their heads in the extravagance of Oriental grief, and imploring them to avenge their murdered sister and remove the awful menace of the maneater. The husband and family of the dead girl were loudest in their lamentations and appeals to them to slay her slayer and give her spirit rest. And with their shrill cries ringing in his ears Stuart passed on to his task of vengeance.

When they drew near the spot where the tragedy had occurred the *mahout* halted his elephant and, whispering to his companions to follow his example, crouched down and covered himself with his blanket, in which he had cut out holes for his eyes. Loading their weapons Stuart and the Pathan imitated him and lay flat on the pad. Then Shaikh Ebrahim turned off into the jungle, his animal bursting her way through the dense undergrowth, her riders having great difficulty in preventing their blanket-coverings being torn off them.

Further in from the road the ground vegetation, deprived of sunlight and air, was much thinner. The great trees, teak, *simal* and *sal*, monsters of astounding girth, rose up branchless for some distance from the ground, spreading out their leafy tops in thick foliage that shut out the sky and let the light filter through in green gloom. Their thick limbs were matted with the glossy leaves of orchids from which drooped long trails of lovely mauve and white blooms. Hanging from the highest boughs, twisting around the stems and biting deep into the bark, swinging between the giant trunks, writhing, interlaced, blending in inextricable disorder, were creepers in tangled confusion, some stouter than a battleship's hawsers, wound round each other, interwoven and forming an almost impassable network. Shaikh Ebrahim, peering through his peepholes, deftly guided his animal so as to avoid these obstacles when possible; and elsewhere the sagacious elephant tore away the obstructing natural cordage with her trunk. The undergrowth of high bushes was not continuous; and here and there under the overhead canopy of foliage were glades filled with bracken.

The avengers moved parallel to the road. Suddenly the elephant stopped short; and under the blanket

Ebrahim's hand groped to touch Stuart significantly. The Sapper pushed the covering a little away from him so that he could see the ground below. On it were unmistakable evidences of the passage of the tiger and his prey. The track of a dragged body, bamboo-grass stems pressed down, fern-fronds splashed with blood, a scrap of coloured cotton fluttering on a thorny bush—there was no doubt of it. And, when the elephant moved along the dread trail, in one patch of sandy soil clear and distinct were the pugs—footprints—of a tiger. Stuart felt his leg gripped by a strong hand, and Khitab Gul whispered loudly and excitedly:

"*Wuh hai, sahib! Yeh bagh hai!*" (That is he, sir. That is the tiger!)

And the officer had much difficulty in silencing him.

Now the elephant moved on with surprisingly little noise. Occasionally a dry twig cracked under her heavy foot; but Ebrahim restrained her from tearing down the creepers, and the intelligent animal, seeming to understand the necessity for silence, pushed the great hanging network out of her way quietly, or moved to one side to avoid it. The trail did not fail them. Here and there the signs of it were wanting; but invariably a little further on the traces of the dragged body and smears of blood or the footprint of the murderer reappeared. In one spot it was clear that the tiger had laid his victim down and stretched himself beside it to rest.

Presently the undergrowth grew noticeably thicker and ranker, indicating to the old *mahout's* trained eye the nearness of water; and again he reached back and touched Stuart warningly. His heart beating violently with the fierce excitement of the chase, the soldier brought his rifle readier to hand and crouched lower Still along the pad.

As the elephant pushed its way through a dense thicket of tall bushes a low growl rumbled through the forest. It was the sleepy tiger, resenting the disturbance and the intrusion on his privacy.

CHAPTER II

THE AVENGER

EBRAHIM promptly guided his animal a little to one side of the spot whence the sound seemed to proceed, and slowed it down almost to a stop; and, as if entering into the spirit of the game, it began to feed carelessly, breaking off branches, tearing down trailing creepers and cramming them into its mouth, while it barely forged ahead in an apparently purposeless way. Again the growling was heard; and Stuart, peering eagerly through the eye-holes of his covering, tried in vain to discern the quarry. Vivid as is a tiger's colouring, bizarre as seem its markings, the black bars across the bright yellow imitate and blend marvelously with the shadows of thick jungle or the blinding glare and the shade in the brilliant sunlight in the open. And, strain his eyes as he might, near at hand as the growling seemed, Stuart could not see the animal from which it came.

But a touch of Ebrahim's foot under its ear made the elephant blunder with apparent carelessness in the direction of the sound; and with a louder grumble of annoyance the tiger rose into view from under a bush not ten yards away and walked sulkily into thicker undergrowth a few feet farther on. In it his head and shoulders disappeared before Stuart could disentangle himself and his rifle from under the blanket; but he took a snapshot at the striped body further back and fired.

A loud roar of pain told that the bullet had got home. The tiger's hindquarters were dragged into the dense vegetation which was agitated by a wild commotion, while grunts, groans, and the harsh breathing of a stricken animal showed that the brute was badly hit. Ebrahim forced his elephant through the undergrowth to get past the tangled vegetation in which the tiger had taken refuge, while his two companions sat up with rifles ready. Moving around the dense thicket they came into a clearer space where a cup-like hollow showed, filled with water. It was the forest pool.

Suddenly out of the bushes the tiger came, dragging himself painfully forward on his forelegs. The bullet had paralyzed his hindquarters; and with a badly-wounded animal's instinct he was making for the water near at hand. Clear of the undergrowth he saw his enemies; and, helpless but defiant, he sat down and snarled savagely at them.

The hideous, barred mask of the fierce face, ears flattened against the skull, whiskers bristling, the lips drawn back to show the great fangs in the slavering red mouth, was a terrifying sight, set as it was in the scowl that mesmerizes victims and frightens foes. But Stuart's arms were rigid as he pressed the rifle-butt to his shoulder and fired coolly. Shot through the brain the tiger fell over on its side, the powerful limbs relaxed, the tail twitched feebly, the beautiful body quivered, and then all was still. Khitab Gul, covering the stricken beast with his gun, had no need to fire. The dead woman was avenged. Her murderer had paid the penalty of his crimes.

"*Shabash! O shabash, sahib!*" (Well done, sir!) cried Khitab Gul excitedly, his face glowing.

Stuart, more composed, but with dark eyes shining with pleasure at his good luck, turned round on the pad and shook hands heartily with his orderly, who was almost even more delighted than he at his success. The *mahout* smilingly joined in the felicitations, knowing that copious reward in shining rupees would be his for his share in compassing the tiger's death.

That it was the maneater admitted of no doubt. For in the hollow by the pool lay the half-eaten corpse of the wretched girl. The clothes had been shredded off, the thighs and part of the body had been devoured. It was a ghastly sight; and Stuart and the Pathan averted their eyes. But Ebrahim, neglecting her slayer, brought his elephant close to the corpse and stared down at it intently. Finally he shook his head and murmured half-aloud in Urdu:

"This is not the Devil-Tiger's work."

Stuart caught the words, but was too anxious to inspect his prize to pay attention to them at the moment.

"Let me get down, Shaikh Ebrahim," he said.

"*Nahin*, sahib. Patience," said the old man. "Let us be certain that he is truly dead. Tigers have a trick of shamming. Peyton Sahib loft his life through it at Alipur Duar."

He broke off a withered bough and flung it at the prostrate beast. It struck the bleeding skull but elicited no movement. Khitab Gul followed it up with a cartridge; and Ebrahim threw the heavy iron *ankus*—the goad shaped like a boathook head. But the animal never stirred. Then the elephant cautiously approached the striped body and, having smelled it, touched it with her forefoot. But the murderer's career was ended. Never again would he flash out of the shadow on luckless travelers and bear them off to a terrible doom.

Stuart and Khitab Gul now dismounted and examined with intense interest their first dead tiger, marveling at its size and strength, at the powerful limbs bowed out with masses of muscle. The *mahout*, shackling his elephant's forelegs and leaving it to graze in the undergrowth, set off on foot to the tea-garden to bring back help to 'pad' the maneater and inform the dead woman's relatives and caste-fellows of the finding of her corpse.

It was an hour or two before he returned; but to Stuart, absorbed in admiring his bag, the time did not seem long. The Pathan, when he had wearied of looking at the stricken tiger, went to gaze again at the body of its victim, but turned away from the contemplation of it with a shudder.

"A pity, sahib, that this devil was not content to fill his belly with the flesh of men or of these monkeys that pass for men in this country," he said, and spat contemptuously on the ground. "The women are the only things in Bengal of any worth. Of a truth when young they are soft and alluring. If ever the tribesmen of my land swoop down upon this country, may I be there to bring back a score of these Hindu girls to fill my zenana!"

Stuart laughed.

"How many wives have you already, Khitab Gul?"

"Four now, sahib. But one is childless and with a venomous tongue. I shall divorce her when next I go on leave. I want only women who can bear sons to fight for me in the tribe when I grow old."

Shaikh Ebrahim brought back fifteen coolies with him, which Stuart thought a needless number to lift the dead beast on to the elephant's pad. But a well-grown tiger weighs three hundred and fifty pounds; and to raise a limp body of that weight, which sags like a feather bed, takes many hands, as the Sapper found. But the task was achieved at last; and he and Khitab Gul started off for the garden ahead of the elephant.

On their way they were met by the wailing mourners; and the dead women's relatives flung themselves in the duft of the road before Stuart, clasped his legs and kissed his feet in gratitude. When he had disengaged himself with some difficulty they raised again their wild cries of lamentation, and plunged into the jungle to seek the poor remains and carry them back to the burning-*ghaut*.

In the tea-garden the coolies, men, women and children left their work to rush and acclaim the officer and his orderly, salaaming and thanking them for slaying the brute that would have proved a terrible menace to the neighborhood. Stuart escaped from them as quickly as he could; but Khitab Gul lingered behind and accepted their thanks and congratulations calmly, smiling with lordly condescension on the soft-eyed, nose-ringed Hindu wo-men as they timidly admired from a respectful distance this imposing being, who seemed to them a marvelous specimen of manhood compared with their own under-sized and effeminate men.

Murray hurried over to the bungalow from the factory to congratulate his fellow-countryman on his success; and together they entered the sick man's room, where Stuart told the story of the chase in full detail. Barter, in spite of his fever, listened with deep interest. The Sapper thanked him warmly for the loan of his elephant and *mahout*, without whom he could not have succeeded in killing the maneater.

The mention of Ebrahim's name brought back to the officer's mind the words that the old man had uttered over the woman's mangled corpse.

"*Shaitan Bagh* means 'devil tiger', doesn't it?" he asked. "Your *mahout* said, as he looked at the girl, '*Yeh shaitan bagh ha kam hahin hai*,' 'This is not the devil tiger's work.' What did he mean?"

"Well, a *shaitan* in this case is a devilish, malignant

sort of ghost rather than a devil, as we understand a devil. In these jungles there is supposed to be—you say the body was half-eaten?"

"Yes."

"Well, the natives round here have a legend of an evil spirit in the shape of a tiger that kills women and sucks their blood, but does not devour their flesh. I've only heard the tale by accident; for they dislike talking about it—they fear mention of it would bring them bad luck, perhaps in the shape of a visit from the ghost-tiger. I think the folk here are fuller of strange beliefs than elsewhere in India. Tibetan and Chinese superstitions drift down from the mountains to add to their own."

"What gave rise to this legend?" asked Stuart.

"I have been told, ever since I came to this district, of native women, always women, killed by a tiger and their bodies not being eaten, though left drained of blood. Of course such a thing might well happen if the beast was scared away from his kill. And no European saw the corpses, which were burned on the funeral pile by the relatives as soon as possible. The colour of the beast supposed to be the ghost-tiger was grey, not yellow. But any old animal's hide goes grey."

Murray shook his head.

"There's not much I'd disbelieve in this country, Barter," he said. "I'm not very superstitious; but in the years I've been out here I've known strange things happen—things I couldn't account for."

The Forest Officer wiped his face, on which a healing sweat was breaking out, and said:

"In the jungle one could credit anything. Perhaps the loneliness gets on your nerves when night after night you sit in an isolated bungalow in the heart of it and listen to uncanny things moving about outside, and weird noises that no animal ought to make. In the hills I've shot a strange beast like a white wolf—the natives denied its existence and tried all they could to prevent me from hunting it—that sobbed and muttered and, I could almost swear, talked like a man in pain after I had wounded it. Yes, in the wild forest you're ready to believe things that you'd laugh at in the smoking-room of your club in London."

Murray, sitting by the bed, nodded assent, and said:

"If one-half the tales they tell of the gypsy tribe that comes regularly to Morton's tea-garden be true, the wildest ghost-stories that even a Highland nurse could tell you, Stuart, would be tame in comparison."

The fever-stricken man shifted restlessly on his bed.

"Their ordinary crimes are quite enough without their practicing the Black Art, as people say they do," he observed wearily. "They are daring poachers. In the last two months my forest guards have found five elephants dead in pits dug, I'll swear, by them. Three were cows, but two were bulls. The tusks had been hacked out of their skulls. As you know, killing elephants in Government Forests is very strictly forbidden and punishable by law. But, though I'm sure it's these gypsies, we can seldom catch any or prove anything against them."

"Whenever they come into this district," said Murray, "there are always cases of highway robbery, and

women and children are found murdered for the silver
ornaments they are wearing. And the devils seem to bring
other evils in their train. It's a curious fact that, when
they are here on Morton's garden, many more people are
killed by maneaters than at other times. And the Ghost
Tiger walks oftener. The brutes apparently keep company
with the human beasts."

"Morton? That's the sour-faced, sallow chap at the
club, isn't it?" asked Stuart. "Why does he let those
gypsies come to his garden?"

Murray laughed grimly.

"Why? Because they're his own people," he replied.
"His grandfather was the first man to come to this district
when it was ceded to England by Bhutan after the war of
1864-5. He started a cinchona plantation. He had a
mistress from that gypsy tribe—she was the mother of
Morton's father, who in his turn kept up the family
tradition and connection by having one, too."

"What? Is this Morton the son of a gypsy?" asked
Stuart.

"I believe so. His father went to England and married there. He brought his unfortunate wife out to India,
but as the poor girl was always ailing the brute soon
wearied of her and kept a gypsy mistress openly in their
bungalow. She had a son, whom the father tried vainly to
pass off as the Englishwoman's child."

"Mrs. Morton had a tragic ending, hadn't she?"
asked the Forest Officer.

"Yes, she was killed by a maneater. The story goes
that it was Ghost Tiger, and that her body was found

uneaten, but with the blood drained through a wound in the throat and never a drop on the ground."

"Was that true?" said Stuart, deeply interested.

"I don't know. It was before my time," replied Murray.

"So Morton has a strong touch of the tar-brush," observed the Sapper. "I thought he looked like it. I've only seen him a few times at the club."

"He doesn't come there often. He's not very popular, though some fellows pretend to like him, but I think it's because they owe money to him."

"Yes, I've heard he's a bit of a Shylock," said the sick man. "He's pretty well off, isn't he?"

"Yes. His estate is very profitable. His father gave up cinchona for coffee-planting at the right time, and later went in for tea and did well. The present man has made a lot of money, and spends little."

"So he owns his estate?" said Stuart. "I thought all those tea-gardens belonged to companies in London."

"They do, except his and the one next his. That belongs to Webb, whose father was the earliest planter here after the Mortons. You know Webb. You were playing tennis at the club last week with his daughter."

"He's not doing as well as his neighbour, is he?" asked Barter.

"No. He always has bad luck. And he's a thriftless devil. Good-natured chap, certainly, but careless and weak. He has no go in him and lets his garden run to seed. I'm afraid he'll go under if we have another bad season. I'd be sorry, not so much for his sake as for his wife and daughter. Mrs. Webb is a sweet woman, and Margery's a thoroughly nice girl."

"I wish it were Morton who was in danger of being ruined," said Barter vindictively. "If he left the district we might keep those cursed gypsies out of it."

"No such luck. The Devil looks after his own; and Morton's his favourite child," growled the planter.

"His pals the gypsies are certainly Satan's children," said Barter. "I believe they're devil-worshippers; and the natives firmly believe in their powers of magic. My forest guards are often afraid to interfere with them, I'm sure."

Voices outside the house reached the three men in the bungalow; and Murray, going to the doorway, lifted the bamboo *chik* hanging over it and looked out.

"Here's the elephant with your tiger, Stuart," he said. "And just come and look at that confounded orderly of yours strutting up the road like a peacock, with half the women of the garden at his tail. By the way, I wanted to speak to you about him. He's a good chap, I know; but you'll have to keep him in order. There'll be trouble over him if you don't, for my male coolies are complaining of his attentions to their wives."

"Yes, he's a devil of a Lothario," said Stuart, laughing. "But I'll warn him."

He followed the planter on to the verandah. Up the road between the orderly rows of tea-bushes came a procession headed by Ebrahim and his elephant, on the pad of which was tied the tiger's carcass. Behind it swaggered Khitab Gul, who had gone to meet them. He was surrounded by a crowd of admiring women, their mankind from factory and plantation following at a respectful distance the tall Pathan, whom they feared and hated. For the moment, however, they were so overjoyed at the maneater's death that they swelled the chorus of praise acclaiming him as the tiger's slayer.

While the two Britishers on the verandah awaited the arrival of the elephant, Murray raised his hand and pointed upward.

"Look there!" he said.

From the great clearing of the tea garden where the forest trees no longer shut out the sky could be seen, the mountains rising in tumbled masses, climbing one above another to the clouds, the foothills beginning hardly two miles away from the bungalow. Along this giant rampart of India ran, six thousand feet above the sea, the invisible frontier-line of the little-known Buddhist land of Bhutan that borders Eastern Bengal and is almost the last country in Asia to preserve its mysteries from the profane gaze of the intruding white man. A few political or military officers, sent on diplomatic missions to its rulers by the Government of India, are the only Europeans who have ever entered it.

But Murray's pointing hand was not directed towards the mountains, but to the blue sky overhead. There high in air above them floated a minute speck that gradually grew larger and revealed itself as a great bird, planing down in wide circles, while from all points of the compass similar specks came into sight at immense heights and swept swiftly downwards.

"How quick those vultures are to spot a dead beast!"

exclaimed Murray.

Then, as the elephant was halted under the solitary banyan and the tiger's body lowered to the ground, while the natives gathered round it to abuse their fallen enemy, the air above was filled with scores of huge circling birds and the rushing sound of mighty wings. Sweeping nearer and nearer in wheeling flight, some more daring than the others almost touched the treetop as they flew past. At last one, then another and another, came to rest on the highest branches. More joined them. With angry squawks and shrill, petulant cries, quarrelling, hustling, pecking each other, these foul scavengers of India, loathsome to look upon with their bald, red, mangy heads and necks, impatiently awaited their share of the feast.

The coolies surrounding the tiger fell back to allow the sahibs to pass as Murray and Stuart descended the verandah steps, the former carrying a tape measure in his hand. Ebrahim and Khitab Gul stretched out the carcass on its side; and the planter ran the tape along from nose to tip of tail.

"Nine feet, six inches. A fine beast, Stuart," he said admiringly. "What a powerful brute he was! Just look at the immense muscular development of his forelegs."

"I'm surprised that his skin is in such excellent condition," replied the Sapper. "I always thought that maneaters were aged, mangy beasts, too old and feeble to hunt down deer and cows, and so driven to killing human beings as a last resort."

"That's not so, I believe. They are generally cattle-slayers that are used to the sight of man and so have lost their fear of him. Probably one day in attacking a herd they've been interfered with by the native in charge of it and killed him. Then, realizing what an easy prey man is, they go for him in preference ever after. But they've no objection to a cow if one comes in their way."

As the white men drew aside and the natives again closed round the carcass to revile it, one of the coolies who had accompanied Ebrahim arrived after the rest of the party and came salaaming towards the planter.

"Sahib," he said in Urdu, "when leaving the jungle I found the bones of a man killed and eaten by that *shaitan* there." He pointed towards the dead tiger. "And on the road I met two men from the village near the river. They were looking for their father, who had set out yesterday to this garden and had not returned. I showed them what I had found. Around in the jungle were strips of cloth which they recognized as part of their father's garments. So they carried away the bones to their village."

"By Jove, two kills in two days!" exclaimed Murray to his companions. "It's lucky you got the brute."

From the village the professional flayers had been summoned to skin the tiger; and, as they cut and stripped off the gaudy hide, the women streamed back to their huts and, returning with baskets, cloths or pots, sat down to wait like the vultures in the tree and with the same object. For it is a native belief that the flesh of a tiger will endow the man who eats it with the dead beast's vigor, courage and strength; and with this object a Hindu wife will eagerly procure a piece, cook it and give it to her husband.

When the skin was lifted from the carcass Stuart marveled at the masses of muscle and the thick layers of firm white fat that were revealed. The animal was indeed well fed. Shaikh Ebrahim carefully cut away and collected the fat for boiling down, for it gives an oil that natives believe to be a sovereign remedy for rheumatism. Then Khitab Gul borrowed his knife and, hacking the flesh off in lumps, distributed it with somewhat indelicate jests to the waiting wives, who smilingly thanked him and bore their prize away. The skin was carried into the sun and, stretched out and pegged to the ground hair downwards, carefully scraped clear of flesh and fat and covered thick with wood ashes. It was to be left for a couple of days to be dried, and thus temporarily cured and then would be sent to a professional taxidermist in Calcutta to be properly treated.

When the last human beings had left the neighbourhood of the tree the vultures flopped down heavily to the ground and, hopping awkwardly to the hacked carcass, fell upon it with talon and curved beak. And soon of the slayer of men nothing was left but a well-picked skeleton.

CHAPTER III

THE JUNGLE CLUB

THREE DAYS after the maneater's death Murray and Stuart pulled up their sweating ponies on the bank of a swift-flowing river of clear water running down from the mountains and cleaving the forest on its way to pass on through the level plains of Eastern Bengal to its junction with the sacred Ganges. Dismounting, they threw their reins to their syces, who had preceded them, and hailed a ferryman on the far bank. His boat was pulled up on the sand at a spot on the opposite side where the big trees were drawn back some distance from the water's edge and the low and tangled vegetation had been cleared away, leaving an open space. In this stood a roughly-built, single-storied wooden building with a high and wide verandah to which a flight of broad steps led from the ground. Nearby several ponies were picketed, a few Ford cars were parked, two or three dogcarts rested their shafts on the earth, and syces sat in groups in the shade of the building. Despite the heat of the sun—for it was noon—white-clad figures moved swiftly about a tennis-court in a vigorous game watched from the verandah by a dozen or more spectators, among whom were a couple of ladies. A strange sight to see in the heart of the jungle.

It was a tea-planters' club. These lonely pioneers are

scattered in twos or threes on widely separated estates strung out in a loose chain in the Terai Forest along the foot of the mountains. The only solace of their solitary lives is found in weekly gatherings in such an institution as this. In each district a rough wooden one- or two-roomed bungalow is built in a spot as equidistant as possible to most of the gardens as a meeting-place for the few European residents for ten or twenty miles round. Here on one day a week they come for a few hours to see others of their race, talk, eat and drink together, play tennis and sometimes polo, until the setting sun warns them to outride darkness back to their lonely homes and escape being benighted on the dangerous forest roads. Each one in turn undertakes to act as host, sending from his house miles away the necessary food, drink, crockery and cutlery by coolies or bullock-cart.

At Murray's hail a half-naked boatman squatting on the beach before the club rose up and pushed his flat-bottomed craft into the water; and, as the swift current caught and swung it round, he picked up a long bamboo and deftly poled the boat across to the two waiting sahibs. Stuart's syce placed a suitcase for his master in the boat, which the ferryman pushed off as soon as his passengers embarked.

Its progress across the stream was watched by two ladies seated on the club verandah on either side of an elderly, dark-complexioned man with greying head. Their strong likeness proclaimed them mother and daughter; and, although the elder's hair had not the golden lights that shone in the brown tresses of the younger, the dark blue eyes were the same, and the rounded cheeks almost as soft and rosy. Twenty years before the mother had been as pretty as her daughter was now; but her face lacked the strength and character that the latter's possessed.

As, leaving Murray speaking to the boatman, Stuart walked on ahead to the club-house, the girl waved to him and, rising, leant over the rail of the verandah.

"Congratulations on killing the maneater, Mr. Stuart!" she called out as he approached. "Well done!"

The elderly man beside whom she had been sitting looked up at her ill-humoredly.

"I didn't know that you ran after men, Margery," he said acidly.

"Yes, dear, you really should wait until he shows that he wants to speak to you," echoed her mother in a distressed tone. "Mr. Morton is right. You don't know Mr. Stuart very well, and he might think that you were running after him."

The girl turned and patted the older woman's cheek affectionately.

"You dear, simple, old-world mummy," she said, smiling. "Why shouldn't I speak to him? We're quite good friends already; and I know he'd like to talk to me."

"These Army men are ready to think that every girl is running after them," grumbled the elderly man.

"Nonsense, Mr. Morton," replied the girl with a careless laugh. "You are really as early Victorian as mamma, I believe, and imagine military officers to be terrible monsters ready to devour every innocent maiden they meet.

You needn't be afraid for me; and Mr. Stuart's quite harmless, I assure you."

And she walked along the verandah to meet him as he came up the steps.

Mrs. Webb looked after her helplessly.

"Margery is quite beyond me, Mr. Morton," she said. "I don't understand the girls of today. They're so different to what they were in my young days. We never thought of speaking to a man unless he addressed us first."

The sallow-faced planter scowled as he looked at the girl and the Sapper talking and laughing light-heartedly.

"It was a mistake her going to Oxford, I've always said," he replied irritably. "Those colleges ruin girls, make them independent and fast."

The mother turned almost indignantly on him. Mild and sweet-natured as she was, she refused to allow her daughter to be unfairly criticized.

"Oh, but Margery is not in the least fast, Mr. Morton," she said almost angrily. "Independent she may be; but of course I'm hopelessly antiquated in my ideas, I suppose, and not used to the freedom that girls have nowadays."

Her face softened as she looked at her daughter and the young officer. They were chatting with animation and as frankly and naturally as comrades of the same sex. Even to eyes less prejudiced than the mother's they were a handsome pair; and their very contrast in colouring as in character made them seem as though designed by Nature to be mates. It was small wonder that to the mind of the mother—to whom the happy marrying of her daughter was a natural and constant preoccupation—the fugitive thought should occur that perhaps this man was destined to be the girl's husband. She greatly liked the little that she had seen of Stuart, whose frank and open nature appealed to her as much as his courteous and pleasant manner.

Certainly the young couple made a charming picture. Margery, slight but well formed, was not quite as tall as the man. The sunlight had caught her hair and turned it to gold; and she looked adorably pretty as she stood with her face upturned to her companion, her blue eyes looking into his dark ones, her fair colouring contrasting with his swarthy complexion, just as the natural gaiety of her disposition did with the gravity of his quieter character.

Murray now came up the steps and joined them. Shaking hands with the girl he asked:

"Is your father here today, Miss Webb?"

"No: he was too busy to accompany us, so mother and I came alone."

"Are you never afraid to drive back by yourselves through the jungle when night is falling?" asked Stuart. "You might bump into a bear or a tiger, as happened to Mainwaring and Mayne."

The girl laughed.

"Not in the least; I'd do as they did—drive right at the beasts and scare them by wild shrieks," she answered. "But, seriously, the only thing I'm really afraid of meeting is a rogue elephant."

"Yes; that's the animal you'd be most in danger

from," said Murray. "If you were riding you could wheel your pony round and outstrip the elephant if he chased you. But in a trap you'd be in a nasty plight, particularly if you came across the brute in a narrow part of the road where you couldn't turn easily."

"Let us hope that we won't meet one, then," said the girl, smiling. "Fortunately there have been no rogues in our part of the district lately."

"What is a rogue elephant, exactly?" asked Stuart.

"A tusker that has abandoned the herd and taken to a solitary life temporarily or permanently, usually only the former," replied his friend. "Whether it's the want of the soothing influence of feminine companionship or not, I don't know; but he becomes a crusty old bachelor and turns dangerous."

"But what causes his enmity to human beings?"

"Sometime or other, perhaps, he raids the patch of cultivation around a jungle village, the inhabitants of which try to drive him out of their fields by shouting, beating tom-toms and waving lighted torches at him—for he usually comes at night. Angry at being disturbed over his feed he turns on them and kills one or more. And after that he seems to have a grudge against humans and attacks them on sight whenever and wherever he meets them."

At that moment a hand was laid on Stuart's shoulder and a cheery voice cried:

"How's ma bonnie Heilan' laddie? So it's taking to killing tigers you are?"

The Sapper turned and shook hands with the newcomer, a red-faced, elderly man with a hearty manner, and with two other planters who had come up with him.

"Hullo, Beresford, how are you? I've brought my bag and am ready to go along and stay with you, as you kindly asked me to do last week. As for the tiger, yes, I had a bit of luck the other day."

"It was a good thing you put a stop to the brute's career so soon," said another of the newcomers, Carey by name. "We had one that devastated our district and killed thirty or forty people in two years. Everyone was terrified; and coolies refused to leave their huts and go to work on the garden unless one of us stood guard over them with a rifle. Luckily Baynes of the Police got it at last."

"It was worse on Newton's plantation ten years ago," said Beresford, who was one of the oldest residents of the district. "A tiger took to coming into the village at night and carrying off people, until the coolies abandoned the place in a body. There was no one left to cultivate the garden and the year's crop was lost."

"Confound the brutes!" ejaculated Carey. "There's always one or two about. Last cold weather we often couldn't get our letters, as a maneater had established himself on the road from Tukawari and killed two postmen. Has the Ghost Tiger been walking lately?"

The other planter laughed derisively.

"Hullo, Carey, do you really believe that old woman's tale?" he asked.

Beresford shook his head.

"It's all very well your jeering at it, Smith," he said seriously. "You've been too short a time in India to know all about it yet, haven't you? You won't find the older hands here laughing at Ghost Tiger. Eh, Murray? What do you say?"

"I offer no opinion," said the cautious Scot. I've been too long out in this country to believe or disbelieve anything."

"Oh, come; surely the yarn's too silly," expostulated Smith. "A vampire-tiger centuries old, that drinks human blood, and all that rot."

"Well, we won't argue about it," replied Murray. "What about lunch? Who is host today?"

"Cartwright. There he is at the bar. He's calling us to have a cocktail before lunch. Come along, you fellows," said Carey.

And the planters trooped off, leaving Stuart, who had laughingly declined the invitation, alone with the girl again, to which he was not averse, for he had already a strong liking for her.

Margery Webb had been born on her father's tea-garden in the Terai and, until her tenth year, had never stayed longer in England than a few months during her parents' infrequent visits home. But when she had reached that age they left her behind at a Brighton school, where she remained for five years. Then she went to India for twelve months and returned to the same school until she was eighteen, when she went to Somerville College, Oxford. Always full of the joy of living she was particularly happy there, for she was intelligent and intellectual without being in the least a blue-stocking. Though fond of learning she enjoyed the hours spent in games or on the river quite as much as those in the lecture-room. But she would have preferred to Study hard and make a career for herself in England rather than return to India and await matrimony there. For she was very much a modern girl, frankly fond of men's society but not dependent on it, and far from desirous of marriage for the mere sake of marrying. Without believing Woman to be Man's superior, or even quite his equal, she would not admit her to be his slave and personally was not prepared to give either to father or husband a blind and servile obedience. At Oxford and in London, or wherever she spent her holidays at the homes of girlfriends, she had boated, played tennis, danced and flirted with men. But she met them always on equal terms; and, although she had had one or two proposals, she did not leave her heart behind when, secretly reluctant, she had obeyed her parents' desire that she should give up her studies and return to them in the Terai a year before Stuart had come to it. She was then twenty-one. She had since had several more offers to change her state; for she was the only English girl in the district, and a planter's life is a lonely one.

But indeed she was pretty and attractive enough to win hearts even in civilized places where more competition existed. Her mother, fearing to lose her only child too soon, yet anxious to see her well settled in life— for the poor lady was not ignorant of her husband's financial embarrassment—was puzzled at her daughter's attitude to men; and even the year together had not accustomed and reconciled her to it. A generation behind the modern girl, Mrs. Webb could not understand Margery's independence of chaperonage and her utter frankness and freedom with men, which, in the mother's young days, would have been characterized as being shockingly fast. But she was content to trust her, because she knew her child's innate purity and intense self-respect; for the two were as close friends, *confidantes* and companions as it was possible for persons of such different characters to be. The mother had already come to lean on the daughter's Stronger nature. She knew that Margery, who indeed made no secret of it, liked the Royal Engineer greatly, seldom as she had met him. For Stuart was an intellectual, educated and deeply read man, and as such appealed to her. Mrs. Webb, while approving of him herself, was apprehensive of her daughter's growing to care for him, lest the affection might not be returned.

At lunch the Sapper took his seat beside Miss Webb at her frank invitation, much to the ill-concealed annoyance of Morton, who had placed himself on her other side. At table the conversation at first consisted of an interchange of news and happenings on the various gardens since the last weekly meeting at the club, the condition of the crop, the state of the tea-market and enquiries after absent members of the little community. Tales of the depredations of wild animals brought the talk naturally to Stuart's tiger; and the story of its death was called for and told modestly by its slayer.

While congratulations and compliments were being showered on him by the other planters Morton made a sneering remark as to Stuart owing more to luck than to good sportsmanship. Beresford, between whom and the half-caste existed an enmity of long-standing, overheard it and resented it so hotly that a fierce dispute between the two men was averted only by the efforts of Mrs. Webb and her daughter.

To turn the conversation Margery said:

"How is your quarry getting on, Mr. Stuart?"

"Very well, thanks. The coolie camp is built and the men to fill it are beginning to arrive. The railway company has made good progress with the temporary extension of the line that's to be run up to the quarry to carry away the stone. In the meantime, I'm to be allowed by Government a couple of tame elephants to carry up supplies. I'm very delighted at this, and hope they'll be animals that will be good to shoot from, as I'll have a lot of time on my hands."

"Ask them to send you tuskers, then," said Carey. "Males are much better for shooting—pluckier, you know."

"I'm not so sure. I prefer females on the whole," said another.

And in the discussion that ensued on the respective merits of bull and cow elephants for shooting from, the danger of a quarrel at table between Beresford and Morton was averted.

CHAPTER IV

THE DEVIL TIGER'S PREY

AN HOUR or two after lunch Margery and the Royal Engineer played tennis together. Morton watched them for a time jealously, then went to the long bar running down the side of the one room of the building, where most of the planters were standing in groups chatting and drinking. None of them invited him to join them, for he was anything but popular in the district. However, he went up to two young assistant managers leaning against the bar next a circle of men around Beresford and, asking the servant behind the bar for a drink, began to talk to them. He was sure of his reception with them, for they were both in his debt.

Murray, joining the group about Beresford, said to a member of it named Keighley, who was the honorary secretary of the club:

"Stuart wants to know if there's any objection to his becoming a full member of the club. Of course we've made him free of it; but, as he will probably be a long time in the district, he'd like to pay his subscription and his share of expenses as we do."

"That's very decent of him," said the Secretary. "Of course we're very glad to see him here as a guest; but, if he feels like that, I don't see any objection to his joining as a full member. What do you fellows say?"

All in the group agreed; and Keighley, turning to the three next them, asked their opinion. Before his companions could reply Morton broke in rudely:

"I object strongly. I don't see that Stuart has any claim to be a member or that anyone has a right to make him one. This is a Planters' Club—he's not a planter."

Beresford, angry at a friend of his being objected to by the man whom he hated most in the district, turned on him hotly:

"What the devil have you got to say against it? Do you call yourself a planter?"

"Yes; what do you call me?" said his enemy, scowling.

"A cursed money-lender."

Morton's sallow face flushed darkly.

"You lie."

Beresford sprang furiously at him, seized him by the throat and half-strangled him before the others separated them. Morton staggered back against the bar gasping for breath, while his angry antagonist was dragged away by his friends.

"You'll be sorry for this someday," the half-caste hissed after him, as soon as he could speak; and it took half a dozen men to prevent Beresford attacking him again.

Even the men who owed Morton money showed him little sympathy; for his opponent was the most popular member of their community, and Stuart had already made himself liked in the club. So, turning to the bar, he called for a glass of brandy and, draining it, went out on the verandah, where he stood alone, jealously watching Miss Webb and the Sapper on the tennis court.

Later in the afternoon when Stuart and Murray sat at tea with the girl and her mother, the half-caste went down the back steps of the building with the stealthy gait peculiar to him and ordered his syce to put his pony in the trap. As he stood waiting Beresford saw him. The elderly Irishman was in a calmer but not more repentant mood. He, too, went unobserved down the steps and approached Morton, who shrank apprehensively from him.

Beresford laughed grimly.

"Don't be afraid. I'll not dirty my hands on you again," he said. "I've come to have a word with you alone. I know why you dislike Stuart. I know what you want, and why you've schemed for years to get Webb into your power. But I'll spoil your game, my friend. I'll not let a beast like you get hold of little Margery, whom I've known since she was a baby. You're not the only one who has money. I've saved a tidy bit, and I'll stand by my old friend Webb and get him out of your clutches, you Shylock. I'll see that tomorrow night he'll be free from his debt to you. That'll hurt you more than my grip on your throat."

With black curses on his lips and a face like a devil the half-caste climbed into his trap and struck his pony savagely with his whip. Beresford, chuckling, watched him drive off, and then, firm in the resolve that he had suddenly taken to baffle his enemy's schemes and save the girl whom he loved as his own child, returned to the club and, going straight to Mrs. Webb's table, said as he sat down:

"Will you tell your husband without fail that I'll ride over to see him tomorrow morning on very urgent business?"

"Certainly. You'll stay to breakfast then, of course," replied Mrs. Webb.

"I'll see that Mummy doesn't forget, Uncle Pat," said Margery, handing him a cup of tea.

"Thanks, I'd like to, Mrs. Webb," answered Beresford. "But Stuart here is coming back with me this evening to stay for two or three days—"

"Won't you bring him over with you, then?" asked Mrs. Webb hospitably. "You'll come, Mr. Stuart, I hope? You've never been to see us yet. Our garden, Malpotha you know, is next to Mr. Beresford's—only about four miles from it."

"Thank you very much," replied the Sapper. "I shall be delighted, if Beresford will bring me over."

The Irishman nodded.

"Right. Expect us both to breakfast then, Mrs. Webb. I say, Margery, will you drive me back this evening and drop me where my garden road turns off the main one? Stuart can come along in my trap with my assistant, Lane, and pick me up there."

"I'd love to, Uncle Pat. I haven't had a chat with you for ages," replied the girl.

A little later the setting sun gave warning that it was time to depart. For all present had a long way to go, and the jungle roads are dangerous in the dark, when the night-prowling beasts haunt them. So after a final drink at the bar the party began to break up. Murray and the planters who lived across the river went over in the ferry-boat; while the others rode or drove off.

Beresford, sharing the backseat of the Webbs' dog-cart with their syce, called out to his assistant, who was standing with Stuart and two or three others on the ver-andah.

"Hurry up, Lane. You'll never catch us up if you don't get a move on; and I don't want to wait an hour for you at the crossroads or have to walk from there home. Buck up, my lad."

And he shook his fist playfully at his grinning assis-tant, as Margery drove off.

Lane finished his cocktail and said resignedly to Stuart:

"Come along. The dear old man will swear like a trooper at me if I keep him cooling his heels at the crossroads. Hi, *syce! Gharri lao!*" (Bring the trap!)

When the Sapper had shoved his suitcase under the seat he climbed up after Lane; and they started. The slanting shadows of the trees fell across the white road as the strongly built trap rattled along in the deep ruts made by the heavy bullock-carts that conveyed the packed tea-cases or brought the food supplied for the thousands of coolies in the villages on the various estates.

Lane, a cheery, sociable individual, sang snatches of comic songs or cracked jokes as he whipped up his pony; until the sight of a long strap dangling uselessly below the shafts made him pull up with a groan.

"That infernal buckle's broken," he said in dismay. "Heaven knows how I'm to fix it! And old Beresford will bite my head off, for we'll be awfully late."

There was more damage done to the harness than was at first apparent; and the repairs took him some time. While he laboured with much profanity at his task and the syce held the pony's head, Stuart sat smoking in the trap, thinking of nothing in particular and lazily happy and comfortable.

Suddenly a strange, miserable feeling came over him. Fear gripped him, fear nameless, undefined, fear of some calamity, some terrible danger—not to himself, but to someone for whom he was concerned. It was so strong, so real, that he told Lane of it, half-ashamed of it even as he spoke.

"Nonsense, old chap, that's a bit of Scotch superstition," replied the other, looking up with a laugh. "You haven't got second-sight, I hope; otherwise it might mean that we're going to run into a rogue elephant and get smashed up. But I wish you'd had a presentiment about this strap before we started. Then I'd have looked to it at the club."

When at length he climbed back into the trap, having first lighted the lamps, he said, as they started again:

"Thank goodness there's a moon tonight. I don't relish the chance of meeting a wild elephant; for, if the pony bolted, this rotten harness would never hold."

The short Indian twilight faded; but the moon, not yet at the full, lit up the road between the black shadows of the trees. Lane was silent now as they drove along, keeping a keen lookout ahead for possible wild beasts in their path; for the danger of encountering a rogue elephant, which would inevitably attack them, was a very real one.

When they reached the junction of the main road with the private one leading to his garden he heaved a sigh of relief when he saw that Beresford was not waiting for them.

"Thank Heaven! he has given us up and walked home," he cried. "The dear old bird will be in a better temper after a drink or two before we get to the bungalow."

He broke into a song and made up for his previous silence as they drove through the mile or two of jungle that separated the tea-garden from the main road. He let the reins lie on the pony's neck; and the animal, nearing its stable, trotted on briskly.

Suddenly it shied so violently that it almost upset the trap.

"What the blazes—? Hullo! there's a coolie lying drunk in the road," exclaimed Lane, tightening the reins and trying to soothe the pony, which had stopped and, with forelegs planted, refused to pass a prostrate figure lying half in the shadow of the trees, its legs and feet in the moonlight.

Stuart peered down at it.

"That's not a native," he said. "He's got trousers and boots on."

He jumped down and, approaching the prostrate man, struck a match and bent down to look at him.

"Good God!" he cried. "It's Beresford. Dead! My presentiment!"

He flung himself on his knees beside the body. Lane sprang down, tore a lamp out of its socket and ran to him, while the syce went to hold the terrified pony.

The corpse was lying chest underneath; but the head was twisted round in an unnatural position with the face upturned. Lane held down the lamp. It was indeed Beresford—dead. The sightless eyes stared up unseeing; the usually rubicund countenance was wax-white; the contorted features were frozen in a look of terror.

Reverently the two men turned the body over. The head rolled and waggled horribly—the neck was broken. Lane held the lamp closer; and both men drew back in horror. From chin to collarbone the throat was torn away in a ghastly, gaping wound through which life must have instantly fled.

"Who—what—has done this?" cried Lane aghast. "There's no blood . . ."

The edges, the interior of the horrid rent were red, the clothing was bedabbled; but no blood oozed, nor where the body lay was there any on the ground, though from such a wound it should have poured in torrents.

An awful suspicion dawned in each man's mind. Lane, pale as the corpse, rose and by the light of the lamp closely examined the ground.

In the dust there showed plainly what seemed the footprints of a giant cat. The young planter looked at them and then at the bloodless wound.

"The Ghost Tiger!" he gasped.

CHAPTER V

IN THE TOILS

A COUPLE of months had gone by since Beresford's strangely mutilated body had been laid to rest in the little cemetery of a Santal Mission village twenty miles away, where the burial service was conducted by the white-haired missionary named Saunders, who had worked for nearly forty years among the natives. The mystery of the Irishman's death was never solved. More than ever the inhabitants of the district believed in the existence of a strange and supernatural beast which nourished itself on the blood of human beings; and the tales about it grew as they passed from mouth to mouth. Nor was it only the Indians who credited them. More than one planter secretly put faith in them or at least did not deny the possibility of the incredible thing.

Stuart, aware of his Highland tendency to super-stition and determined not to give way to it, sought for a natural explanation of the tragedy. At daybreak on the morning following Beresford's death he visited the spot where they had found the body. It occurred to him that the absence of blood might be explained by the unfor-tunate man's having been struck down further away, and his body carried some distance from where he died.

But Beresford's footprints were plainly visible in the thick dust of the road to the very spot where he had been found; and the Sapper saw in the undergrowth unmistakable signs of where the tiger had lain in wait, as well as marks of its fatal rush. No; the planter had undoubtedly died where his corpse had been discovered.

Rifle in hand, Stuart searched the jungle alone and on foot for hours in the hope of coming on the slayer and avenging his friend, but in vain.

When he met the Forest Officer sometime after the funeral he talked the matter over with him at length. Barter told him that it was not only unusual, almost unheard of, that a tiger should suck the blood of its victim, but also a matter of extreme physical difficulty. Yet soon after Beresford's death several native girls were killed in the same way. Barter began to wonder if their slayer were not human; and, as the footprints of a tiger were always found near the body, the Forest Officer suspected that the assassin was shod in the skin of the legs and feet stripped from a dead tiger or in shoes made to resemble such an animal's paws. But the crimes seemed so purposeless that he dismissed the idea.

But Stuart was left unsatisfied to brood over the mystery of his friend's death, the shock of which greatly affected his sensitive nature. He had looked on dead bodies by the score on the battlefield with far less horror than on this solitary corpse. Beresford's fate cast a gloom over the scattered community of the planters. Independent of the fact of his universal popularity, the loss of one of their small number and the manner of his taking off naturally depressed them. Mrs. Webb and Margery, who regarded the big-hearted Irishman almost as a dear relative, were heartbroken.

But there was one exception to the general sorrow. For Morton was not grieved at the disappearance of one who had not only been his avowed enemy for years, but had also declared his intention of checkmating the other's most cherished plans. He realized with gladness that Beresford's death happened most opportunely for him. The sudden removal of the menace of the Irishman's interference rejoiced him; and he had no tear to shed for the terrible fate of his foe. The strong strain of native blood in him endowed him with the true Asiatic spirit of long-enduring, revengeful hate and of unwearying, if tortuous, persistence in the accomplishment of his desires.

He was thinking of these desires as he sat in a room in his bungalow. Before him on the floor squatted an old woman whose sharp, hawk-like features bore no resemblance to the faces of any of the native races of Bengal or indeed of any province of India. But their like might be seen in every country in the world in the tents and caravans of the allied tribes of gypsies, *gitani*, *zingari*, or by whatever name these Ishmaelites are known. She was very old; but her spare frame was full of vigor, and the eyes looking affectionately at Morton were bright and clear. She was his mother, and loved him with the fierce devotion of a wild animal.

"So, my son," she said, "as I foretold, the danger that threatened you has passed. Will you persevere"

"Aye, mother, that will I," replied Morton emphatically, in the gypsy patois that she employed. "Neither man nor devil shall stop me. The girl must be mine. Can you not aid me? Can you not turn her heart? Have you no spells, no charms, no drugs?"

The old woman shook her head.

"You know, Son of my Heart, that evil I can work, but not good. Death I can give. Drugs I have to cause madness, spells to bring a curse, to wreak revenge, to gratify hate. But Love—no. Only He can help you."

The planter moved uneasily in his chair.

"What has He done for me so far? I have worshipped Him. I have sacrificed to Him. Much have I wrought for Him and His—to what result? I begin to lose faith in—"

The gypsy held up a warning hand.

"Beware! Do not blaspheme! He is the All-Powerful One. In His own good time will He aft."

Morton choked back an angry reply. After a pause he said:

"I see I can only rely on myself. The girl grows colder to me day by day. I begin to suspect that cursed soldier is really the cause. Were I sure of it—"

He broke off with a fierce oath. His mother grinned fiendishly. After a while, Morton went on:

"But if she will not favour me, then her father must make her. I have him in my power. As that dead fool guessed, for this I have schemed; my plans must bear fruit now. Shall I succeed?"

The old woman leaned forward and, taking his hand, first kissed and fondled it, then opening it gazed in silence at the palm. She traced its fines with her withered forefinger, and said:

"Obstacles there will be in thy path, my son; but thou'lt surmount them. There will—what's this? I see danger to thee, but I cannot tell its nature. Yes—'tis of metal. But which metal? Is it steel of knife or lead of bullet? Nay, neither can harm thee. Thou'rt charmed. Ha! I see. 'Tis silver—silver coin. I cannot understand. But there it is, son. Beware of the peril that lurks for thee in money."

Her son smiled grimly.

"Money is my friend, mother, not my foe. Leave me now."

The old gypsy nodded and, rising, left the room.

Morton sat motionless in his chair, thinking. For years his fixed idea had been to make Margery his wife. Even in her early girlhood he had desired her; and with infinite cunning he had plotted to get her father into his power so that eventually he might possess her. Webb, unsuspicious and weakly good-natured, believed firmly in his neighbour's disinterested friendship, speculated blindly on his advice and, when the inevitable losses followed, accepted Morton's financial help gratefully. Bad seasons and careless management of his garden had plunged him deeper into his supposed friend's debt. Cursed with an easygoing disposition which led him always to shirk trouble, he had resolutely shut his eyes to the truth, content to go through life without worrying himself.

The following day found Morton seated with Webb

in the latter's bungalow after breakfast. The host's face was anxious and troubled, as he nervously turned over a pile of papers on the table before him. He had just had brought home to him the realization of the large total of his indebtedness to Morton, coupled with a quiet intimation from his creditor that repayment was at last required.

"On my word, my dear fellow, I'd no idea I owed you so much," he said, gazing helplessly at the documents. "But you surely don't want it at once, do you?"

"I'm sorry; but it happens I do. I've a chance of a splendid investment; and you should remember that in this debt of yours I've locked up a good bit of capital for years."

"But—but, really, I don't know just quite where to lay my hand on the money at the moment. You wouldn't mind —you'd wait a bit, old chap, wouldn't you?"

Morton shook his head.

"It isn't fair to ask me, Webb. And it's no use. I must have the money," he said firmly.

Webb stared at him in surprise. He could not realize that his old friend could be so obdurate. He pointed out, at first half jocosely, then with increasing earnestness, the difficulty, nay the impossibility, of raising sufficient money to pay the debt at once, as he had little security to offer, since the estate was mortgaged for it to his present creditor.

After a while Morton appeared inclined to relent. Webb, seeing this, pleaded more earnestly still and pointed out that with the security of the property the money was safe.

At last Morton said slowly:

"I see one way of arranging the matter."

"Yes? What is it?" cried his host eagerly.

The other hesitated. Then he said:

"I'll settle the money on Margery as a wedding gift."

Webb's face lighted up and he broke in impetuously, as the other paused:

"By Jove, that's good of you!"

"When she marries me," concluded Morton.

Webb stared at him in blank amazement.

"What? Is she going to marry you?" he exclaimed. "I've never heard a word about it. But Margery is a strange girl—goes her own way and tells me nothing of what she does."

Morton laughed a little grimly.

"You needn't blame her. She doesn't know it herself. But I've meant it for years. Look here, Webb.

He lowered his voice with an instinctive fear of being overheard and went on to point out how desirable for the girl and how advantageous for her parents the match would be. The father, conscious only of relief at the passing of the cloud over him, saw nothing incongruous in the idea of such a marriage. He liked his neighbour in his lazy, careless way; had easily persuaded himself that the man was really the son of his father's English wife, and thought that he would make a sensible, steady husband. The girl would be well settled in life and would still remain near her parents. So when Morton left the bungalow he had Webb's promise to convey his offer to

Margery backed up by all the paternal influence. It had, moreover, been clearly intimated that her refusal of his suit would mean the foreclosure of the mortgages on the estate.

With such an alternative it was not to be wondered at that Webb espoused his neighbour's cause warmly when he informed his daughter of the proposal. And, conscious only of its advantages, he was genuinely surprised at the reception that it met with. The girl was at first astonished and incredulous; but unbelief was speedily followed by annoyance and a very decided refusal of the offer. The father, who was secretly somewhat in awe of his independent daughter, dropped the matter for the time being. But when he found that his wife agreed with Margery, and regarded the idea of such a marriage with horror, he explained the situation fully to her, and showed her that the future of them all depended on their child's answer.

Mrs. Webb was deeply distressed, and at first could not agree to the girl's being sacrificed for them. But, when she fully realized that ruin menaced them all equally, she gave way and promised to do her best to persuade her daughter to look more favorably on their neighbour's suit.

Then began for Margery the most unpleasant period of her life. She had to resist the entreaties of her much-loved mother, the arguments and appeals of her father, and to endure with apparent resignation Morton's odious attentions. His courtship consisted in haunting their bungalow, and overwhelming the girl with fulsome and ridiculous flattery at all times and on all occasions. He

only succeeded in making himself hateful to her; and it
needed all her mother's prayers to induce her to endure
his society.

Perhaps the fact that about this time she began to see
a good deal of Stuart, whom she frankly liked, helped her
to ignore the annoyance of Morton's attentions. The
Royal Engineer had much leisure just then, as work on
the quarry was at a standstill until the completion of the
temporary line from it to a railway which entered the
forest and served to carry away the produce of the tea-
gardens of the district. One transport elephant for his
camp had arrived and, when not required to bring up
supplies, served to take him out shooting, always
attended by Khitab Gul. Much of his leisure time the
Sapper spent with Barter, accompanying him about the
large section of the forest in his charge, learning much
jungle lore from him and getting a great deal of sport.
Dotted about the district were three or four wooden
bungalows, intended as official residences for the Forest
Officer to enable him to supervise efficiently every part of
the broad stretch for which he was responsible.

For certain reasons Barter had of late passed much
of his time in one of these, which was fairly close to the
tea-garden of which Beresford had been manager. Lane
had been appointed by the company to succeed the
Irishman; and, as he had a warm liking for Stuart, he
frequently invited the Sapper to visit him and his wife,
who had recently come out from England to join him. As
Mrs. Lane and Margery were close friends, it followed
that the girl and Stuart met much oftener than her father

guessed. For she judged it best to keep her own counsel on the matter, as she found that Webb, inspired by Morton, frowned on her friendship with the soldier.

Of this the latter knew nothing. He was openly glad to see more of the frank and attractive girl who had appealed to him from their first meeting. Mrs. Lane, with a woman's natural instinct for matchmaking, did all she could to bring the young couple together, and invited them to meet at her bungalow whenever Stuart was in the neighbourhood with Barter, who of late seldom left this section of his district.

For the Forest Officer was paying particular attention to it just then, owing to a series of incidents that had recently occurred in it. First, there had been a recrudescence of poaching, and three or four elephants had been found dead in deep pits dug to trap them. Only one was a tusker; and his ivory had been hacked from the skull. Then several forest guards had been attacked at night by mysterious assailants, the huts of two others had been set on fire during the dark hours; and, finally, the corpse of one had been found shot through the back. As all these men had been at various times instrumental in bringing home offences against the Forest Regulations to members of the gypsy tribe now camped once more after a long absence on Morton's estate, suspicion naturally fell on these nomads.

But there were even worse happenings. The Ghost Tiger had begun to walk again. Three young girls were found dead at different times near jungle villages, each with the ghastly throat wound, and the strange absence of blood that were regarded as the hallmarks of this mysterious animal.

"Beast or devil, I'm determined to hunt it down," declared Barter to Stuart.

And the young soldier, who had developed a warm friendship for his host, and who also was consumed with a passionate eagerness to avenge Beresford's death, pledged himself to help.

"You've got no clues to the brutes who committed the outrages on your forest guards, I suppose?" he asked.

Barter shook his head despondently.

"None. It's those infernal gypsies, of course; but— we'll never bring it home to them. Simpson, the Deputy Superintendent of Police, is on his way here to investigate; but he'll do no good. Yet he's a keen energetic fellow, who knows the natives well."

"It's a shame that the Government Station no police anywhere in the forest," said Stuart. "Just think of the few white planters—ladies, too, among them—on those scattered gardens, with hundreds, thousands of coolies around them, scoundrels like these gypsies wandering about, and Bhuttia outlaws along the Bhutanese frontier a few miles off; and yet there is no protection for them. I suppose the nearest help they could get is from the Military Police Outpost up in the hills there at Ranga Duar. And that's fifty miles away."

"They're only to guard the frontier. Of course, they'd aid in an outbreak. But against ordinary crime we're helpless. There are no civil police within thirty miles—not that they're much use, thieving, corrupt Bengali cowards that they are."

Simpson arrived two days later. Stuart, who found him very interesting, and gathered much instruction about native life from him, accompanied him when he went out to pursue his investigations. The D.S.P. paid special, if unobtrusive, attention to the gypsy colony, but could find no proof that its members were responsible for the outrages. Yet he fully shared Barter's suspicions and, under the pretext of shooting, haunted the jungle in the neighbourhood of Morton's garden on Stuart's elephant, accompanied by its owner.

One day in public forest land on the confines of the half-caste's estate, they came upon a crowd of gypsies gathered in a large circle around two men seated on the ground. Approaching, the Europeans saw that the couple were a *yogi*, a Hindu mendicant priest, and his *chela*, or disciple. The latter was bending reverentially before his superior who, with glassy eyes fixed in a meaningless stare, gazed unseeing before him. The priest, like his disciple, was naked but for a loincloth, his face and his whole body smeared white with ashes, his long hair twisted into a knot on top of his head. On his forehead was painted in vermilion a caste-mark, a small, semi-circular line with a round patch in the middle.

Whenever the *chela* bowed the gypsies prostrated themselves in mute admiration; but the *yogi*, absolutely motionless, paid no attention to them. He seemed as if carved from stone.

Stuart stared at him for a time.

"The man looks as if he were in a trance," he said.

"He is in one, I think," replied the Police Officer. "I've heard of him. He is a sort of priest of these gypsies; and I wondered at a Hindu ascetic, as he is supposed to be, having any connection with them; for they are not Hindus. But you see the caste-mark painted on his forehead? That is the tilaka of the *Saktas*, a caste of Hindus whose beliefs and ceremonies are bestial and obscure. They are supposed to indulge in human sacrifices when they can, go in for gross and revolting practices, and revere demons. As apparently the only religion that these gypsies have is a sort of devil-worship, I think I see the connection between them and this *sanyasi*."

The adoration of the immobile priest had gone on hitherto in silence. Suddenly the disciple raised his arms in the air, called out a name three times and began a loud chant in Bengali, a language of which Stuart understood very little. Seeing that Simpson was deeply interested the Sapper whispered, when the *chela* paused for breath:

"What's he saying?"

"It's rather curious. He says that the *yogi's* spirit or soul is now in Benares, and that we are merely looking on its untenanted shell, his body. Certainly the man seems in a catalepsy. I've often heard of this sort of thing, but I've never seen a case before."

"But surely you don't believe it?"

"I don't know. Listen!"

The *chela* began again. Simpson translated.

"He says that at this moment the *yogi* is applying the torch to the funeral pyre of his dead father on the banks of the Ganges."

"A difficult thing for a disembodied spirit to do, isn't it?"

"Well, the belief is that in these cases the wandering soul takes on its body's double and so can be seen—and felt—in two places at the same time. But only one of these bodies has life—or, at least, power of action. Let's get down and see if the *yogi* is really in a trance or only shamming."

At a word from him the *mahout* pressed the point of his iron goad into the nape of their elephant's neck and the animal sank to its knees. Slipping to the ground from its back the two white men made their way through the ring of worshippers. Facing the motionless priest, Simpson gave him the respectful salutation that Hindu reverence considers the due of these holy ascetics:

"*Ra! Ram! Shri Maharai!* Greeting in the name of Rama, O King!"

The *chela* looked up at him sullenly.

"He cannot hear you. He is far away," he said.

"How can that be, *O chela-ji?* We see him before our eyes."

The disciple scowled and drew a knife from his loincloth.

"Behold, thou unbelieving one!" he cried, then, leaning forward, drove the blade deep into the arm of the priest and left it quivering there.

CHAPTER VI

A NIGHT OF HORROR

A GROAN of wonder rose from the worshipping gypsies. The disciple, content with the demonstration, sank back again on his heels. Simpson stepped forward and drew out the knife. In the priest's flesh there remained the gaping hole, and he could see the raw interior of the cut, but no blood flowed from the wound and the blade was unsullied.

Throwing the knife down, the Police Officer turned away.

"It's beyond me, Stuart," he said. "Come, let us be off, or I'll begin to believe in magic."

And they mounted the elephant and moved away through the jungle; and the dense undergrowth closed behind them.

Two days later a coolie arrived at the bungalow of the Forest Officer bearing a letter from Mrs. Lane inviting him and his two guests to dinner at her house that evening. She mentioned that Miss Webb was to be present. Barter was suffering from one of his periodic attacks of fever and could not accept; but he insisted that Stuart and Simpson should go. Accordingly, after protesting against leaving him alone, they rode off before sundown along the jungle path that led towards Lane's tea garden.

They had not long started when a forest guard arrived at the wooden bungalow and asked urgently to see Barter. He was so emphatic that he was admitted to the sick man's room, and there, salaaming repeatedly, reported that he had just found in the jungle the dead body of a native girl, apparently killed not an hour before. And the corpse bore the awful mark of the Ghost Tiger.

Ill as he was Barter rose from his bed and, despite the remonstrances of his old and faithful 'boy', gave orders for his elephant to be got ready and insisted on being helped to dress. But he was so weak that he had to sit down every few minutes while putting on his clothes. He swallowed a very strong dose of quinine. The medicine and the fever made his head swim; and the buzzing in his brain prevented him from thinking clearly. With shaking hands he put his rifle together and pasted a long strip of white paper between the barrels to show up the sights in the dark; for he meant to watch by the corpse all night, as the moon was at the full.

Again and again his servant tried to dissuade him from an effort that seemed clearly beyond his powers; but Barter scarcely heard him.

Before sunset he started on the elephant on his way to the spot where the tiger's victim lay; but he was so feeble that the forest guard had to hold him on. Behind them on the animal's pad was strapped a *charpoy*, a native string-bedstead which was to be tied up in a tree above the corpse as a machan or platform from which Barter could watch for the possible return of the slayer. In saner moments he would have remembered that the Ghost Tiger never came back to eat the flesh of its 'kill'.

The guard guided them to a clearing in public forest land which, although they did not know it, was the spot where Stuart and Simpson had seen the *yogi* and his worshippers. On the branches of the trees around it scores of bald-headed vultures sat silent and motionless, unlike their usual habit of squawking, squabbling, jostling and pecking each other viciously. Their unwinking gaze was fixed on a dread something that lay at the foot of a large tree, and from which a crowd of flies rose up as the elephant approached. It was the corpse of a young Hindu girl, a red flower withering in her shining black hair, and cotton bodice torn aside showing the rounded breasts. For she lay on her back; and the horrid wound in her throat was at once apparent. But to Barter's blurred vision it was not clear until he had dismounted from the elephant and, supported by the guard, tottered over to the corpse.

It was a hideous sight; and, shaken as he was, he could not bear to look at it. He threw himself wearily on the ground behind the trees, which hid the body from his eyes; while the *mahout* and the forest guard, both badly scared, pointed out to each other the *pugs* of a tiger round the body.

Ordinarily the vultures would have been feasting on such a banquet spread for them; or at least, if the striped slayer lay too close to it for them to venture to tamper with his prey, they would have shown their impatience by cries and irritable movements, by swooping down as near the corpse as they dared, and rocketing up into the air again at the tiger's menacing growl. There was something uncannily impressive in the silent, immobile watch of the foul birds.

Their unusual behavior was not lost on the two forest-bred natives, to whom the jungle was an open book; and it added to their terror. Hastily they climbed the tree, at the foot of which the dead girl lay, and with a rope pulled up the wooden-framed *charpoy* which, with trembling fingers, they tied in a stout fork about thirty feet from the ground. Then with cut leafy branches they screened it from view from below.

After this was ready for his occupation they had to help their *sahib* up to it—no easy task. For he was so weak that he could make no attempt to climb even with their assistance; and, one pushing, the other pulling, they had to try to drag him up to the *charpoy*. But their efforts were fruitless; and, seeing his feebleness, the two men begged him to give up the idea of watching for the tiger and to allow them to take him back to the bungalow.

A sudden access of fever lent him artificial strength; and suddenly, almost unaided, he climbed up to the *machan* and lay at full length on it, shaking with ague so violently that the screen about the *charpoy* trembled as if composed of aspen leaves. His followers handed him up his rifle and water-bottle. Then he bade them go; but, terrified though they were at the possible near presence of the legendary Devil Tiger, they were yet reluctant to leave him in the state he was. But his orders were peremptory; and they mounted the elephant, which disappeared with noiseless tread into the jungle.

The sun was setting; but there were none of the usual forest sounds and sights of such an hour. No birds twittered in the foliage; no jungle cocks crowed their evening challenge, no troops of monkeys swung through the leafy airways among the boughs on their way to water for their final drink of the day or huddled together for the night in the topmost boughs. The vultures still sat silent and serried in the trees. Nothing broke the uncanny hush of the forest save the drone of the multitudinous insect-life and the horrid buzzing of the countless flies about the corpse.

But Barter was deaf and blind to everything as, almost unconscious of his surroundings, he lay on the *charpoy* shaking with fever. The quinine made his head swim; but it had not brought down his temperature. With difficulty he raised a burning hand to his aching forehead and tried to sit up. The effort was almost beyond his Strength; and he only succeeded after two or three attempts.

Daylight died on the mountaintops, and the swift-coming Indian night fell on the forest. The full moon shone down on the clearing, leaving blackest shadow under the trees. But one ray struggled through the leaves and quivered on the face of the corpse; and to Barter's fevered eyes it seemed as if the dead woman was gazing up at him with a mocking grin. As he stared down fascinated he fancied that she stirred; and fear seized him at the awful thought that she was about to rise and ascend to him.

A cloud came over the moon; and the body was lost to view. But delirium mounted to the sick man's brain. He believed that he heard the corpse climbing the tree; and he gripped his rifle by the barrel, ready to fell it with the butt. But the moon shone out and he saw that the body lay still.

The world grew dark again; and suddenly it seemed to him that the eyes of the vultures huddling on the trees around shone with phosphorescent fire, and the great birds themselves, though in deepest shadow, became visible and took other and more dreadful forms.

A wind swept down from the mountains, and heavy clouds passed across the face of the moon. In the swift succession of light and darkness the ground appeared to the delirious man to be covered with creeping things. The flickering shadows became moving, gruesome forms, and the moan of the wind the wail of lost souls. He could have sworn that the corpse stirred, half rose to do battle with hideous shapes that thronged about it, then sank back again and lay still.

The torment of his fever grew unendurable. Agonizing pains racked every limb. The throbbing pulses beat like drums through his aching brain. His body shook and alternately froze with the ice of the Arctic and burned with the fires of hell. He no longer knew where he was or why he had come there.

A heavy cloud lingered over the moon. It passed; and the clearing was lit up again. To Barter's wild fancy it was now crowded with human forms, among which moved strange shapes, half fiend, half animal.

The sky grew black again. A dense pall was drawn over it. Swiftly lights began to burn on the ground. A sudden blaze of leaping flames lit up the open space and showed it crowded with living beings. Men, women, children, they seemed, all holding torches in their up-lifted hands.

To Barter in his delirium there was nothing strange in this desolate spot in the jungle being thus tenanted; and he nodded gravely when the wavering lights showed that all the mysterious beings bore the features of gypsies.

Suddenly a blinding burst of brilliant flames leapt up to the level of the treetops from a space left clear in the center of the thronging crowd. Plainly revealed four figures stood out before it. At that instant Barter's fever seemed to drop from him; and he gazed at them steadily. One was a crone with wrinkled features and sparse white locks, old, very old, yet her withered frame was strong and vigorous. Beside her stood a tall, thin man with gypsy features, strangely light eyes and a disfiguring harelip. The other two were almost naked and ash-smeared Hindu ascetics. The four lifted their arms and cried out a name, then flung themselves on their faces, and all the crowding beings around them did the same.

At once the torches were extinguished and the flames died out as swiftly as they were born. After the glare the darkness was opaque, intense.

Suddenly it was rent asunder by a dazzling flash of lightning that seemed to strike the clearing. In its momentary glare the watcher in the tree saw every detail of the scene, the silent vultures on the branches that bent beneath their weight, the corpse below him, the prostrate forms of the worshipping crowd. And, horror in their midst—a gigantic, terrible form, hideous, devilish, satanic, more dreadful than the horrible nightmare idols of Tibetan and Chinese shrines or the awe-inspiring gods that guard the gateways of Japanese temples.

Demoniac, awful, incredible, it towered above the worshippers in the blinding glare of the lightning. Then darkness fell on the world again.

But an appalling peal of thunder crashed overhead and echoed, a hundred times repeated, from the great wall of mountains so near at hand, then died away in distant rumbling among the giant hills.

The great fire blazed up, the torches gleamed, and fever seized Barter once more. Without surprise he gazed unmoved upon the hideous apparition—colossal idol or veritable demon, he did not trouble to speculate which— that the lights revealed again. It towered in all its terrifying hideousness; and to the sick man's delirious gaze it appeared endowed with life as its awful visage grinned fiendishly on its adorers.

It seemed to Batter that the air was filled with the wheeling shapes of giant bats, the flapping wings of foul vultures and flying things more dreadful still. And beyond the prostrate bodies of the human worshippers were strange and awful beasts in endless throngs, while giant serpents writhed on every branch of the trees above them.

The four detached figures rose up from the ground and lifted their hands to the Awful Being. They knelt, stood up again, bowed and appeared to be performing some sacrifice to the horrible thing. Their voices rose in a wild incantation and, kneeling, they placed on the ground at its feet a large and deep golden bowl.

Then to Barter's excited fancy, the Demon nodded its horrid head; and the four celebrants and the bowed worshippers stood up and turned their faces towards the tree in which he hid. An awful fear gripped his heart, and his burning blood froze in his veins. But the staring eyes were directed below him; and he looked down. Horrible! Over the body of the dead girl stood a tiger that in the uncertain light showed gigantic, incredible in its size.

As Barter, horror-stricken, gazed at it the tiger bent its head and its jaws closed on the frail corpse which it lifted and bore with ease towards the Demon God. The worshippers parted to give it passage, but betrayed no fear of it. As it neared the great blaze the light showed that its hide was grey between the black bars on the skin.

At the feet of the Devil Thing it stopped and dropped the corpse. Then, horrible to relate, it bent its head over the great golden bowl, and from its slavering mouth spewed up blood until the gleaming vessel was full. The *yogi* and his disciple, the old woman and the tall gypsy, dipped their hands into the red liquid and flung it towards the awful Devil God, then turning, threw it on each other and on the worshippers who had fallen on their knees.

The fevered watcher in the tree went mad at the sight.

"Ghost Tiger! The accursed Ghost Tiger!" he gasped.

Then he sprang up on the *charpoy* and frenziedly tore aside the leafy screen that hid him.

"Beast! Devil! Devil-Beast!" he shrieked in his madness, as he stood revealed.

An appalling crash of thunder shook the forest. Barter was conscious in his delirium of a sea of eyes glaring up at him, from the terrible flaming orbs of the Demon-God, the fiery eyes of the tiger, to the flaring optics of the crowd.

Unheeding, he began to climb down from the *machan* with the insane idea in his distraught brain of strangling with his bare hands the accursed beast where it stood at the feet of the Devil-Monster. With the sudden strength of fever he dropped from bough to bough until he reached a great limb of the tree ten feet from the ground. Here he flopped and faced the terrible audience again. His brain reeled, everything danced before his blood-shot eyes. Nothing seemed real, the trees, the flames, the awful shapes in the air or on the ground. All he was conscious of was the gaunt grey beast that through the parted multitude came slowly, stealthily, towards his tree, its barred face set in a fiendish snarl that showed the great white fangs bared between the tightly-drawn lips.

The sick man stood as firmly on the rounded wood as though on a level floor, though it seemed that the universe spun round with him, that he was caught up in a maelstrom of wind and whirled through endless space peopled with yelling, taunting demons.

But always he could see the awful form of the Ghost Tiger; and in frantic rage he cursed it, he raved, he threatened. Thunder crashed overhead; the air, the forest, were filled with clamor. The spectral beast came stealthily on and seemed to swell to fantastic stature as it crept nearer and nearer. It reached the foot of the tree and flattened to earth, while the man above shrieked curses at it.

There was a sudden, awful stillness. Then the crouching beast sprang—and as it did the madman above with a wild shriek leapt through the air to meet it.

CHAPTER VII

LOVE AND DEATH

STUART sat with Margery on the verandah after dinner, while in the drawing-room Simpson and their host stood over Mrs. Lane at the piano, chorusing to her accompaniment a comic song half-forgotten in London, but new to the exiled dwellers in the Terai. Their voices rang out loudly into the silent night, but the man and the girl never heard them. They were far away in another world, a world of their own, isolated, apart, divided from the rest of humanity by a golden wall.

For, though they were unconscious of it yet, their mutual liking had deepened into love; and they heeded none, needed none, other than themselves. Perhaps of the two the girl was nearer to understanding the truth; for

Love is never far from a woman's thoughts, since it means so much more to her than to the other sex. Stuart only realized that Margery was the sweetest, most delightful woman that he had ever known, that her society was all-sufficing, all-absorbing and for the moment he wanted no more. She was so companionable, so understanding.

She was good to look at. It was delightful to lean back in his long-chair and watch the light from the verandah lamp shine on the golden-brown ripples of her hair, to see the play of expression on her pretty face when she talked, to look into the dark depths of the lovely eyes, their blue changed to blackness in the shadow. He grew impatient at the recollection that he must soon ride away to the lonely house in the jungle. It would be pleasant to know that he would see the girl again on the morrow and the next day and the next. What a charming picture she made as she sat in the lamplight! How delightful it would be to be able to look on it whenever one wanted!

But on the whole he was lazily content as he lay back smoking. In the drawing-room the singing had stopped; but the tactful Mrs. Lane, determined that the couple on the verandah should not be disturbed, played on and kept her husband and Simpson inside. The dreamy melody did not jar on the peaceful stillness of the night. The moon shone on the wide stretch of the tea-garden, silvering the long, regular rows of low bushes and showing the distant dark wall of trees of the encircling forest. An occasional mosquito humming about Stuart's head all that marred the serenity. Margery and he had lapsed into the understanding silence of perfect companionship, as they

listened to the haunting music that floated out into the
still air. It was good to be alive on such a night, in such
company, thought the Highlander.

But gradually, imperceptibly, his happiness and content seemed to ebb from him. A strange feeling of
oppression, of dire foreboding, a sense of discomfort, of
disaster, crept over him. He tried to shake it off, to
capture again the blissful peace that had possessed him,
but in vain.

Margery, watching him with eyes sharpened by
affection, was conscious of his disquiet.

"Is there anything the matter, Mr. Stuart?" she
asked, with a little anxiety.

He started.

"Eh? Oh, no. Why?" he stammered in surprise.

"You look troubled."

"Do I? Well, I—it's absurd, I suppose, but I've
suddenly got the same uneasy feeling, the same sense of
some evil happening that came to me on the night of poor
Beresford's death."

"Strange. What can cause it?" said the girl
reflectively.

Being a woman she could understand such feelings
of gloomy apprehension better than a man and had no
inclination to make light of them, as Stuart had feared
that she would.

"Oh, it's nothing. But, try all I can, I can't shake it off.
It's a curious feeling—as if some evil threatened someone
I liked. It can't be—"

He stopped.

"What?"

"I wondered if anything was happening to Barter—if he has suddenly got worse. But it's only one of his usual attacks of fever, and he's safe in bed. I've got to like him a lot, so I suppose it's natural that I'm anxious about him. Hullo! there's a storm coming."

A peal of thunder sounded from the mountains.

"A storm in the hills! Curious, at this time of year," exclaimed the girl. "How dark it's getting!"

A flash of lightning lit up the distant sky.

"Perhaps it's the electricity in the air that makes you depressed," she continued.

"It may be. But, somehow, I don't think it's that," replied Stuart.

He got up and walked to the verandah rail to look out. The moon shone above them clearly again, but towards the mountains the sky was black as ink. Again it was rent by a vivid flash that seamed the dark pall with a jagged line of fire. The girl rose and went over to her companion. From the drawing-room the others came out and joined them.

"It's strange to get a thunderstorm at this time of year," remarked Lane. "It's lower down than I thought and moving this way, apparently. Well, a little rain would do the crop good. Oh, by the way, if it comes, you fellows had better stay here for the night. Miss Webb is stopping, but we can find you a shakedown."

Simpson approved of the idea.

"Thanks. I'd like to stay," he replied. "I don't feel inclined to turn out after the excellent dinner you gave us,

Mrs. Lane. And I shouldn't be sorry to be spared the ride back at this hour through your beast-haunted jungle. It scares me. Well, what do you think, Stuart?"

The soldier said impatiently:

"It's very good of you, Lane, but I want to get back. I'm uneasy about Barter and don't like leaving him alone all night."

"Oh, I forgot him," exclaimed Simpson. "Yes, we'd better get back."

With such a reason for their going Lane did not press them to stay and complied with Stuart's request to have their ponies brought round.

"Well, if you're going you'd better start at once and race the storm," he said. "Did you bring a rifle with you, Stuart?"

"Yes, I don't like being out in the jungle at night without one."

"I don't wonder, after what we've seen," said Lane. "Poor old Beresford. God rest him!"

Ten minutes later the two guests cantered away from the bungalow. Stuart's mind was filled with a medley of regret at being obliged to bid farewell to Margery and losing the opportunity of seeing her on the morrow and of vague and oppressing fears of some indefinable disaster. Simpson, finding him averse to talking, sang loudly the songs that Mrs. Lane had played for them, and shouted the choruses through the silent forest in the hope, he explained, of scaring any dangerous beast that might be lurking in their path. The thunder drowned his voice at times; but no rain fell.

His companion seemed to have forgotten the possibility of any peril to themselves as, urged on by an increasing anxiety, he galloped recklessly along the track cut through the jungle from the main road to the Forest Officer's house. Simpson's appeals for a slower pace were unheeded; and he had to ride hard to keep up with his companion on the dark path which the moon could not reach.

But they arrived at the bungalow without mishap. The flames from a fire in the clearing behind it shone on two elephants, shackled by their hindlegs to trees. The great beasts were restlessly shifting their weight from leg to leg, swinging their trunks, or with them picking up one of a pile of cut branches behind them, stripping the leaves off it and cramming them into their mouths. Around the fire a group of men were seated—Khitab Gul and Barter's servant, Shaikh Ebrahim and Stuart's *mahout* Kadir Baksh and the syces. They rose as the sahibs rode up and the syces ran to take the ponies. Stuart handed his rifle to Khitab Gul and before going into the bungalow, enquired from Barter's 'boy' how his master was.

When the latter told them that their host, whom they had left on a sickbed, had gone out into the forest to 'sit up' for a tiger, neither of the two white men could believe it at first. But when they realized that it was a fact both were distressed, and the Highlander was convinced that his dread premonition was true, as it had been before, that some terrible disaster had befallen his friend. He wanted to start at once in search of him, and was only prevented from ordering the elephants to be got ready at once by Shaikh Ebrahim's declaring that he would not be able to guide them by night to the spot where his master was watching. The forest guard had gone off to his home. The Sapper was forced to content himself with bidding the *mahouts* be prepared to leave at daybreak.

He could not go to bed; and he had so infected Simpson with his fears that the latter, after tossing sleeplessly for an hour, listening to the thunder that still rumbled among the mountains, got up and joined him in the one common room of the bungalow. Here through the night the men sat smoking, trying by their talk to rid themselves of their gloomy fears, and pausing nervously every now and then to listen for they knew not what. The servants had shut themselves in their huts and were asleep.

The forest was very still, yet to the two watchers it appeared full of strange sounds. They seemed to be aware of furtive beasts prowling around the bungalow. At times they could have sworn that a stealthy footfall crept along the verandah—they could hear the planks creaking under it. A hand tried the door. A heavy body dragged itself, sighing wearily, up the sloping roof. So unstrung were their nerves that the eerie cry of an owl almost sent them to their feet; and at the tinny shriek of a distant wild elephant Stuart sprang up and seized the loaded rifle lying before him on the table. In the awesome hush of the dark hours the great forest is never truly silent, and he was used by now to its weird noises; yet this night it seemed full of menace, of threatening sounds and presences, such as he had never before been conscious of.

Suddenly a distinct tapping on the unshuttered window looking on to the verandah startled them. Breathlessly they gazed; and each man gasped as the tapping began again and he saw a white finger pressed against the glass. Stuart picked up his rifle and rushed out on to the verandah. The light from the window showed it untenanted; and utterly mystified he slowly returned and closed the door. Hardly had he sat down when the tapping began again, and the finger was distinctly visible.

Stuart rushed out on to the verandah once more, only to find as before that there was no one there. Rifle in hand he ran round the house, but saw no one. When he reentered the room Simpson was standing at the window, and with a laugh showed him the cause of their alarm. Clinging to the glass a small, white-bellied *gecko*, the little lizard that takes up its abode in Indian bungalows, was seizing in its mouth the moths that attracted by the light inside, were fluttering against the window. To kill them it beat them against the pane, and from a few yards away its white throat looked like a fingertip.

Laughing shamefacedly at their fears, yet with an inward feeling of relief, the two men sat down again. Simpson was lighting his pipe, when suddenly a wild, bloodcurdling shriek with an infinity of agonized misery in it rang through the silent house, seeming to come from Barter's sleeping-apartment. Horror-stricken, they sat paralyzed for an instant. Then the Police Officer seized the lamp, and they rushed to the room.

But it was empty. They searched the bungalow, aided

by Khitab Gul and the servants, who had come running with lanterns. For they had been aroused by the mysterious cry. So appalling had it been that, like the two sahibs, their nerves were unstrung. When the strictest search provided no explanation of the uncanny sound the natives withdrew, visibly terrified, to the butler's quarters, where they huddled together for company during the remainder of the dark hours, telling ghastly tales of *shaitans, bhuts* and other dread visitants from beyond the grave. And the two white men were left alone to their dreary vigil.

The night passed at last. At the first streaks of dawn in the sky Stuart insisted on starting. He and Khitab Gul sat behind Kadir Baksh on his elephant Jumna, while Simpson went ahead with Shaikh Ebrahim on the Forest Officer's. Under the dense canopy of foliage it was still as dark as midnight; but the *mahouts* followed a path through the jungle that led them roughly in the proper direction. When the light grew stronger, Barter's *mahout* went confidently through the dense undergrowth in as straight a line as possible.

Presently he stopped his elephant and held up his hand in warning. Kadir Baksh brought Jumna alongside, and together they pushed out through the screen of bushes into the open.

A simultaneous cry burst from the lips of the five men. For in the center of the clearing on which they had emerged Barter lay motionless. Over him stood a gaunt tiger with lean flanks and grey hide that told of old age. It was looking straight at them, the hideous mask of its cruel face set in a fiendish snarl, the ears flattened to the skull, the whiskers bristling, the tightly drawn lips baring the gleaming fangs, while from the reddened jaws blood dripped freely.

Quick as lightning Stuart threw up his cocked rifle and fired both barrels, but the great grey beast leapt unhurt across the clearing and, before Simpson or Khitab Gul could load, disappeared into the screening undergrowth.

Furious at his bad shooting, the Sapper jerked out the empty cases and thrust fresh cartridges into the breech, urging Kadir Baksh to follow into the jungle.

But a shout from Simpson arrested him. The Police Officer pointed to Barter, and Stuart remembered that his first duty was to his friend. Shaikh Ebrahim brought his elephant to his knees for the D.S.P. to dismount; but the soldier, without waiting for his animal to kneel, dropped impatiently from the pad and, running to the prostrate figure, flung himself down beside it.

It lay on its face. Trembling with fear of what would be disclosed, Stuart gently turned it over. A cry of joy burst from his lips when he saw that the throat was intact, that the dreaded wound was not there. But the face was white and distorted, the eyes fixed in an unmeaning stare.

"Has he fainted?" he asked, looking up anxiously at Simpson, who had a fair surgical knowledge.

The D.S.P. knelt down and thrust his hand inside Barter's shirt. He could not feel the heart beating. He held a polished silver cigarette case to his lips. No breath tarnished it. He raised the lids and gazed into the eyes.

Then he straightened himself and took off his sun-helmet.

"He is dead," he said slowly.

"No, no! He can't be! Look! he has no wound," cried Stuart frantically, tearing open the shirt and baring the chest.

Simpson touched the flesh and gazed into the face again. On it was frozen a look of awful horror, of mortal terror.

"He died of fright, I think. He has been dead some hours," he said simply.

Stuart covered his face with his hands; and a sob burst from his throat. Was there a curse on him, he wondered, that his friends should be taken from him one by one like this?

Then the thought of vengeance filled his brain. With a fierce oath he picked up his rifle and, springing to his feet, was hurrying blindly into the jungle on the tiger's trail, when Simpson and Khitab Gul seized him and held him fast.

"It's useless. The brute is far away by now," said the Police Officer.

Stuart struggled fiercely for a few moments, then collapsed with a groan.

"The accursed beast! Did you see it? Old. Grey. There is truth in the strange tale, then. It was the Ghost Tiger. And I missed it. Fool! Fool that I am! How could I? An easy shot like that!"

"You fired too hurriedly. You were too excited," said

Simpson soothingly.

He knelt down by the body and examined it again. Struck by a sudden thought, he cried:

"I say! Do you remember? The brute's jaws were dripping blood. Yet poor Barter has no wound. Where did the blood come from?"

Stuart's gaze was still fixed on the spot where the tiger had disappeared. He scarcely heard the question.

"Eh? What? I don't know. I suppose it killed something else."

"Yes; but—By the way, where is the corpse of the girl?"

He turned to the three natives, who were standing at a respectful distance. The tears were streaming down Shaikh Ebrahim's face; for he had loved his master. Simpson repeated the question to him. The *mahout* led the way to the tree under which the corpse had lain. It was no longer there. But plainly visible above was the *machan*. Simpson climbed up to it, carefully scrutinizing the boughs as he ascended. On the *charpoy* were Barter's cocked rifle, water-bottle and hat. The Police Officer, unloading the weapon, handed it and the other articles down to Khitab Gul, who had followed him up the tree. Then climbing down he said to Stuart:

"It's very strange. Barter must have got down to the ground unarmed after his men left him. I wondered if by any chance the tiger could have dragged him out of the *ma-chan* by a sudden spring, but there's no sign of a struggle or marks of the brute's claws on the bark of the tree."

The five men separated and searched the clearing. A cry from Kadir Baksh brought the others to where he stood at the fringe of the undergrowth. At his feet lay the dead girl.

Stuart pointed to the terrible throat wound.

"You see? It was the Ghost Tiger. And I had the devil-beast point blank before me—yet I missed!"

Again they moved about the clearing. Then Shaikh Ebrahim called the rest to him and pointed to the earth at his feet.

"Sahib, there is much blood scattered here on the ground. And see! Many people were gathered together here last night."

Even to less trained eyes the traces of this were evident.

"What does it mean?" demanded Stuart eagerly, turning to his companion. "Who could have been here? Were men concerned in this? Is it foul play—these cursed gypsies, perhaps?"

But Simpson asked the *mahout* cautiously:

"Are you sure it was last night?"

The old man laughed contemptuously.

"Am I blind, sahib? Ask Kadir Baksh." He turned to him. "Tell us, brother, are these tracks fresh?"

The other *mahout* nodded.

But the cautious Police Officer shook his head doubtingly. He had not sufficient skill in tracking to be able to confirm or contradict their statement.

"I wish I could tell myself if they're right or wrong," he said in English to Stuart. "The tracks may be old and easily accounted for. Don't you recognize this spot?"

The Sapper looked around.

"No, I don't. I—yes, I do, though. This is where we saw the *yogi* in the trance, isn't it?"

"Yes. It's close to Morton's garden; and the gypsies probably gather here frequently. By the Lord! I wonder if—No, it's not likely."

"What?"

"Nothing. Just a wild idea."

Kadir Baksh had been scrutinizing the ground closely.

"Sahib, what Shaikh Ebrahim said is true talk. Many men there were here—and by night. For they carried torches. See, where the lighted droppings have burned."

The other *mahout* had meanwhile been examining the edges of the clearing and the tracks leading to it.

"Sahib, there were women and children in this gathering," he said.

Kadir Baksh agreed with him; but the white men could not make out anything for themselves.

"This is utterly beyond me, Stuart," said Simpson. "I've puzzled out some strange mysteries in this extraordinary country; but I'm baffled now. I had a wild idea a minute ago. Could Barter have disturbed these damned gypsies in some of their devilish rites? But, then, what killed him? And there's the tiger to account for. I'm beaten. Come, we must bring the poor fellow back. I'd give all I've got to know the secret of his death."

Sadly, tenderly, the white men and black raised the body and fastened it on to the pad of the elephant on which the Forest Officer had ridden so often in life. Simpson joined the others on Jumna. In silence they brought Barter back through the jungle realm to the lonely bungalow, where the Police Officer watched reverently by his corpse.

Stuart, after sending a note by a coolie to Lane telling him the news, and asking that the Chinese carpenter on the garden might make a rough coffin, cantered off on a long ride to the Santal Mission village for the second time in a year, to warn the old clergyman there that on the morrow he must lay another friend in his little burial ground.

CHAPTER VIII

A MODERN GIRL

WEBB shifted uneasily in his chair, and looked for support to his wife seated at the other side of the drawing-room of their bungalow. But he found no encouragement in her anxious face and the appealing eyes that she turned alternately on him and on Margery. He was not fitted to play the stern father; and his daughter's calm and direct gaze made him feel uncomfortable and not a little ridiculous in the part.

But with an effort he looked severely at her, and said

pompously:

"It's all very well for young people to think that they know more than their elders; but I must beg you to remember, Margery, that I am your father."

"Well?"

The uncompromising monosyllable checked the flow of his measured discourse.

"Well? Well? It's easy to say 'Well?'" he said irritably. "You don't seem—I mean that—well, all I've to say is that I think Morton is perfectly justified in feeling hurt."

"Why?"

"Because you're not treating him properly in seeing so much of this young Stuart. And you've been so deceitful about it. You never mentioned a word to me about his being so often at the Lanes'. I'd have known nothing about it if Morton hadn't found it out."

"So he has been spying on me?"

"No, no. But you know how natives will talk; and it got to his ears."

"How is it didn't get to yours when you live so much nearer?"

"I don't listen to natives' talk."

He saw that he was practically condemning his friend's conduct, and went on hurriedly:

"But you've no right to be encouraging Stuart when you have promised to marry Morton."

"I've done nothing of the sort," she said indignantly.

The planter again shuffled nervously.

"Well, I did for you," he said.

"You had no right to do so."

"You seem to forget that I'm your father, Margery," he began, with an assumption of haughtiness. "And as—"

The girl calmly cut him short.

"Don't be absurd, Daddy. I don't do anything of the sort. But we're not living in an age when English parents can promise their children in marriage as natives do. We've got past that, thank goodness."

Her mother broke silence for the first time, and said reproachfully:

"Oh, darling, remember that your father must know better than you."

The girl looked at her with a wealth of love in her eyes, but replied playfully:

"No, mummy dearest, he can't know better than I, whom I do or don't want to marry."

The planter lost his temper.

"Are you or are you not going to marry Morton?" he demanded.

"Certainly not," replied Margery coolly. "I never thought of it for an instant."

"Well, you shall marry him! I insist on your doing so!" he almost shouted.

The girl sat straight up in her chair and regarded him calmly and steadily. Her light, careless manner fell from her and was replaced by an air of cool determination that was not without its effect on the irate man. It was a riddle where she got her strength of character from, considering the natures of her parents.

Now, as her mother looked appealingly from one to the other but did not dare to intervene, Margery said firmly:

"Well, father, we may as well have this out. It has been going on long enough and making us all uncomfortable, I might say miserable as far as I'm concerned. Understand once for all, please, that under no circumstances whatever will I marry Mr. Morton. I never liked him much; though as I've known him since I was a baby I was used to him. But now I hate him. Please let this end. I repeat, I will not marry him."

"You shall, you disobedient girl," cried her angry father. "I will make you."

Margery was not in the least afraid of him. She rose to mark the close of the debate.

"You know you can't, Daddy. As I said, all this sort of thing's out of date. And you're not cut out for the stern parent. I am of age and my own mistress. I don't want to leave Mummy and you; but if this persecution—for that's what it's becoming—doesn't end, I'll go back to England. My old tutor, Miss Newman, has been appointed Head of the new girls' college near Rugby, and asked me in the letter I got from her last mail to join her."

"Oh, Margery, could you leave me?" cried her mother pathetically.

"No, darling, I don't wish to. But don't you see that father wants me to do so by marrying me to a man whom I detest?"

The planter gazed at her in helpless wrath. He was not really an unkind man and would not willingly have made his daughter unhappy. But like many other parents he considered that he was better able to judge what was good for his child than she was. But he realized his powerlessness. In the face of her determination his weaker will wavered; and he said irritably:

"Very well, you must have your own way, I suppose. And I hope it'll please you to know that you're turning your father and mother out to starve in their old age."

The girl, who had gone over and bent down to caress and soothe Mrs. Webb, who was sobbing silently, looked up in astonishment.

"What do you mean? Turning you out to starve? How am I doing that?" she exclaimed.

"What do I mean, my dear?" replied Webb, shrugging his shoulders. "I mean this—the garden's mortgaged to Morton, and he'll foreclose and turn us out if you don't marry him."

The girl gasped and fell on her knees beside her mother.

"It isn't true! It can't be true! Oh, Mummy, tell me it isn't!"

In the presence of her child's anguish the elder woman forgot her own troubles. She folded her daughter to her breast and kissed her tenderly as she said:

"Never mind, my darling. Your life must not be ruined. It was cruel of me to agree for a moment. And perhaps, after all, Mr. Morton won't be so hard."

"Then it's true," cried Margery.

"Oh, it's true enough," said Webb wearily. "I owe him a lot more than I can ever hope to pay him. He's willing to settle it all on you if you marry him. But you must have your own way; and we can go to the workhouse or whatever's its equivalent in India. That's the selfishness of the young nowadays."

But to his surprise his usually docile wife suddenly asserted herself.

"No, James. It is not selfish. The child has a right to her own life, a right to lead it her own way, to choose her own husband. We ought not to ask her to sacrifice herself for us."

The girl had sunk down dejectedly beside her mother's chair. Her first impulse had been to cry out that she yielded, that she would save them by marrying Morton. But instantly her whole being revolted at the thought. She was no mere child ignorant of what matrimony meant, of the physical contact that it involved; and she sickened at the thought of surrendering her body as well as her soul to a man as repulsive to her as the planter was. Her father's accusation of selfishness aroused her.

"Yes, father, I have a right to control my own life," she said firmly, as she rose to her feet. "And you are the last who ought to charge me with selfishness. I am not blind. That you are in debt to Mr. Morton is only your own fault."

"How dare you speak to me like that, Margery?" blustered Webb. "Are you blaming me, your own father?"

"Yes, I am. For you *are* to blame. Since I returned home I couldn't help seeing how you have neglected the garden, which should be as profitable as any in the district. Of course no one has dared to say anything against you to me; but scraps of talk I've chanced to overhear at the Club have told me what others think of you for letting the estate go to rack and ruin. And more. You are to blame for *this*. This sort of thing has swallowed up the money that you borrowed needlessly from Morton."

She pointed to a pile of papers and opened envelopes on the table near her father. They were circulars that the last mail had brought him— prospectuses of companies of goldmines in Peru, or rubber plantations in Siam, of oil-wells in Bolivia, all the wildest schemes that found a ready believer in Webb.

The planter endeavored to look like a just man falsely accused, and said reproachfully:

"I have tried to make provision for your mother if anything happened to me—aye, and for you too, you un-grateful girl."

But he winced as the accusing voice continued:

"You should have done so by devoting yourself to looking after the estate and not by indulging in wild speculation."

Distressed at the dispute between the two beings that she loved best in the world, Mrs. Webb broke in:

"Oh, hush darling. Your father did it all for the best. He wanted to provide for us. He thought only of you and me. Everything's been against him. He has had such bad luck with the garden. The crops have not been good for years, the market low, everything to make it hard for him. He hasn't got lots of money behind him like the big companies that own most of the estates in the Terai."

Margery put her arms round her and kissed her tenderly.

"Yes, mother, I know. I don't want to be hard or undutiful. I'd do anything for you but this. I can't—I won't marry Morton. I'd sooner die."

Then she stood up again and stretched out her hands appealingly to her father.

"Oh, Daddy, dear, why need we quarrel?"

"I don't want to, God knows, Margery," said the harassed man. "I'm sure I don't want you to be unhappy."

It was true; for in his own way Webb loved his daughter.

"But I would be, awfully, if I married Mr. Morton. Can't you find any way to pay him?"

"How can I? I can't raise money anywhere. No; we must go out of Malpotha where I was born, where you were born, too. I must starve in the streets in my old age."

His voice quavered in his intense self-pity. But, torn and tortured as the girl was, she did not falter in the defense of her womanhood.

"I cannot believe that Mr. Morton would dare to do a thing that would be condemned by the whole district, and defy public opinion by taking our garden from us, even if he has the right."

"Can't you? I can. You don't know him," remarked her father bitterly.

"I'll write by the next mail to Miss Newman and accept her offer. She wants me to be her first assistant. I should have a good salary—for she is well off and only teaches for the love of her work—and a little house in the grounds all to myself. So Mummy can live with me, and you too, Daddy, until you find something to do."

Webb laughed bitterly.

"I find anything to do in England at my age?" he cried.

But his wife, charmed by their child's loving thought for them, saw nothing unpractical in the scheme, and drew the girl to her in a fond embrace.

Then the father got up to go to the factory, though he grumbled that it was useless his devoting any more time to it, and left them together. The two women clung to each other lovingly, cried a little and whispered the tender little speeches that come so naturally and meant so much to two as devoted as they were. Margery bore up better and strove to seem less affected, seeking to console and hearten the elder woman.

After a while the girl reminded her mother that she had promised to ride over to breakfast with the Lanes, and went out of the room to change and order her pony. The truth was that she was suffering intensely and in her misery wanted to get away from the house and out into the silent forest to think, wanted to go to her one woman friend in India, sure of her sympathy and understanding. She had not seen Stuart for a couple of weeks, and she longed for news of him and to hear his name spoken, as she would certainly do at the Lanes' bungalow.

The gallop along narrow animal-paths through the jungle and over the soft, unmetalled roads of the gardens blew away some of the misery from her heart and mind. Yet, when she was alone with her friend and confidante in the latter's cozy little boudoir opening off the drawing-room, she broke down and cried bitterly in Hilda Lane's affectionate embrace as she told the story of her troubles. When the voice of some importunate servant drew the mistress of the house impatiently out on to the verandah, the girl laid her head on her arms, resting on the back of a settee and sobbed her heart out.

As the usually mild-tempered Mrs. Lane scolded the tactless servant who had obtruded himself on her attention at such a moment, she chanced to glance out over the garden and started in joyful surprise. For up the broad way between the serried rows of tea-bushes came a white man on an elephant.

It was Stuart. She did not pause to wonder what good fairy had sent him at such a psychological moment, but as Jumna sank on her knees and the Sapper slid to the ground Mrs. Lane took a sudden resolve. Heedless of the hot sun she ran bareheaded down the steps to meet him, and before he could utter a word of greeting, said breathlessly:

"Oh, Mr. Stuart, you mustn't on any account go into my boudoir. Poor Margery is there, crying her eyes out."

"Margery? Crying? Why?"

"I oughtn't to tell you, I suppose. But I know you're her friend. Her father owes heaps and heaps of money to Mr. Morton, who has a morgage on his garden and is going to turn the Webbs out to starve unless Margery marries him."

The lover's eyes blazed with anger.

"What? Margery marry that brute?" he cried.

His Highland impetuosity swept him away. Without a word of apology to Mrs. Lane he sprang up the steps of the verandah and, rushing through the drawing-room, burst like a whirlwind into the boudoir.

How it happened neither could ever explain afterwards. But in a minute Margery was crying on his shoulder instead of the back of the settee, while he kissed her wet face and swore that she should never marry anyone but him. The modern girl is after all not very different from her great-grandmother.

And Mrs. Lane sat contentedly smiling to herself in her bedroom, and did not send repeated messages to her forgetful husband at the factory that breakfast awaited him, as was her usual habit.

But even lovers have moments of reflection. And presently Margery remembered that her being engaged to marry Alan Stuart—as she realized with a start that she now was—would not preclude Morton from foreclosing. And her homeless parents could hardly come to live with her on a Royal Engineer subaltern's pay. But the soldier laughed her fears away and bade her be of good cheer, for he promised that all would come right in the end. And Margery, under the soothing and narcotic influence of Love, felt her troubles fall from her and was content.

But her father was not when, on her return to their bungalow, she told her parents the surprising news of her engagement with as many blushes and as much hesitation as any Victorian girl. The planter had not the same sublime faith in Stuart's power to sweep away their troubles and mend their broken fortunes. He shrank from facing Morton's anger when their creditor should hear of the death of his hopes. Webb had no illusions as to the half-caste's being prevented from ruining them by fear of the opinion of their little community. So he hailed with relief the news of his neighbour's sudden departure on urgent business to Calcutta, as it postponed the awkward moment of explanation.

He could not refuse to receive Stuart into his house; but he frankly told him that he did not approve of the engagement, although he could not prevent it. The usually proud and rather touchy Highlander—Alan had the faults as well as the virtues of his race—was not affronted, and only smiled at his future father-in-law's plain speaking. Margery, who had feared that he would take offence, was relieved and astonished at his behavior and at the gay and light-hearted manner that replaced his usual grave reserve. He seemed to be constantly enjoying a subtle joke all to himself.

A week later she began to understand better when he came again to their bungalow on his elephant. This time he was accompanied by a much older European, whose deeply lined face bore a strong resemblance to her lover's. Alan presented him to her as his uncle. The old man looked long and searchingly at her before his hard features softened suddenly, and he said with an accent as strong as if he had only left his native land a month before:

"Alan boy, you've gude taste."

And he kissed the embarrassed girl on the forehead.

Margery was astonished at the respectful warmth of her father's greeting to him. For she had not seen the letter from her lover asking for an interview in which he would be accompanied by his uncle, and stating who that uncle was. The name "Angus Stuart of Stuart, Mackie and Forsyth, Calcutta", would have conveyed nothing to her. But it spoke volumes to her parent, for it belonged to one of the merchant princes of the commercial capital of India; and the firm with its branches in Bombay, Rangoon, Singapore, Hong Kong and Sydney, was a leading one in Greater Britain.

So Webb's reply had been a warm invitation to both Stuarts to come and stay at his bungalow. And Margery was astonished at his jovial spirits at dinner that night after a private talk with the uncle. He cracked jokes and bubbled over with mirth in a genial mood that his wife and daughter had long forgotten him capable of.

The girl had taken an instant liking to Angus Stuart. She was already prejudiced in his favor, for Alan had often told her of his uncle's goodness to him and how he had been a second father to him ever since his own was killed in action, when the boy was not five years old. Angus had been the eldest of three brothers, the second of whom, Malcolm, was also alive and a general on the active list in England. The youngest, Alan's father, had been the first to die; the others had lavished on his son the love that they had felt for the dead Ian since they were boys together.

The old man had asked Margery to show him round the estate in the cool of the afternoon and explain to him the mysteries of a tea-garden. During their ramble he did not speak much, but he seemed extremely kind and sympathetic; and the girl's heart went out to him when the few words that he said about Alan betrayed the old man's deep love for his boy, as he called him. She had no idea that his quiet, simple manner hid one of the keenest intellects in the business world of the Empire, and that all the time that he listened interestedly to her explanations in the garden and the factory he was summing her up shrewdly.

But that his judgment of her was wholly favorable was evident on their return to his nephew, who knew the old man by heart; and he did not need, to tell him that his choice had been approved, the friendly pressure of his uncle's hand on his shoulder and his whisper:

"Alan boy, I like your lassie."

The Stuarts only stayed two days, as the elder could not spare more time from his business and Alan had to return to the quarry, where he now had some hundreds of coolies at work piling up stone in readiness for the coming of the railway, which was expected to take place before long. But when they departed they left behind them a changed man in their host. For Webb was happy in the knowledge that the burden of debt was to be lifted from his shoulders. The rich merchant had promised to place to his credit in his bank in Calcutta a sum that would pay off Morton and save the estate. Yet in deference to the wishes of the cautious old Scot, who was strongly opposed to hasty unions, there was no question of the marriage taking place for some time.

News travels slowly among the scattered community on the tea-gardens of the Terai; and when the planters next gathered at the club in the jungle the Lanes and

Murray were the only ones who were aware of the engagement. But when it was announced, Margery and Alan were puzzled at observing that no one appeared at all surprised at the intelligence.

None ever knew what Morton thought or said when the news was conveyed to him in a letter from Webb— who lacked the courage to face him—together with a communication from the latter's solicitors regarding the paying off the mortgages. For he henceforward avoided the weekly gatherings at the club and did not again visit the Webbs' bungalow, which was the only one in the distal to which he had ever been welcomed. But he was rumoured to be indulging in wild orgies and fearful debaucheries among the gypsies on his estate; and his cruel treatment of the coolies working on his garden drove them to desert in scores.

CHAPTER IX

BEASTS OF PREY

To be divided between Love and Duty is a trial that falls to the lot of many men; and Alan Stuart had to experience it now. Long and weary were the miles between the rocky amphitheatre in the hills where he had made his quarry and Malpotha, where his betrothed lived. But Love found a way to shorten them. As his elephant was a slow means

of transport he supplemented his two ponies by a third
procured from Calcutta, and with them established a
system of relays—laid a *dak*, it is called in India—between
Murray's bungalow, which he still shared, and the
Webbs', stationing one pony with its *syce* midway in a
bamboo and grass-thatched stable behind the club.

By this means he was able to go quickly to Malpotha
whenever he could get away from his work; and the ferryman by the clubhouse learned to look for the young sahib
who used to dash up to the riverbank on his pony, hustle
the old man until he was landed on the other side, and
then gallop off on a fresh animal as if all the *shaitans* in
Hindustan were at his heels.

It was a Celtic poet who sang:

> "There's nothing half so sweet in life
> As Love's Young Dream."

And Alan, with all the romance that dwells in the
Highland glens and hills filling his soul, found it true.
Margery in love was an even more delightful companion
than the calm, heart-whole Margery that he had first
known. Her nature seemed changed, softened, her self-
reliance transformed into a delightfully flattering depen-
dence on her lover; and her air of practical common sense
had given place to a romantic tenderness that Alan at
least thought became her better.

They made an ideal couple; and Hilda Lane used to
watch them with a sense of proprietorship, as one who
knew that the match was all of her making. And Mrs.

Webb, who had always secretly regretted that she was not the mother of a son, felt that she had gained one now in the young man whose heart went out in affection to her who was ready to replace the mother that he had lost so young, dead of a broken heart six months after her adored husband's death.

Stuart was delighted to find that Margery, among other tastes that they had in common, shared his passionate love of the jungle. Although so much of her life had been passed surrounded by the great forest, yet it was almost a sealed book to her. For only on a trained elephant could one venture into it off the main road or the tracks along the broad fire-lines; and no one in the district, except an occasional Government official like the Forest Officer or the Settlement Officer, possessed such an animal. On foot movement through it was impossible save along the few paths made by wild beasts, owing to the density of the undergrowth and the tangled network of creepers between the trees. And one entered it afoot in peril of his life, for, to say nothing of other animals, wild elephants abounded in that part of the Terai. More dangerous even than the largest herd were the solitary rogues that wandered alone, always ready to attack a human being unprovoked.

But, when Stuart brought Jumna, Margery never feared to go with him on fascinating expeditions into the enchanted recesses of the forest. To her it was a joy beyond words to sit behind her lover on their great steed's broad back and be borne without effort under the high green canopy stretched above the fluted columns of the huge *sirnal* trees and the tall pillars of *sal* and teak festooned with the graceful curves of the creepers swinging from bole to bole.

The elephant surged through the sea of dense vegetation, shouldering it off as a stout ship throws off the clambering waves from her glistening sides. The wind that swept down from the mountains passed over the tree-tops, but never penetrated below them; and the fronds of the high bracken and the white bells of flowering bushes were never stirred by it. The solemn hush of the forest was broken only by the sudden crowing of a jungle-cock or the measured beat of the wings of a hornbill flying overhead.

Margery had never known the excitement that fills the sportsman when some great quarry falls to his rifle. But, in spite of her natural womanly pity, she felt the thrill of it now when sometimes a tall sambhur stag crashed to the ground with Stuart's bullet through its heart, or a graceful spotted deer, racing across an open glade in light timber, checked suddenly, pitched forward among the ferns and lay still.

The estate of Malpotha ran up to the lower slopes of the foothills of the Himalayas, where the big trees gave place to smaller growths, and higher up only the tall, feathery plumes of the bamboos or an occasional sago-palm rose above the undergrowth of densely-matted bushes. Then the rounded foothills gave way to jagged peaks and rocky precipices draped with the waving white veils of waterfalls. Here was the haunt of the herds of *gooral*, the pretty little wild mountain-goats. And here, too, prowled in search of them the sleek, sly panthers.

Anxious to shoot a *gooral*, Alan Stuart set out on foot one morning with Margery across the garden in the direction of the hills. When they reached the northern boundary of the estate, his companion guided him towards a wooded spur jutting out from the wall of mountains and thrusting down the forest below. Margery followed a steep and narrow path which led up and across it.

"This is a short cut between Malpotha and Mr. Morton's garden," she told him. "Natives passing from one estate to the other often use it, as it saves at least two miles on the way round by the road. We must be careful, though; for it is also a favourite route for wild elephants climbing up or down the mountains to or from Bhutan, the frontier line of which is up there six thousand feet above our heads."

There was another reason for proceeding with caution along the path; for in places it ran dangerously near the brink of rocky precipices two or three hundred feet deep. Stuart, nervously anxious for Margery, was relieved when she turned sharp off it up an almost invisible track that led straight up the face of the mountains.

"I don't know where this will bring us," she said," but it seems to go in the right direction. And apparently a native has just passed up it. Look!"

She pointed to the fresh print of a naked foot in a dusty patch. It was curiously short and broad; but unfortunately Stuart did not glance at it.

The track was old and failed them in places, being completely overgrown; and they had frequently to move off to one side or another to find a way through the bushes. It was a stiff climb, made harder by the thorny plants that caught their garments and held them back. Stuart was further hampered by his rifle and the necessity of guarding against a twig catching the trigger; for he was afraid to uncock it in such a place. He fell some distance behind his guide and was trying to overtake her when he was securely hooked by a thorny bush. He was impatiently endeavoring to free himself when he was startled by an agonized cry for help from Margery, who was out of sight ahead.

Bursting free from the clinging grip of the thorns he scrambled wildly up the steep slope, and his heart seemed to stop when he saw her rushing down towards him. For close behind her shambled the huge, hairy bulk of a monster Himalayan bear with vicious eyes and open, slavering red mouth. At the very moment that Alan caught sight of her the girl stumbled and half fell into a thorny bush. And the ferocious brute rose on its hind-legs and, towering over her, raised its great paw for the deadly downward, skull-smashing blow. Leaping past Margery, Alan sprang in between her and the bear and, thrusting the muzzle of his rifle against the animal's breast, fired both barrels into it. As the brute staggered back he dragged the girl aside, and the dying animal collapsed and fell heavily on the very spot where she had crouched.

Alan hastily reloaded. But there was no need; the bear never moved again. Then Stuart turned to Margery who, pale and trembling at her narrow escape from death, yet managed to smile feebly and thank him in a shaky voice. But when his eager arms went round her and she saw the concern in his eyes she gave way and cried a little, lying exhausted in his clasp for a few minutes. Then, summoning up her courage, she tried to free herself and apologized for her weakness.

But her lover was even more shaken than she. The danger to her had unnerved him; and it seemed to him that he had never really known how dear she was to him until the awful moment when he had so nearly lost her. He pressed her to his heart and kissed her passionately.

Margery, the less highly-strung of the two, was the first to recover. She struggled from his arms and wanted to approach the bear to examine it, where it lay huddled up among the bushes. But Stuart shuddered at the mere thought of her going near it, and held her back lest there should be life still in the motionless beast. And, afraid of exposing her to any fresh danger in the jungle—for it was probable that the dead bear had a mate close by—he insisted on their returning at once to the bungalow under the pretext of sending men to skin the animal.

As they reached the path over the spur again he examined the footprint to which she had called his attention on their way up; and he cursed himself silently for not having looked at it then. For he saw that it had been made by the bear, although the marks left by such an animal are sufficiently like the print of a man's bare foot to excuse Margery's mistake.

It was agreed that nothing should be said of the

danger that the girl had escaped, as the knowledge of it would have distressed her mother; and with an air of unconcern they answered her greeting from the verandah as they drew near the bungalow and merely told her that Stuart had shot a bear. Her husband called out to Alan from his room:

"A coolie has just come with a wire for you from the telegraph office on Keighley's garden, which is ten miles away. It arrived there last evening; but of course the post-master could get no one to bring it here in the dark."

The Sapper tore it open and found it to be from his head-clerk at the quarry, informing him that an urgent appeal for help had come from the encampment of coolies working on their branch railway extension through the forest; for a rogue elephant had attacked it twice and killed several men. The work was at a standstill. Stuart was wanted to kill the brute.

Usually the prospect of encountering such a splendid quarry would have roused him to enthusiasm; but, after so nearly losing her altogether, he found it hard indeed to part so soon from Margery. But it had to be done. There was nothing for it but to return at once to Baghpota, get his elephant and go to their aid.

He would have ordered his pony and started imme-diately, had not Mrs. Webb with motherly care insisted on his breakfasting first and putting a cold lunch into his haversack. As he meant to travel fast and wanted to be unencumbered he left his rifle at the bungalow. Then, his farewells said, he swung himself into the saddle and set off on his long ride. He cantered across the garden and turned to wave a last goodbye to Margery and her mother on the verandah before he disappeared from their sight through the wall of trees. Instead of going by the cart-track through the estate to the main road he aimed for a narrow path that led to the latter through the jungle, and would save him a couple of miles. It wound tortuously through the undergrowth, and he had to slacken his pace along it. Lost in thoughts of the girl that he was leaving behind he let the reins lie on the neck of his pony, the Waler that he had got from Calcutta. The animal, not yet used to the forest, trotted slowly along the track, nervously starting at every flutter of a leaf or rustle in the undergrowth.

But in a reverie Stuart paid no heed to it and let it go its own pace. He roused himself sufficiently to take out his case, extract a cigarette and, dropping the reins altogether, strike a match. But at that very moment when he was least prepared for it the pony shied so violently that he was flung to the ground, and struck so heavily against the huge trunk of a *sal* tree that he lay half-stunned at its foot.

To his horror, a few yards further on the head and shoulders of a tiger were visible, thrust out of the under-growth, and the fierce face, set in a savage snarl, stared straight at him. The pony swung round and bolted; while Alan, unable to move, watched the beast emerge stealth-ily from the screen of vegetation and, clear of the bushes, crouch for the fatal spring. And the man's blood froze in his veins as, unarmed and helpless, he recognized the gaunt frame and grey hide of the grim brute that he had

seen standing over Barter's dead body. Was it the Ghost
Tiger in truth?

He made a desperate effort to rise, in the wild hope
of climbing the tree above him or arming himself with a
branch torn off somewhere to do battle for his fife with
the frail weapon. But to his horror he found that the
shock of the fall seemed to have paralyzed him; and the
awful fear shot through him that he had broken his spine.
Helpless he lay and gazed fascinated at the devilish beast
that, belly to earth, crawled stealthily towards him. The
cruel eyes in the barred mask of the face set in that
terrifying scowl that deprives a victim of volition mesmerized him as slowly, imperceptibly, the Striped Death
drew nearer and nearer.

He felt no fear, only a vague wonder if the end would
be painful. In a few seconds it would be all over, his
corpse, the throat torn out, the lifeblood drained away,
would be lying motionless in the jungle that he had loved
so well. The thought of Margery came to him; and his
eyes grew misty, not for his own fate, but for her sorrow
when she knew him dead. He grieved for his uncle, too.
How hard a blow it would be for the old man who loved
him so! But for himself he felt no pity. If only the end
would come swiftly!

As if in answer to the wish the powerful limbs were
drawn up under the lean body, the muscles quivered beneath the striped grey hide, the tail flickered, as the beast
gathered itself for the final, the fatal rush. Then with a
coughing roar it sprang. Over the prostrate man it
seemed to tower, the sharp talons curving out of the great

paws, the white fangs glistening in the red mouth. And Stuart, fascinated, undaunted, looked up steadily.

A miracle happened. At the instant that the claws were about to rend him, the slavering jaws close on his throat for the neck-breaking twist, the tiger checked— checked in mid-air, it seemed, and leapt back with a dismayed roar. Snarling savagely the great cat retreated slowly, reluctantly, with a strange appearance of fear, uttered a loud howl and, turning suddenly, sprang into the undergrowth. And Stuart, stupefied, heard the bushes give way to the passage of the heavy body until the sounds died away in the distance.

Amazed he lay and looked about for what had saved him. What had scared the tiger? Was it some beast more terrible still? Was it a man? But he could see nothing. And it had seemed to him that to the last the brute's eyes had been fixed on him only.

In bewilderment he strove again to rise and found to his joy that, bruised, sore and shaken though he was, he was not crippled; and after a painful effort he dragged himself to his feet. Unnerved as he had been when Margery's life was in danger he was not unstrung by his own past peril; and he thought coolly of what was best to do. There seemed but one course to pursue—go back to the Webbs' bungalow to which the terrified pony had probably returned, reclaim it and set his friends' fears at rest.

But he had not hobbled a hundred yards along the path before to his relief he found the animal mad with fright, striving to free itself from the tangled thorny undergrowth in which the trailing reins and one stirrup-leather were caught and held fast. Stuart soothed and released it, then, climbing painfully into the saddle, turned its head away from Malpotha and resumed his journey. Before he reached the river the stiffness had worn off and, although still sore, he kept steadily on his way until by evening he reached Murray's bungalow.

There he told his astounded friend the tale of his almost incredible escape, while Khitab Gul massaged his aching limbs.

"Then you think that it was a real tiger?" asked his host, when he had finished.

"Yes, I'm satisfied that there's nothing supernatural about the brute. It's a genuine flesh and blood animal. I'll never stir out again without a rifle."

"And you've no idea what scared it."

"Not the least. That's the only mysterious thing about it. But it must be the beast they call the Ghost Tiger. I'll swear it was the animal I saw by poor Barter. Well, when I've bagged this rogue or had a good try to, I'll go after the other brute again and never rest until I've got it."

At daybreak Stuart started off on Jumna with Kadir Baksh and Khitab Gul, and was glad to be able to stretch out his bruised body on the broad pad instead of having to sit in a saddle again. The sun was still shining, though near its setting, when they reached the head of the railway extension.

It was marked by the broad swathe through the forest, where the axe had felled the giant trees to make a way for the straight track of brown earth on which the shining rails lay, by the piles of sleepers and construction material lying about, and by the mushroom village of bamboo huts thatched with grass. No one was at work. The hundreds of coolies were gathered despondent and afraid in the encampment, huddling in crowds together for company in affliction.

Someone saw Jumna approaching and shrieked an alarm. Panic ensued. Men, women and children bolted from the camp, screaming frantically. Some tried to climb the trees, others flung themselves into the undergrowth to hide, many, insane with fear, running aimlessly about.

Even when eventually the more sensible recognized that the advancing elephant was not a wild one and bore the white man who was coming to their aid, it was a long time before all the coolies could be persuaded that there was no danger and brought back to the encampment. Then Stuart addressed them and, promising that he would protect them, bade them return to work. With the implicit confidence of the uneducated Indians in the sahib the men cheerfully seized their mattocks and, flocking on to the line, began to labour at once, while the women and children followed with rush baskets to carry the earth away.

The Sapper did not blame them when he heard the full tale of the havoc wrought by the rogue. The audacity of such outlaws of the elephant race is always astounding—they will hold up the traffic on roads through the jungle, attack bullock-carts in the hope of finding them loaded with grain, feed calmly in the cultivation around villages, and fiercely resent the peasants' attempts to drive them off. They will even enter a sportsman's camp at night and trample down his tents. They will attack human beings unprovoked and mete out to them a horrible death.

But the daring of this particular animal exceeded all that Stuart had ever heard; and the recital of its misdeeds roused the Highlander to anger and a stern resolve to put an end to its murderous career. A dozen coolies rapidly erected near the camp a small grass hut for him, into which Khitab Gul put his guns, folding-bed and bath, his store of tinned food, and the other things for his use or comfort, that Jumna had carried as well as her three passengers. The orderly had already established himself and his few belongings, as well as his master's cooking-pots, with Kadir Baksh under a shady tree near the one to which their elephant's hind-legs were shackled. A friendship had sprung up between the *mahout* and the young Pathan, whose swaggering conceit always amused his old co-religionist.

When night fell, Stuart sat smoking in his camp-chair outside his grass hut watching the two Mahommedans squatting by their fire, the white-bearded Kadir Baksh listening with a cynical smile to Khitab Gul's boastful lies about his father's wealth and influence in the wild No-Man's Land beyond the North-West Frontier. The coolies, down-country dwellers all, had gathered after their work to gaze in awe from a distance at Jumna, the only elephant that most of them had ever seen except the terrible beast that had so frightened them.

Next morning the Highlander began his quest for the rogue. Seated with his orderly on Jumna's pad while the *mahout* bestrode her neck, he wandered while daylight lasted about the jungle for miles around the encampment. They tried to follow the traces that the animal had left on its last raid; but these were speedily lost in the myriad tracks of other wild elephants in the forest, and the hunters returned at nightfall unsuccessful. Day after day passed fruitlessly; although once they found a sign of the brute's presence in the corpse of a woodcutter killed by it. The poor wretch's body and skull were trodden to a bloody pulp, and the legs torn from the trunk and thrown twenty yards away.

The sight filled Stuart with horror, and redoubled his determination to slay the murderer. Every day from dawn to dusk he searched the jungle. The pursuit of the rogue became an obsession with him. Waking his thoughts were of it, sleeping it inspired his dreams. He almost forgot at times the girl thinking always of him miles away through the forest.

But Margery was not the only one in whose mind he had a place. Morton, looking ten years older than he did before the failure of his plot to gain her, his haggard face lined deep with the traces of his excesses, sat in his room one day, regarding gloomily its other occupants who squatted on their heels on the floor before him. They were five, all gypsies—three women and two men. One of the latter was a typical Romany; but the second was grey-eyed and lighter complexioned than the rest and had a harelip, an unusual deformity among natives. A close

observer would have noticed that in the face he re-
sembled the planter, which was not surprising, as he was
Morton's illegitimate son by a discarded mistress. This
woman was present, prematurely aged like most Indian
lower class females after twenty-five. She sat beside the
planter's mother, and looked with ill-concealed hate at
the third woman present, a young and handsome girl,
who was the reigning favourite of the hour.

The gypsies sat mute, waiting for their protector to
break the sullen silence into which he had fallen.

At last he spoke:

"He has not come back?" he asked.

"No, my son, he is still following this *budmash* elephant. Perhaps it may save us the trouble."

The young girl laughed derisively.

"Must you ask its help?" she said to Morton. "He has
crossed your path and yet he lives."

"But not for long, girl," snarled the old woman. "That
I foretell."

Morton scowled, but ignored his mistress.

"One prophecy of yours has come true, mother," he
said. "You warned me to beware of money, that it would
vanquish me. You were right. It has."

"But whence came the rupees to pay the debt to my
son?" asked the old crone.

"I know not. But it could only have been from one
man. This soldier. Sometimes these Army sahibs are
wealthy. Yet this cursed Stuart cannot be well-to-do,
otherwise he would not be here."

"I do not see why you should bear him a grudge,"

pettishly exclaimed the youngest woman. "You should be grateful to him if through him you got back your money."

"There is the girl," said one of the men.

She turned angrily on him.

"What of her? Why all this trouble about one girl just because her skin is a trifle fairer than ours? Am I not enough for him?" she cried jealously.

"The white man to the white woman, Daughter of a Noseless Mother," said the cast-off mistress, to spite her young supplanter and please Morton, who even with the gypsies in the wildest debauches in which he shared always insisted on his white race.

The younger woman retorted fiercely, but was silenced by the old hag, of whom all the tribe stood in awe.

"Peace! Peace, ye shameless ones both!" she shrilled angrily. "Our Sahib is judge of his desires."

"My father, I have a plan. The Master of All has inspired me," said the harelipped man. "This old one who has freed himself from your debt is still poor, is he not?"

Morton nodded.

"And the sepoy sahib is not likely to have money to help him again, is it not so?"

The other gypsies nodded their heads in agreement.

"Well, what of it?" asked Morton sulkily.

"Let us cause the girl's father to need money once more, and he may be forced to borrow from you again."

"Yes, but how?" demanded his male parent impatiently. "This is a good season. Even his garden will bear a fine crop. O that the Master would blight it!"

"My father, He will—through me," said his son with a

hideous grin. "I will burn down the factory and the go-downs."

An appreciative murmur came from the other gypsies. It was the sort of scheme that would appeal to them.

But Morton shook his head apprehensively.

"I would be suspected at once," he said.

"Nay, my father, I plan better than that," said his son, with a callous laugh. He motioned towards the other male gypsy. "Motu and I will gather a score of masterless Bhuttias from across the border and lead them to raid Malpotha. Those outlaws in Bhutan look ever longingly at the tea-gardens, for they know of the many boxes of good silver coins that you planter-sahibs bring to pay the coolies. And they lick their lips when they think of the looting there would be in your villages, where these Hindu dogs keep their rupees hidden until the day comes when their contracts end and they can return to their homes."

"Well, if these Bhutanese robbers despoil his coolies, how will that ruin my enemy?" asked Morton contemptuously.

"While the Bhuttias are looting, Motu and I will put a torch to the buildings; and they will get the blame for it. Aye! and we'll carry off the girl for you if you will."

"No, no, that would be dangerous," said the planter hastily. "But there is much in your plan."

He thought deeply for a while.

"Yes, it is good talk!" he cried at last. "You have planned well, Hari. With the factory, engine-house and godowns burnt, Webb is ruined unless I aid him again. Good! I'll have the girl yet. "

CHAPTER X

THE RAIDERS

AS DAWN whitened the sky above the white peaks of the Himalayas, thrusting up above the clouds to catch the first rays of the sun, a group of men lay asleep under a giant teak-tree in the forest near the mountains. Close to them a lightly-shackled elephant fed on the creepers within reach of its trunk, tearing them down noisily and cramming them into its mouth. Perched on a branch high above it a red-plumaged jungle cock crowed; and its shrill *reveillé* was repeated through the jungle by defiant rivals, warning the drowsy monkeys in the treetops and the watchful animals on the ground that day had come. But the men slept on.

For nearly a fortnight Alan Stuart and his two followers had ranged the forest from sunrise to dusk in pursuit of the rogue elephant, suffering hunger, thirst and privation in the relentless chase. Wherever night overtook them they flung themselves exhausted on the earth, almost too weary to prepare the scanty food procured at some rare forest village, if the fire to cook it had not been necessary in the dark hours to scare off dangerous beasts of prey. They would often have gone hungrier if Kadir Baksh's wood-lore had not supplemented their fare by snaring jungle fowl and digging up wild tubers that could be eaten only by starving men. Since below the foothills the river-beds were dry, their only drink was mostly the water secreted in the fortunately very frequent creeper with furrowed, cork-like bark, the *pani-bêl*, that is Nature's kindly provision for the thirsty in the forest.

Only once in their wanderings had they encountered the animal they sought. They had come upon it suddenly one morning. It charged them on sight; but, driven back by bullets from Stuart's and his orderly's rifles which wounded, without disabling it, it turned and bolted. Never again had they come up with it. For several days they had lost its tracks. Their endurance was almost exhausted. Even the white man, strung up to desperate resolve, felt that he was near the end of his tether; and, when they camped on the previous evening, he had, out of pity for his tired companions, agreed that, if they did not find their quarry the next day, he would abandon the search for it.

Now, while they slept, a party of men passed not a mile away along a jungle path leading from the mountains. They numbered over a score of stocky, sturdy individuals, yellow-skinned and with Mongolian features, bareheaded, barelegged and each clad in a single woollen garment, similar in shape to a Japanese kimono, kilted up at the waist. From the girdle that confined it, hung a straight short sword, called a dab.

They moved at a steady jog-trot that took them quickly over the ground and seemed a distressing pace for the two men of obviously different race who toiled wearily behind them. They were gypsies, although one was tall and slight with grey eyes and a harelip. This was Hari, and his companion was Motu. They were bringing the band of outlaws from across the Bhutan border in the mountains to raid Malpotha and throw Webb again into the clutches of their patron.

No inward monitor warned the Highlander as the ruffians went by that there was danger threatening his betrothed. He and his companions slept unsuspecting.

But the raiders in their passage through the jungle disturbed a solitary tusker-elephant which, as it stood drowsily shifting its weight from foot to foot, occasionally scraped up a pile of dust and blew it with its trunk on fly-blown wounds on its head and body.

It was the rogue. Nervous now and easily alarmed, it roused itself at the faint sounds of the Bhuttias passing and turned its head towards the mountains. After extending its trunk and scenting in all directions, it moved off wearily in the direction of the hills and plodded stiffly through the jungle with the hatred of human beings that had long rankled in its small brain increasing with every throb of pain in its aching wounds. And suddenly it saw before it three of the detested creatures lying motionless and unguarded on the ground. They were Stuart and his companions.

The murderous brute's eyes gleamed viciously as it looked at the unconscious men. It saw but paid no heed to the unsuspecting Jumna feeding close by, and with soundless feet and all the cunning of its kind it drew silently nearer and nearer its prey. But the tired men slept on.

Suddenly Jumna scented the danger, looked round and, seeing the tusker, tore herself free from her shackles and bolted in alarm. The crashing in the jungle as she dashed away roused the sleepers. They awoke swiftly, as do men inured to perils, and to their horror saw the rogue not thirty yards from them. It had checked in its advance, and stood for a moment hesitating as it looked after Jumna.

But only for a moment. Its savage gaze came back to the men; and trumpeting shrilly it curled its trunk between its tusks and with ears and tail cocked rushed at Stuart, who was nearest. He was lying on his back with his feet towards the animal.

The other men scrambled up, Khitab Gul looking wildly about for his weapon, which he had carelessly laid down out of reach. But Stuart had not time to rise. In the aft of awaking his hand had closed instinctively on the rifle by his side. He seized it and, still lying on his back with his left hand against the butt-plate near his chin, rested the barrels on his bent knees and fired into the onrushing brute's open mouth. It was the best shot that he could have made in his position, the only one that had a chance of reaching the brain from where he lay.

The mammoth checked in its headlong charge, slid with stiffened legs for a few yards, its toes ploughing up the soil, stumbled and then fell heavily to the ground with an earth-shaking thud almost on its slayer. Stuart barely managed to scramble out of the way in time and, springing up, levelled his rifle at the prostrate animal. The rogue lay still. But the Sapper knew that elephants struck down by head-shots were often only stunned and, if not properly finished off where they fell, recovered and got up again. So he carefully approached the motionless beast and fired his second barrel deliberately into its heart. It was needless. Not a tremor shook the great body; the first bullet had pierced its brain.

Kadir Baksh had disappeared, but the Pathan, as soon as he had got his rifle, ran up to his officer's assistance. But he had not had time to fire. When he realized that the quarry that they had pursued so long and seemingly so hopelessly lay vanquished and dead before them, he shouted in wild excitement, rushed to Stuart, saluted, shook hands with the equally delighted Highlander, and saluted and shook hands over and over again. Then he abused the elephant's female forebears for many generations with all the vivid eloquence of the East. This did not give sufficient vent to his feelings; so, approaching the huge carcass cautiously, he kicked it violently.

A sudden crashing in the undergrowth behind him made him start and swing round with rifle ready to meet any fresh danger. But it was only caused by Jumna being brought back very reluctantly by her *mahout*, whose first thought when he awoke had been of her. He could hardly believe his eyes when he saw the rogue lying without movement on the ground; and he called out to his com-

panions to be on their guard against a sudden return to consciousness.

But when he learned that there was no doubt of its being dead, his joy was almost greater than theirs that the chase was ended; for he was an old man, and the fatigue and want of rest had told more heavily on him. He drove Jumna forward to smell and touch the vanquished enemy; but for a long time she was afraid to approach it.

The hunters examined their prize with interest. The tusks were measured, and proved to be each over five feet in length. As to extract them it would be necessary to remove the flesh along the nasal bones up to the eyes and split the tusk-cases with an axe, Kadir Baksh suggested going at once to the nearest village or tea-garden to obtain implements and assistance. He climbed a huge tree as adroitly as a monkey to try to locate their position. To Stuart's surprise, he called out from the topmost branch that they were not far from Malpotha.

Alan could hardly believe that the fortnight's jig-zagging pursuit in which they must have covered a couple of hundred miles had led them back near the spot from which he had started out. Delighted at the happy chance he bade the *mahout*, when he climbed down, take them at once to the tea-garden. Leaving the dead animal they mounted Jumna and set off; and as she bore the tired but happy trio through the jungle they recalled the incidents of the arduous chase and went over every detail in turn. So absorbed were they that the distance to Malpotha seemed very short; and Stuart was quite surprised when in what seemed only a matter of minutes, he found himself on the path on which he had been attacked by the mysterious tiger. As he was pointing out where the encounter had taken place, they turned a corner and came suddenly on four or five Hindu coolies who, on seeing the elephant, rushed in alarm into the jungle, apparently failing to realize that she was not a wild one. Stuart cried out to them that there was nothing to fear; and first one, then another, peered out cautiously and eventually crept nervously on to the path again.

When they saw a white man on Jumna's back they stretched out their arms and cried:

"Sahib! Sahib! Help! Save us from the dacoits, the murderous robbers!"

It was a little time before a coherent story could be extracted from the panic-stricken men; but eventually Stuart learned to his horror that a band of armed Bhuttias had just appeared on Webb's garden, invaded the village and were torturing the inhabitants to make them surrender their money. Their leaders were two gypsies—at this Stuart started, and wondered at once if Morton were connected with the outrage. As the old *bunniah* had refused to reveal where he had hidden his rupees, one of these men had shot him as a warning to the other villagers.

These few coolies had escaped into the jungle and were fleeing blindly when they had met the elephant and her riders. They could not say whether the raiders had attacked the Webbs' bungalow or not.

Mad with anxiety the impatient Highlander did not wait to hear the end of their story, but bade Kadir Baksh push on, and left the lamenting Hindus behind. The distance to the garden now seemed interminable; and he raged at Jumna's slowness, although the *mahout* was urging her to her fastest pace. Every yard of the way seemed a mile; and over and over again Alan thought of slipping off the pad and rushing forward on foot. But he realized that after all the elephant would prove the faster eventually.

At last daylight through the trees ahead showed that they were nearing the garden. When they reached its confines Stuart bade the *mahout* halt and remain with Jumna in cover. He and Khitab Gul slipped down from the pad and loaded their rifles.

From the screening trees they could see across the tea-bushes the ugly wooden factory buildings with corrugated iron roofs. From one a thin column of smoke was ascending into the still air. But the bungalow was hidden by the engine-house and withering-sheds. The village was visible, but too far away to permit of their seeing what was happening in it; but the keen-sighted Pathan detected that two or three figures outside it were Bhuttias.

A broad belt of cleared ground divided the forest from the trim rows of tea-plants; and across it Stuart and the orderly crept until they reached the cover of the bushes. Through these they moved as quickly as possible, sometimes bending down, sometimes on their hands and knees, until they could see the bungalow, which was only a few hundred yards away. To Stuart's dismay a group of raiders stood in front of it, while others were visible on the verandah.

At the sight he flung caution to the wind and, rising to his feet, dashed furiously forward through the impeding bushes, followed closely by his orderly. They were seen at once. The group outside the house broke up and, shouting a warning to their comrades inside, drew their *dahs*. There were eight of them, and four more ran out of the house and joined them. Waving their swords they advanced against the two audacious intruders.

The soldiers stopped and, raising their rifles, fired together. A Bhuttia, struck in the chest by Stuart's heavy bullet, pitched forward on his face and lay still, while another dropped his *dah* and clapped a hand to his right shoulder.

"An outer, sahib—only two points," said Khitab Gul, with grim humour, as though counting the value of a shot on the rifle-range.

He fired again. A third Bhuttia staggered forward a pace or two and then fell dead.

"A bull's eye this time, sahib," commented the Pathan, smiling.

A fourth raider dropped to the officer's rifle; and the remaining outlaws, waving their *dahs* above their heads, charged with wild yells, leaping into the air as they came. But a fifth and sixth stumbled and fell to the ground; and the survivors, losing heart, turned and fled towards the village, from which a number of other Bhuttias issued at the sound of firing.

From behind the factory buildings, close to which the two soldiers were standing, a couple of men ran out to ascertain the meaning of the shooting. One held a smoking torch in his hand. Stuart saw them and, guessing them to be the gypsies of whom the fleeing coolies had spoken, and suspecting them to be the instruments of Morton's revenge, determined to capture them alive if possible. He hurriedly said so to Khitab Gul and both ran towards them. The gypsies, turning, fled and were lost to sight behind the factory buildings, two of which Alan saw to be afire as he followed the fugitives. When he and his companion got clear of the sheds they saw the gypsies trying to hide in the tea-bushes, for they were afraid of the rifles of their pursuers.

But as the soldiers drew near them they rose and ran. They leapt and stumbled wildly over the furrows and through the impeding bushes, the stems and trimmed twigs of which hurt their bare feet, while the booted men behind them did not suffer. Then, finding their enemies closing on them, the gypsies turned in desperation to fight for their lives like cornered rats.

Motu, armed with a long knife, rushed fiercely on the Pathan who, clubbing his rifle, swung it aloft and brought the butt down with awful force on the gypsy's head. The skull cracked like an egg under the blow; and Motu dropped in a heap.

Hari, facing round, fired two or three shots from a revolver at Stuart when the latter was several yards away. Alan's rifle was unloaded; but he hurled it at his opponent, and the heavy weapon struck the gypsy across the face, and staggered him for a moment. But, before he could recover, his antagonist had closed with him and seized him by the throat. To and fro they struggled fiercely; and Hari, fighting like a wildcat, bit and scratched and tore at the white man's eyes.

Alan released the grip of his right hand and, drawing his arm back, struck his opponent on the point of the jaw with such force that the gypsy collapsed and sank half-stunned to the ground, just as Khitab Gul, having disposed of Motu, ran up to Stuart's help. Between them they tied Hari up securely with his own girdle, for he was dressed like a hillman and wore one. Then they examined Motu and found him to be dead, with his skull fractured.

Alan picked up his rifle; and, running to the factory, they climbed to the upper story of a withering-shed, a wooden building open on all sides where the freshly-gathered leaves are exposed in long trays to dry naturally. Lying on the floor hidden from sight by a ledge that ran round the room where the outer wall should have been, they looked over the garden and saw the rest of the Bhuttias, numbering nearly twenty, streaming towards the factory with drawn swords. When they were less than three hundred yards away the concealed soldiers opened fire on them. Two men fell. The raiders stopped and looked everywhere for the invisible marksmen. A third man was wounded in the leg, a fourth shot through the stomach.

The Bhuttias broke into a run. Two more of their number fell, one dead, the other badly hurt. The survivors halted and flung themselves on the ground among the tea-bushes. But they still could be seen by their hidden enemies, and the pitiless bullets sought them out. Three more were stricken; and the Bhuttias' courage failed them at last. Those who were able to move sprang up and fled towards the forest. A few parting shots quickened their retreat; and another of their number was hit. When they had disappeared in the trees Stuart, bidding his companion return to where the prisoner lay and guard him, rushed downstairs and raced towards the bungalow, consumed with anxiety as to the fate of its occupants.

CHAPTER XI

THE PRISONER

AS he approached the house, to his intense relief Margery and her parents appeared on the verandah. The girl ran down the steps to meet him, and flung herself into her lover's eager arms. "Thank God you are safe, sweetheart!" cried the Highlander, pressing her to his heart and covering her face with kisses.

"Oh, Alan, it was awful to see those men attacking you and not to be able to help you," she said. "If only we'd a gun or a revolver in the house I'd have taken it and come out to your aid."

Her mother and father joined them. Mrs. Webb was crying quietly with joy at the unexpected rescue; and Stuart, taking the overwrought woman in his arms, kissed her and soothed her as a loving son would have done. Webb shook him by the hand and overwhelmed him with thanks, then suddenly remembered the burning buildings.

He ran to the servants' quarters behind the bungalow, where the terrified domestics were still hiding, and with difficulty got them out and led them to save the factory. From the village the coolies were beginning to emerge cautiously; and, seeing that the raiders had disappeared, they came across the garden to help.

Fortunately only two storehouses, both empty, were alight. On one of these the flames had got too strong a hold to be extinguished; but the other was saved and the fire prevented from spreading. Morton's hopes were again doomed to disappointment. The incendiaries had been interrupted only just in time. In another ten minutes the engine-house and other important buildings would have been ablaze.

When the fire had been got under control and his help no longer needed, Alan joined Margery and her mother, who had been watching the operations. From them he learned that the Bhuttias had made no attempt to loot the bungalow or molest its occupants, contenting themselves with holding them prisoners.

As soon as the fire was extinguished Stuart took Webb aside and mentioned his suspicions about Morton being the instigator of the raid; but the planter ridiculed the idea, even when he was told that two gypsies were the leaders of it.

Presently Khitab Gul came through the buildings

with the pinioned prisoner on his shoulders and dumped him down before the white men. Webb stared fixedly at Hari, but said nothing. But, as the coolies gathered round to gaze at the captive, several of them exclaimed:

"Sahib, sahib! That is the man who killed the *bunniah*. That is Ramchand's murderer!"

And an old coolie said:

"Sahib, I have seen that man—I know him by the twisted mouth. He is one of the gypsies on Morton Sahib's garden. He is—"

He faltered and stopped, terrified by Hari's ferocious glance. Stuart was surprised that the planter did not question either the coolies or the prisoner. He himself asked the gypsy who he was, and how he came to be associated with the Bhuttias in the raid; but Hari maintained an obstinate silence. Khitab Gul volunteered cheerfully to make him speak by the application of some effective Eastern torture, and was plainly disappointed when Stuart refused his offer and intimated that he wanted the prisoner kept alive and in good condition. The Sapper sent for cords and lashed the gypsy up scientifically until he was absolutely helpless. Then, leaving him in charge of the servants, he bade the orderly follow him and asked Webb to come with him to inspect the fallen Bhuttias.

Most of them lay where they had dropped, for the timid coolies feared to approach them; but two who could hobble were found to be making their way painfully to the forest. Khitab Gul rounded them up and disarmed the other wounded, who glared savagely at their captors, but quailed before the still fiercer glance of the tall Pathan

standing over them with ready rifle, while Stuart examined their wounds and did what he could to stop the
bleeding. Webb, who had some knowledge of the Bhutanese language, questioned them, and succeeded in eliciting
from one that they had been persuaded by two gypsies to
attack the garden and loot the village.

Giving orders to some low-caste men to bury the
dead and transport the wounded to a storehouse where
they were to be locked up and guarded, Webb and Stuart
turned back to the bungalow, Khitab Gul being left to
superintend operations.

As soon as they got beyond earshot the planter
stopped and said:

"You were right and I was wrong. This is Morton's
doing. The gypsy you captured is his illegitimate son. I've
seen him several times when I've been at his father's
bungalow."

"Is it possible?" exclaimed Alan.

"Oh yes. There's no mistaking that harelip. Now I
understand why he tried to set fire to the factory. His object was to ruin me. The looting of the village was only the
inducement to the Bhuttias."

"Can't we bring it home to Morton?" asked the
Sapper.

The planter shook his head.

"I'm afraid not. My kind neighbor has covered his
tracks, you may be sure. The gypsy will never split."

"What do you propose doing?"

"I'll send off a coolie to the telegraph-office on
Keighley's place with a wire to the police, informing them

of the raid and asking them to come for the prisoners. But they can't be here for a couple, of days at least. How the deuce am I going to guard all these men?"

"If you keep the Bhuttias securely tied and locked up they'll be safe enough. No one's likely to try to rescue them. I shall leave my orderly to guard your bungalow and look after them. He's equal to a dozen Bhuttias. But the gypsy's the trouble."

"Yes; his friends will be sure to come for him. Morton will send all his scoundrelly tribe to get

Stuart thought for a moment. Then he said:

"I'll take him back with me. He'll be safe enough at Baghpota until Simpson comes for him. I must return to-day."

Margery was very disappointed when she learned that her lover was to leave her so soon. The danger that he had encountered before her eyes and the perils that he had risked in his pursuit of the rogue affrighted her; and she clung to him and begged him to stay with her a little longer. Courageous as she was, she trembled for his safety, and still pleaded with him even when he pointed out that he must return to his work after so long an absence and, furthermore, that it was advisable to remove the prisoner out of reach of his tribe.

"I wish I could stay, dearest," he said. "But these brutes wouldn't hesitate to attack your bungalow to rescue him."

"I wish you could, Alan, I wish you could," she said fervently.

"You don't know how hard it is for me to leave you

behind, my darling," he said, with tender solicitude. "I can't stand this anxiety about you. I'm not going to wait much longer for you, Margery darling. When I get back I'll write to Uncle Angus to tell him so and say that we must be married soon."

She looked at him with love-filled eyes.

"Oh, Alan, I hope he'll agree! I want to be always near you. Do you think that I'm not just as anxious about you; with more reason, too, for you are always running into danger? I can't bear to let you out of my sight. I wish they'd give you another post that would take you to some big station or to England, where you'd be safe."

She paused for a moment, and then said sadly:

"But you'll never be safe; for you're a soldier. I used not to be a coward. I am now, I think, I sometimes wish you weren't in the Army; for I feel I'd die if you were ordered on active service. Oh, Alan! Alan! I couldn't bear to lose you out of my life now."

She broke down and sobbed bitterly. They were alone in the drawing-room, and her lover took her tenderly in his arms and tried to console her.

But later, when he climbed up on Jumna's back and sat with his prisoner securely roped to the pad in front of him, the girl bore up bravely and waved him a cheerful farewell before her parents and the salaaming servants. Khitab Gul stood near at the salute, proud of the trust that his sahib had placed in him when he bade his faithful follower guard with his life his future bride.

The elephant lumbered away at its usual lounging gait, followed by a party of men who were piloted by

Kadir Baksh to where the dead rogue lay, their task being
to secure the tusks and bring them back to Malpotha.
Then he turned Jumna's head towards her goal.

When the trees hid her lover from her sight Margery,
who until then had stood with her parents on the
verandah waving cheerfully to him whenever he looked
back, went quietly to her room and there in solitude
broke down utterly before his portrait. Never before had
she realized fully how very dear he was to her, how blank
life without him would be. Never before had the misery of
parting seemed so unendurable. But she had just been
through an agony worse than death when she had
watched him battling to save her. She felt that she could
not bear him out of her sight. She knew of his suspicions
as to the author of the raid; and she dreaded for him the
vengeance of the half-caste and the murderous instincts
of the gypsy tribe. Affection had sapped the strength of
mind, the common sense, on which she had prided
herself; now she was only a timorous, loving woman. She
threw herself on her knees and prayed with all the fervor
of her soul that Alan might be spared to her.

With no fears for himself, but many for her, he was
being borne further and further away from her. Although
his thoughts were busy with the girl he loved, he kept a
watchful eye on the menacing jungle that hid so many
dangers. He held his cocked rifle across his knees ready to
meet an attempt to rescue the prisoner, who lay on the
pad before him, with eyes fixed on him in a look of such
unutterable hate that it sent chills down Stuart's spine.
All through the long journey the gypsy never spoke, but

watched him with the unwinking stare of a cobra.

As dusk fell they reached Baghpota and Murray's bungalow. The elder Scot, warned of the approaching elephant, came out on the verandah and stared in astonishment as his servants and the *mahout* lifted down from the pad the roped figure of a man bound hand and foot.

"What on earth's this, Stuart?" he cried. "I heard you'd gone after an elephant rogue—it looks as if you'd found a human one."

Stuart laughed grimly.

"I have. Where can I put him in security?"

He shook hands with his friend, who had come down from the verandah to inspect by the light of a lantern the helpless prisoner, and told him briefly of the raid.

Murray thought for a moment.

"My office is the safest place. We'll chain him to the safe," he said.

He bade the servants follow him with the prisoner, and led the way to a small chamber opening off the sitting-room. Besides a desk and a couple of chairs it held only an iron safe with short legs embedded in the concrete floor. The planter sent for a padlock and a long steel chain which he wound several times round the gypsy's arms and legs, and then passed about one of the legs of the safe and padlocked it.

"There! He's pretty secure now," he exclaimed. "It would take his pals some time to file through that chain and, until they do, they can't carry him off unless they take the safe and the floor with him."

He ordered his servants to bring some boards from

the factory and nail them across the one window of the room.

"Now, no one can get at him from outside unless they come through the roof," he remarked, surveying the preparations with pride. "But that devil and his pals will certainly try to reach him. They could easily pull those tiles off and get in. You and I must mount guard over him by turns at night. Simpson won't get here at the earliest for two days. Now, have your bath and come to dinner in half an hour."

After the meal Stuart stretched himself gratefully in a long-chair and told in detail the story of his pursuit of the rogue and of the providential chance that led him to Malpotha in the nick of time. Murray punctuated the tale with expressions of wonder, and overwhelmed his sleepy friend with questions until, taking pity on him, he sent the tired man to bed and took the first watch. He established himself with a loaded revolver in a comfortable chair beside the bookcase in the sitting-room, leaving open the door into the office in which a lamp was burning, so that he could see the prisoner clearly. From time to time he lifted his eyes from the book that he was reading to glance at the gypsy, who never moved.

At one o'clock in the morning he was relieved by Stuart, who sat down in the same chair hardly awake, and with a brain still fogged by the confused dreams of battling elephants and men that had haunted his short slumbers. He took down a favourite volume from the bookshelf. It was Kipling's fascinating *Kim*, but his thoughts strayed from it to Margery, and the danger to her and hers that his timely arrival had averted. This brought Morton to his mind, and he wondered what the villainous half-caste would do when he learned that his plans had again miscarried.

He glanced at the prisoner and noticed that the eyes of the prostrate figure on the floor were fixed on him in a penetrating stare that gradually irritated, disquieted him. Alan began to think of him, his race, his origin, the queer existence that he must have led, the cold-blooded crime that would probably cost him his life.

Then Stuart's musings took a strange turn. He began to wonder what the gypsy would do if he were to set him free. Would he attack his captor in vengeful mood or would he be grateful? Would he return to his tribe or disappear from the district in fear of the police? And suddenly the Sapper awoke to the consciousness of almost a desire to set the murderer at liberty. He could scarcely believe that he wished to do so unwise a thing. But gradually the feeling became stronger. It seemed as though someone was whispering to him to fetch the key of the padlock from Murray's dressing-table and release the gypsy. The impression grew so distinct that he actually turned his head to see if anyone were near him. But he was alone, and the impulse began to be over-powering.

To shake it off he rose from his chair and paced the room, angry with himself for his unaccountable foolish-ness. But it seemed to possess him utterly. He felt as if a hand were pushing him towards Murray's bedroom. An almost uncontrollable desire impelled him to fetch the key; and he had actually reached the door when he turned back and glanced at the prisoner. The snake-like eyes were fixed on him in a Steady, concentrated Stare and impelled him again towards the door. He tried to Struggle, but Strength seemed to have left him. Angrily he fought with the impulse—but unavailingly.

Suddenly the thought came to him that he was being mesmerized; and in a rage he forced himself back to his chair again. He made a superhuman effort to regain control of His will. He tried to think of other things, of Margery, of His work, of the thrilling encounters with the rogue elephant—but always his mind came back to the key on Murray's table, the padlock and the prisoner. Some irresistible power drew him towards the door, and he rose from the chair again.

As he did so the book that he had tried to read fell to the floor. He glanced down at the volume and his thoughts flew to its wonderful hero, Kim, and how the country-bred boy struggled against the Simla pearl-healer's mesmeric influence, and saved himself by concentrating his mind on so prosaic a tiling as the multiplication-table. And Stuart sought salvation in a problem of Euclid.

"The line A B is equal to the line D E and the line D C is equal to the line E F; and the angle A B C—" he repeated, forcing his mental vision to see only the image of two-lettered triangles chalked on a blackboard.

The effort seemed to demand all the energies of his soul and his body. The sweat broke out on his forehead. But gradually he conquered. The insane desire weakened, died. He was himself again. And he saw the prisoner's glittering eyes hitherto fixed on him in a burning stare grow dim, the strained face relax, and the head turn wearily away.

In daylight the experience seemed absurd; and Stuart was almost ashamed to mention it to Murray. He did so, however.

The older man nodded his head.

"I am not surprised at it," he said. "I've heard extraordinary tales of mesmerism among the natives. This morning I learned that this man we've got is a sort of priest among gypsies, an acolyte and disciple of their *yogi*. And these *yogis* are not all impostors. Some of them learn in their temples the secrets that the Brahmins have handed down for thousands of years, secrets of the mastery of natural forces of which we Westerns know nothing, at which only a few of our scientists guess vaguely."

"Do you believe in them?"

"I neither believe nor disbelieve. Have you read *Occult Science in India**, by Louis Jacolliot? No? He was the Chief Justice of the French colony of Chandernagore near Calcutta and investigated Spiritism among the Brahmins. He saw strange things done by *yogis*, things that set the law of gravity at naught—a huge bronze vase filled with water, one as big as a bath and so heavy that two men could not move it when empty, rocked wildly on its base and lifted from the ground when no one was near it, weighty stone flower-vases moved through the air, fea-

*See the special appendix to this book

thers fly up to the ceiling of a room where no breeze stirred and stick there, a *yogi* raise himself off the floor and remain suspended several feet above it—"

"Trickery or mesmerism? All rather senseless things, too—the sort that our spiritualists at Home aim at," said Stuart, striving to crush down his tendency to credit the occult.

Murray shrugged his shoulders.

"Perhaps. But I'd like to see them."

That night Alan kept the first watch. Towards morning he was sleeping soundly in his bed when he was awakened by Murray's voice calling him urgently:

"Stuart! Stuart! Come quick, for God's sake!" it cried.

He sprang out of bed and rushed to the sitting-room. Murray stood with outstretched hand pointing a shaking finger to something in the office.

"Look! Look! Am I mad?" he cried.

CHAPTER XII

THE LIVING DEAD

STUART flared amazed.

The massive steel safe was rocking violently from side to side as though moved by invisible hands, its legs being gradually loosened from the cracking cement. The chain had slipped to the bottom of the one around which it was fastened and lay on the ground, so that it could be pulled out if the leg were lifted free of the floor. And the prisoner, lying on his side, was watching it eagerly.

"Good Heavens! This is witchcraft!" cried the Highlander.

"Do you see it? Have I gone mad? Is the safe really moving?" cried Murray.

"Yes; unless I'm crazy, too."

As they looked on in stupefaction the heavy safe tilted to one side as if about to topple over, two legs drew out of the cement, the chain was freed, and the prisoner, rolling away, pulled it clear. The safe settled back and stood without motion. And then the cords that bound the gypsy fell asunder, as if severed by a sharp blade. Only the chain still fettered the captive as he strove to struggle to his feet.

Murray sprang forward to seize him, but recoiled as though repelled by an unseen hand.

He struggled to advance; but an invisible wall seemed to bar the way.

Not understanding, Stuart gazed at him in bewilderment. It looked as if his friend had gone mad, and was hurling his body forward and backward in delirium.

"What's the matter with me? Am I paralyzed?" gasped the planter.

"What is it? What are you doing?" cried Stuart.

"I don't know. I can't move forward. Something pushes me back," replied Murray, ceasing his useless efforts. "What's that noise? Listen."

"It sounds like a file," said his friend.

"There's some invisible devil present," cried Murray. "The chain! The chain! Look at it!"

The steel links that fettered the gypsy's legs fell away, one being cut through; and the man rose to his feet. The heavy boards nailed across the inside of the window fell to the floor with a crash. The casement was open.

The gypsy turned towards it. Murray tried again to rush upon and seize him. But he could not move.

"He will escape!" he cried.

Stuart tore the pistol from his hand and sprang forward. It seemed to him as if a thick hedge was interposed for an instant between him and the prisoner. It gave way before him and he reached the harelipped man, who turned savagely upon him and tried to free his still manacled hands.

The Highlander gripped his shoulder, pressed the muzzle of the revolver to his chest, and cried in Urdu as though to an unseen auditor:

"If he moves he dies!"

Through the room resounded a loud moan that seemed to voice an agony of disappointment. It did not come from any of the three men. The prisoner collapsed and sank unconscious to the floor.

And miles away the *yogi* of the gypsies awoke from a trance, and said to the watching group about him in Morton's bungalow:

"I have failed. Some stronger Spirit has prevailed."

Throughout the remainder of the night Stuart sat pistol in hand over the prisoner lying motionless on the cemented floor. Murray, the viewless barrier removed, found no longer any difficulty in entering the office; but his companion insisted on keeping guard until sunrise. And one or other watched the captive, who lay as if dead, until at noon a motor-car came up the soft road through the estate, and from it two English Police Officers and three native constables armed with rifles descended before the bungalow.

It was Simpson with his junior and some of his men. The rest, who had started two days before in bullock-carts, were still some distance away.

When the D.S.P. heard Stuart's story he ordered his subordinate to leave at once in the automobile with the gypsy and the three constables and not to stop until the prisoner was safely lodged in a jail a hundred miles away. The younger man had been inclined to smile at the recital of the past two nights' happenings until his superior, showing himself visibly impressed, bade him keep, like Stuart, his pistol always pointed to the captive's heart until their destination was reached. Then he began to think that there might be something in the surprising tale after all; for he had the greatest respect for his senior's intelligence.

When eventually the remainder of the police arrived at Baghpota, Simpson gave the bullocks a rest, let the men cook and eat their food, then, borrowing a pony from Murray, took them on again. They reached Malpotha the next day. There had been no fresh happening. The Deputy Superintendent's enquiries revealed nothing new. He did not find anything that incriminated any other gypsies, much less Morton himself. So, placing the wounded Bhuttias in the carts, he started back with his party, Khitab Gul accompanying him as far as Baghpota.

In due course the prisoners, charged with the murder and dacoity, were tried by the Sessions Judge at Sanapur Duar, a small town lying just outside the southern boundary of the Terai Forest. It held only two Europeans, the Sub-Divisional Officer of the district and his wife; but it boasted a jail, a sub-treasury in charge of a Brahmin official, and a courthouse. The Bhuttias, unused in their country to anything like justice and astonished that their lives had been spared, made no defense and were sentenced to transportation for life to the Andaman Islands in the Bay of Bengal, India's convict settlement, which had recently been reopened.

But Hari was defended by the ablest native pleader that money could bring from Calcutta. The lawyer made a great fight for his life, and earned his fee well. But the evidence was overwhelming; and the murderer was sentenced to death.

When he heard his fate he only smiled at his mother and the few gypsies present at the trial. He had no fear that he would be left to die on the gallows.

Morton, though he was careful not to appear interested, in secret spared no effort or money to save him. An appeal was lodged; and the High Court of Calcutta ordered the case to be retried before it. Hari was removed to the jail in Alipore, a suburb of Calcutta.

Then peace settled again on the little community of planters in their isolation; and life with them went on seemingly as tranquilly as before the upheaval. But Margery was consumed with fear on Alan's account, convinced that Morton and his accomplices would revenge themselves on him for the failure of the raid and the disastrous results to its two gypsy leaders. There is an element of maternal anxiety in every woman's love; and she craves to mother and take care of her man, certain in her heart that, no matter how wise, strong and fearless he may appear to others, he is never quite capable of looking after himself, and needs her guardianship. Even though days passed with no appearance of danger to Stuart the girl's fears were not lulled.

He seemed to have no apprehension of the danger to himself, but was as anxious for her safety as she was for his. He worked on her mother's fears until she persuaded her husband to have iron bars fixed on every window of their house and the outer doors, usually never closed in an Indian bungalow, strengthened and provided with good locks and bolts. Stuart, on his frequent visits, insisted on superintending the work himself.

"Dearest, it is very good of you to be so concerned about me," said Margery to him one day, while they were watching the estate blacksmith at the task. "But I wish you would take as much care of yourself, Alan. You are in far greater danger."

"Not I, darling," he answered, smiling. "No one has any wish to carry me off."

"No; but they want revenge. And, what's more, they'd like to prevent you from giving your evidence against Hari at his retrial. Don't you realize that Morton and his gang would stop at nothing to get you out of the way now?"

"Oh, I don't doubt that they would. But Khitab Gul and I are a match for twenty of these cowardly gypsies."

"Yes, Alan, I know all that," she said impatiently. "Of course you are in fair fight. But they wouldn't fight you fairly. They'll try to murder you somehow. Oh, I wish you could leave the district. Couldn't you get your Colonel to recall you to the regiment, and send someone else to take on your job here?"

"Not likely, sweetheart. Run away like a cur and leave you here? No, I'll stay until I can take my wife with me when I go. Think of it, darling! Doesn't it sound well? My wife!"

But the words failed to thrill her as they usually did; for she was too overcome with fear for him.

She was right in dreading the undying animosity of his enemies. Morton's hatred of him had reached a pitch of sheer madness, yet it scarcely equaled that felt for the

Scot by Muda, Hari's mother. She was like a tigress robbed of her cub. All the love of which she was capable was given to the man who now, thanks to Stuart, lay in the shadow of the gallows. The old woman, Morton's mother, was consumed by a savage hatred of the one who stood in the way of her son's desires. Only Ula, the youngest of these three women, had no reason for enmity to him, indeed had cause rather to be on his side, since he loved and strove to hold the girl who was wanted to oust her from her position. But she was careful not to let the truth be suspended, and pretended to hate the white man as bitterly as did the others.

One day the forest clearing where Barter found death was crowded with gypsies and the coolies of Morton's garden, ringing round an open space in the center, in which a small, domed shrine had been roughly built of sundried bricks. Before its low door, bolted and padlocked on the outside, the half-caste planter was seated in a chair. On the ground beside him squatted three women and a man, his mother, his cast-off mistress and her supplanter, and the *yogi's* disciple, whose body, naked but for a loincloth, and face were plastered with ashes. Near him lay the begging-bowl and tongs, the mark of the mendicant priest all over India.

The other gypsies and the coolies were drawn back to a respectful distance from the group, and out of hearing of the animated, but low-toned, discussion between its members. Their attention was given to the closed shrine, on which the gaze of all was fixed, except when eyes were turned towards the sky as if to judge the time by the position of the sun, which was nearly overhead. The two elements of the crowd kept apart, and their attitude was very different. While the coolies, men, women and children, chatted, laughed and appeared to have gathered for entertainment, the gypsies were silent or spoke only in low tones, and seemed absorbed in anxious expectation of some momentous happening.

The group around Morton looked at him as he drew out his watch.

"It is not yet time," he said. Turning to the ash-smeared *chela*, he added, "Have you no fear whatever for the Holy One?"

The disciple laughed scornfully.

"For him? None. What is a week's interment to one who has lain in the grave for a hundred years and lived? It was but to convince those of ye of little faith that he has suffered us to entomb him now."

Morton protested hastily.

"No; no. I never doubted his power to be buried and come to life again. Has he not promised me that at his intercession the Master of All will make me, too, immortal? Yet I cannot help being nervous, afraid of the least mishap. For without him, who would plead with the Master for me?"

"Let your mind be at rest! The Holy One will return to us as he has promised when the sun is highest on this, the seventh day of his burial. He is with the Master. He will come back filled with the spirit of prophecy, foretelling the Future."

"You know well, Ragu, that soon Hari will be tried

for his life again," interposed the old woman, "and if the Master aid him not he will be hanged."

"Aye, my boy must die if that accursed white man testify against him," hissed Muda savagely. "Why should he be allowed to live to do it? I ask for the hundredth time, why do you not bid our men slay him?"

"I told you why, woman, and tell you again for the hundredth time—and the last," answered Morton sternly. "It would be all the worse for our son if this brutal soldier were murdered before the trial, for it would be plain that he was killed to prevent him giving evidence. That would prejudice the judges against Hari."

"But you have money. Can you not bribe them?" asked Ula.

"Do not be foolish, girl," replied the half-caste. "These English judges are not to be bribed. If Stuart could die by accident—or what seemed an accident— But how can that be done? He is well guarded. That devilish Pathan, whom all our men fear, watches over him day and night."

"If the men are afraid of this accursed hillman, one woman, at least, is not," said Muda fiercely.

"He is as deadly a witness against my child as the other. Let me kill him. I shall find a way."

"If you were younger and better looking it would be easy; but not as you are now," sneered the old crone. "Your beauty would not lure him into danger, fond as he is of women. If the husbands and fathers among Murray Sahib's coolies were men, instead of sheep, he would have died long ago. They say that no wife or maid in the village on that garden is safe from him."

The *yogi's* disciple joined in:

"Yes, a woman might trap him." He looked significantly at Ula. "There is one of you handsome enough to tempt him—"

Morton broke in on him jealously.

"Ula is not the one for the task. We must—"

He was interrupted by a loud murmur from the crowd that swelled to a shout. He looked round. All eyes among the gypsies and coolies were turned to the sky. He pulled out his watch and glanced at it.

"They're right. It is noon!" he cried.

He turned to the throng. All had risen to their feet and were pressing forward. He beckoned to a gang of men holding picks, crowbars and mattocks.

"Bring your tools!" he called out.

They ran forward. Pointing to the shrine he ordered curtly:

"Pull it down!"

They rushed to the little building and began to demolish it with vigorous blows, while scores of coolie women behind them removed the rubble in shallow baskets. They worked so well that in a very short time all trace of the shrine had disappeared, and a brick flooring lay exposed to view. The chela waved everyone back; and using a small crowbar he carefully loosened a couple of the bricks and lifted them out with his hands. Then he directed the removal of the rest, one by one, until the flooring had vanished and a small vault was laid bare to the sky.

Morton and the women moved forward eagerly to look down, and were almost pushed into it by the pressure of the surging crowd behind them, all as equally anxious to see what it contained.

On the pounded earth floor of the small chamber lay an apparent corpse, the emaciated, almost naked body of a man, the nose and mouth tightly bound up in cotton bandages. It was the *yogi*. In this hermetically sealed vault he had lain for seven days, buried alive by his own command to prove to doubters his power over life and death, the power given by Him whom he worshipped—no god of Hinduism, but the very Spirit of Evil, the Master of Ill.

He lay now before the eyes of all to every appearance a corpse; and Morton, staring down at him in despair, felt an icy hand grip his heart as he saw the one who had promised him that he would never die, that his half-caste, disciple would be as immortal as himself, now wearing the very semblance of death.

The *chela* dropped down into the vault, which was about six feet deep, and with ease lifted the wafted body. It lay rigid on his upraised hands as he held it up to Morton who, assisted by two gypsies, reverently drew it out of the vault and laid it gently on a sheet spread on the ground by his mother. Then he turned in an agony of despair to the disciple, whom eager hands had pulled up to the surface again.

"Surely he is dead!" he groaned.

The *chela* paid no attention to him, but angrily drove back the crowd with curses and threats. As soon as all save Morton and his three women had withdrawn a dozen paces, he threw himself on the seeming corpse, his face against his master's. Forcing open the stiff mouth he breathed into it several times, then made passes over the forehead, muttering incantations and verses from the Vedas.

After a while he rose to his feet and drew back a pace from the motionless body. All eyes were fixed on the emaciated face of the apparently lifeless *yogi*. It was the face of a corpse.

The deathlike silence was broken only by Morton's despairing groans. The half-caste saw his promised immortality vanishing.

Suddenly the ghastly features of the priest quivered. Then from the opened mouth a sepulchral voice issued, a voice terrifying in its non-human tones.

"Thou shalt not die as a man!" it said.

CHAPTER XIII

THE WOMAN WITH TWISTED FEET

MORTON staggered back in amazement. Then in a revulsion of joy he flung his arms up, and shouted aloud in glee.

"I shall not die! I shall never die!" he shrieked.

The *chela* seized him roughly and silenced him by

placing a hand over his mouth.

Once more the hollow voice spoke:

"Against one I cannot prevail."

"Who? Who? Is it the white man?" whispered Ula eagerly.

The *chela* angrily signed to her to be silent.

For the third time came the ghostly voice:

"One a dead woman shall destroy!" it said.

An awful silence ensued. Then a tremor ran through the *yogi's* wasted frame. Slowly he drew breath. His eyes opened gradually.

Women screamed.

"He lives! He lives!" shrieked voices in the crowd.

The *chela* flung himself on his knees beside his master and began to massage the body vigorously. Slowly, stiffly, like an automaton, the *yogi* sat up and stared straight before him with glassy eyes. The disciple rose and, bending down, raised him to his feet.

Then all the terrified onlookers threw themselves on their faces, Morton first of all. But very soon first one lifted his head to look, then another, then all. Slowly they rose to their feet; and cries of wonder, of worship, burst from their lips when they saw the *yogi* standing unassisted, his arms crossed over his bony chest. Then like an automatic figure he moved away feebly, jerkily at first, but gathering strength with every step. Preceding his disciple with bent head the priest passed from among them and vanished in the forest.

No one dared follow him.

Through the widely-scattered coolie villages on the

various tea-gardens separated by miles of dense forest the news of the miracle spread like wildfire. It was discussed, debated, exaggerated throughout the Duars, the vast district of the Terai lying below the mountain passes into Bhutan.

As Alan entered the sitting-room of Murray's bungalow on his return from the quarry in the afternoon, two days after the event, he found his friend drinking a cup of tea.

"Hallo, laddie, back again? What'll you drink?" asked his host. "Beer, whiskey and soda or tea?"

The Sapper dropped with relief into a comfortable easy-chair.

"Tea, please," he replied. "I'm tired."

The planter shouted for his butler and gave the order.

"Have you heard the yarn about the latest stunt of Morton's tame holy man?" he went on.

"Who? The *yogi* that Simpson and I saw?" asked the soldier.

"Yes. The story has come through to our coolies from Morton's. It is said that the old scarecrow swami let himself be buried for a week, and was dug up alive and well at the end of it."

"Really? Do you believe it?" asked Stuart, interested.

The cautious Scot replied slowly:

"I don't know if I do or I don't. I'm never sure how much truth there is in any tales about these *yogis*. Who's to say there's nothing in Eastern magic? You and I saw things happen here the night that we held the gypsy murderer a prisoner—things that few folk would believe if we told them."

"You're right. That young policeman with Simpson thought us crazy when we described what had occurred. Europeans will not credit stories of the magic powers of Brahmin priests and Buddhist lamas. Yet these men have inherited the knowledge of their predecessors who studied occult science for thousands of years in temples and monasteries. But Englishwomen pay their guineas to any swindling fortuneteller in Bond Street, or half-crowns to another in Edgware Road—and believe their nonsense. Today ignorant Oriental and savage races regard wireless and flying as our magic—and not long ago we ourselves would have laughed at the possibility of them."

The planter nodded agreement. "I've heard before now of fakirs being buried for days and being alive when dug up. It's said they bind up their mouths, plug up their nostrils and put themselves in a cataleptic state—such as you saw Morton's yogi in—in which they can exist without breathing. Maybe it's all a fake, yet—Well, perhaps we don't know everything in Europe, though we think we do."

"I'd like to hear more about this miracle of the *yogi*. I'll swear there was no fraud about his state when Simpson and I saw him. I can't help thinking that there must be knowledge stored up in these old Indian temples and in the Tibetan convents that would astonish us moderns if it were revealed to us."

"I don't doubt you're right, laddie," said the planter. He lit a cheroot and went out on to the verandah. "Hullo!

there goes your orderly, Khitab Gul, with Kadir Baksh to the coolie village. Off to court some of the women there, I suppose. He's a regular Don Juan. I wonder the husbands stand for it. But they're all afraid of him."

Stuart joined him and watched the two Mahommedans disappear.

"It's no use my talking to him about it. He thinks all Hindu women are fair game for the Moslem. However, I don't know if he is after the ladies this time. He usually dresses up in his best when he is—gold-embroidered vest, baggiest breeches and most imposing *puggri*. But now he's wearing khaki with ammunition boots."

The Pathan and his companion passed out of sight among the trees. They were going to the village to buy food supplies at the *bunniah's* shop. Khitab Gul usually chose for such visits the hour at which the women went to the well to draw water for the evening meal, so that he could meet and pass them in review. This day he had left it somewhat late; and the last of the long line of barefooted Hindu wives and daughters were disappearing into the thatched huts as the Moslems approached.

But before the two men reached the village the Pathan's quick eye caught sight of the graceful figure of a girl crossing the open sandy space between it and the trees of the untouched forest on the side opposite to that where lay the tilled acres of low tea-bushes. She was going towards the jungle and stopped for an instant to look back at the two men, giving the handsome Pathan a coquettish glance before ostentatiously pulling across her face the cotton *sari* that draped her head.

The susceptible hillman grasped his comrade's arm.

"Did you see that, Kadir Baksh? A beauty! I have never seen her before, yet I thought I knew every woman in the village, by sight at least. She is lovelier than any of them. Did you see her eyes?"

"Fool's talk, O Pathan! I have come to buy flour from that accursed Hindu robber, the *bunniah*, not to look at women," grumbled the practical old *mahout*.

"Son of an owl! You have less sense than your elephant, retorted Khitab Gul. "Who is she, I wonder? Where is she going? It is late for a woman—and, such a woman—to go into the jungle. *Abré*, brother! She has looked back at me again. I must go to protect her. Harm might befall her. It is not safe for her to enter the forest alone."

"Safer for her than to go into it with you," growled the *mahout*. "Come on! Oh, go, then. Follow her if you will, O hunter of women. I shall not wait for you."

As the Pathan turned to stride swiftly after the disappearing figure, the older man walked on grumbling into the village. He bought his provisions after long and acrimonious bargaining with the fat Hindu dealer, who sat surrounded by sacks of flour and grain in his small palm-thatched shop. When Kadir Baksh emerged from the village there was no sign of Khitab Gul; and, used to the Pathan's disappearances on such occasions, he did not wait for him but went back to his one room in the outhouses behind Murray's bungalow.

After dinner Stuart, when his orderly had not presented himself to ask for the next day's orders, as was his custom, bade the butler send for him. But Khitab Gul was not to be found in the servant's quarters. Kadir Baksh, on being questioned, told of the Pathan's disappearance in pursuit of the Hindu woman. Alan, with a feeling of uneasiness gradually deepening into a sense of deep depression that seemed to him a harbinger of ill, said to Murray:

"I'm rather worried about the chap. I am beginning to think that something serious has happened to him."

The planter looked thoughtful.

"Aye, it's gey queer. For even if he was having an intrigue with one of my coolie women, she would not stay out of the village as late as this."

Stuart rose from his chair.

"I'd go and search for him if I had any idea where to look. Do you think I'd find anyone to give me information if I went to the village now?"

"Certainly not. You know that at this time of night every hut is shut up and its occupants asleep."

The Sapper paced the room nervously.

"Of course. But—but—I say, Murray, I've got one of those fits of depression and sense of misery and foreboding that I had when Beresford was being killed, when Barter died. I'm sure some evil fate has befallen Khitab Gul."

Murray was too much of a Celt to laugh at his fears.

"I hope not. Perhaps he has managed to— Anyhow, we can do nothing tonight. He'll probably be back at dawn; for if any lady is entertaining him in her hut, he'd have to get out before daybreak to avoid being seen and ruining her reputation."

He paused and thought for a moment.

"If he's not back early in the morning we'll go and look for him," he continued. "Let's get to bed now; and I'll tell my boy to call me at sunrise."

"I won't be able to sleep. But don't let me keep you up, old man. Good night."

In his room Stuart did not undress. He tried to sit down and read; but the black feeling of evil happening weighed too heavily on him, and he walked restlessly up and down. After half an hour he went out of the bungalow and tried the door of Khitab Gul's room in the servant's quarters. It opened at a touch. There was no one inside; so he returned to his bedroom to wait impatiently for daylight. The sense of ill grew stronger, more oppressive each hour. Two or three times more during the night he went without result to the Pathan's quarters. The man was still absent.

As soon as the first streaks of dawn showed in the sky he slipped a loaded revolver into his pocket. He tried Khitab Gul's room again unsuccessfully, then went and knocked on Murray's door.

The planter's voice answered him at once. Impressed by Alan's foreboding he had slept little better himself.

"Is that you, Stuart?" he cried. "Come in! What's the matter? Any news?"

"None. I'm sorry for waking you so early, Murray; but I can't rest. I must go to the village and look for Khitab Gul. As sure as I stand here something awful has happened to him."

"Wait a minute. I'll go with you," said the planter, springing out of bed. "Give me time to put on some clothes."

He began to dress hurriedly while Stuart went out and roused Kadir Baksh with more difficulty. He needed the *mahout* to show them where he had last seen the Pathan. On returning to the bungalow he found Murray drinking a cup of tea brought him by his butler, and forced himself to do the same. The planter had already sent his servant on before them to the coolies' huts to make enquiries.

When he, Stuart and the *mahout* reached the village it was waking to life. The butler met them outside it. He was looking perturbed.

"Sahib, there is a coolie who has a strange story to tell about the orderly," he said.

"What is the tale?"

"I have sent for the man. Here he is."

A foreman of the garden was approaching with a coolie—a small, wizened creature in an obvious state of fright.

The former salaamed respectfully to his master.

"This miserable liar, sahib, told us a fool's tale about the Pathan last night before we slept," he said.

The coolie bent down and touched the dust with his fingertips, then straightened himself and raised his joined hands above his head.

"Forgive me, O sahib, forgive me!" he pleaded whiningly. "Do not be angry with me. But it is true—true the tale I told them. I swear it by the Water of the Sacred

Ganges, by the Holy Name of the Goddess Kali!"

Murray asked him testily:

"But what is this tale of thine? Didst thou see the hillman?"

"Yes, sahib. I saw him as night was falling when I was hurrying back to the village from the jungle, where I had gone to gather firewood for my evening meal. For I have no wife, no daughter, and must make fire and prepare my own food."

"Well, well? Where was he?"

"What was he doing?" broke in Stuart impatiently.

"O sahibs, be not angered. I saw the man from the hills on the path that leads through the trees to the nursery where you grow the young tea-plants."

"Well, go on! Speak, fool!" cried Murray, as the man hesitated.

The coolie bent his head to his hands.

"The Pathan was—was walking into the forest with—with a—with a woman," he faltered.

"A woman? A woman of the village? Did you know her?"

"No, sahib, no! Oh, it was a woman—but not a woman."

"What do you mean, Fool, and Son of a Fool?" demanded the planter angrily. A woman—and not a woman?"

The man shook with fright. He looked wildly about him and touched an amulet hanging on his chest.

"O sahibs, it was a devil. A *churel!*"

"What does he say?" asked Stuart. "What was she?"

"A *churel.* Some sort of demon in their silly superstitions," replied Murray. He turned to his butler and enquired in Bengali, "What is a *churel?*"

The man looked scared; and the other natives trembled visibly.

"Sahib, a *churel* is the worst of devils," replied the
butler, in a frightened voice. "It is the ghost of a woman
who has died in childbirth. Such a one haunts the neighbourhood of villages at nightfall in the shape of a lovely
woman and smiles at men, enticing them to follow her
into the darkness. If they do, they are never seen again—
alive. Their corpses are found—but torn to pieces by the
devil and her sister-devils."

"Aye, sahib, it is true talk," chimed in the foreman.
"Such a one cannot be mistaken by those who are not
blinded by her beauty. For if they look down they see that
her feet are twisted backwards, so that she walks with her
heels to the front."

He turned to the trembling coolie.

"Was it such a one you saw?" he asked him.

"Yes. O yes! As they came towards me, looking into
each other's eyes, I feared the Pathan's anger if he knew
that I saw him; so I slipped off the path and hid in the
undergrowth. As they passed I glanced at the woman's
face to see if I knew her, if she were from my village. But
it was the face of a stranger. My eyes fell—and, oh! sahib,
my liver turned to water. Her feet were twisted so that the
toes pointed backwards. Then I knew her to be a devil—a
churel!"

Murray translated to Stuart what the coolie said.

"Oh, it's ridiculous, isn't it?" exclaimed the Sapper. Yet despite himself a tone of doubt crept into his voice.

"Of course, absurd. I suppose he sat talking horrors with the other men of the village last night, conjuring up all the devils that Khitab Gul was likely to meet in the jungle in the dark, until at last he persuaded himself that he had seen this monstrosity."

"Of course; that must be it," assented the younger Scot. "Unless he is lying. It really may have been a woman whom he knew, and he was afraid to say who she was. So he invented the ghost."

He called Kadir Baksh.

"Where did you part from Khitab Gul?" he asked.

The *mahout* pointed.

"On the far side of the village, sahib," he said.

"Show us!" ordered Stuart.

Kadir Baksh led the group, now swelled by a number of coolies, round the huts to the open space in which he had parted from the Pathan.

"Here he left me, sahib. You see the marks of his military boots." He pointed to the soft sand, which plainly showed the footprints of a man wearing hobnailed boots, diverging from the tracks of the *mahout's* native shoes.

"See, they lead towards the jungle," said Kadir Baksh, following the orderly's footmarks. The rest crowded after him. "There is where the woman stood."

He walked to the spot.

"There she— *In the name of the All-Merciful!*" he shrieked suddenly. "Look! O look, sahib!"

Cries of terror came from the other Indians. The

elder Scot swore under his breath. Plainly visible were the prints of a woman's bare feet, her toes pointed towards the village; but beside them were the marks of Khitab Gul's boots going towards the jungle. And side by side both ran to the trees towering above the dense undergrowth, as though the woman had walked backward.

Stuart strove to conquer a feeling of superstitious awe.

"It is—it must be mere coincidence. My orderly went towards the jungle and happened to step beside the footprints of some coolie woman, who had previously returned to the village," he said.

"Maybe ye're recht, laddie," muttered Murray, whose native accent always grew more marked in moments of emotion. "But she didna gang to the village, ye ken. She stopped short there, for her tracks go no farther. It's no canny!"

Stuart looked carefully about. There were no other footprints near. At some distance away the loose sand showed where the coolie had crept out of the undergrowth, hurrying to the village.

With a sense of awful foreboding oppressing him Alan, keeping a little to one side, followed the puzzling tracks, the boot-marks of the missing man always beside the little feet that pointed in the opposite direction. A yard or two behind him Murray walked with his eyes glued to the ground; and, their pace slowing down, the Indians came a long way after them.

But when the white men reached the trees the *mahout* and the butler stopped, and the coolies turned and hurried back to the first huts of the village, where they stood to watch.

Fainter, but still discernible, the fatal footprints showed in the dust of the track through the jungle. Two hundred paces in, the two Scots halted suddenly.

"What in Heaven's name is that?" whispered Murray, in an awed tone.

A small clearing opened a few yards ahead of them. The tall trees around it held it in deep shadow, so that their eyes could only indistinctly make out that in it lay several objects. Stuart stared at them, while Murray craned to look over his shoulder. They stood silent, undecided, until a gleam of bright light from the rising sun lit up the clearing. Alan forced himself forward.

But with a cry of horror he drew back when he reached the first shapeless object. Now clearly revealed it lay at his feet.

CHAPTER XIV

THE TERROR BY NIGHT

IT was the head and part of the body of his missing orderly. The sightless eyes were open. The ghastly features were twisted into a horrible grimace. On the distorted face was stamped a look of agonized terror, so awful, so terrible, that Stuart had to cover his eyes with his hands and turn away. Murray was violently sick.

Nerving himself with a strong effort Alan looked again. Scattered about the clearing were the limbs and the rest of the trunk of the wretched man, as if some merciless giant's hands had torn them apart and flung them about in fiendish sport. Everywhere blood lay in dried gouts, in pools. The tree-trunks, the bushes, were splashed with it.

"In the name o'—! What—what happened to him?" ejaculated Murray. "It looks—it looks as if a rogue elephant had killed him. These brutes delight in dismembering a man, in tearing him to pieces. They put a foot on his body and pull his legs and arms off, as a child does with the wings of a fly."

"Yes, yes! It must have been that. No man, no twenty men, could have done this," cried Stuart, eager to escape from the horrible suspicion that filled his mind.

"We'd—we'd better watch out for ourselves, if it was a rogue. The brute may be hiding anywhere around," said Murray.

But Alan carefully scanned the bare sandy soil of the clearing and the path leading into it on the far side. The tell-tale dust would have revealed the huge prints of an elephant's feet had such an animal passed. But it showed nothing save two tracks of human beings—the hobnailed boots, the small, twisted feet of a woman.

Neither Stuart nor Murray ever spoke of the hours that followed or of the awful task that was forced on them. For they were obliged to gather together the dismembered body—their Mahommedan servants, every

whit as superstitious as the Hindu coolies, fled in terror
when brought to view it and flatly refused to prepare the
mangled remains of their co-religionist for interment.
These the two white men had to bury secretly in a spot in
the jungle known only to themselves. For, when Murray
proposed to have a grave for the shattered corpse dug on
the estate, all the coolies, headed by the foremen,
mutinied and threatened to abandon the garden in
superstitious panic. The shock of Khitab Gul's awful and
mysterious death had a great effect on Alan Stuart's
sensitive nature. For the dead man, his faithful follower
for several years, he had had a sincere regard and
affection. It needed all his fortitude and courage to brace
him up against the grief and the depression that the event
caused him. But the fierceness of his anger against the
invisible enemies whom in his heart he believed to be
somehow the authors of the Pathan's terrible fate,
spurred him on to fight them, and made him resolve to
solve the mystery and avenge his unfortunate orderly.
Against his common sense he was convinced in his heart
that some devilry of Morton and his evil gang had
brought death to Khitab Gul.

He and Murray gave out publicly that the hillman
had been killed by a wild elephant. This was the story that
they told the other planters. But the tale of the *churel* had
spread rapidly through the neighbouring tea estates and
soon reached the ears of all the European managers,
assistants and engineers on them; it was the only version
believed by every native in the district. Alan of course
pooh-poohed it when Margery questioned him on the

subject.

But on the day of the finding of the body he had sent a special messenger to Simpson with a letter telling the story in full detail. The Police Officer's answer was to come in person as quickly as he could, arriving two days later at Murray's bungalow in his touring car, accompanied by a slight, dark-haired young man, very Spanish in appearance. The planter welcomed them heartily, and ordered rooms to be prepared for his unexpected guests.

When Simpson got out of the automobile and shook hands with the two Scots, he introduced his companion as the Director of the new Department of Criminal Research, which had recently been started at Simla. His name was Carter, and he had been specially selected for his post by the Viceroy on account of his having skillfully unmasked a widespread criminal and political conspiracy of murder in Bombay Presidency and nipped in the bud the projected armed rebellion of a disloyal rajah, which was intended to be the signal for a big civil war in Western India.

"I hope you'll forgive my turning up uninvited, Mr. Murray," he said, as he shook hands with his host. "But I have been very much intrigued by this unusual affair of the raid of Bhuttias led by the gypsies on your neighbour's garden. Simpson let me behind the scenes and interested me by what he told me."

"You're very welcome, sir," replied Murray heartily. "I'm more than glad you've come. I know you, of course, by reputation, and Simpson's lucky to have you behind him in this affair. Come along in. You'll both need a long drink to wash the dust of our roads out of your throats."

As they mounted the verandah steps Stuart looked with interest at the newcomer, surprised to see one so young holding the important post that he did. But like Murray he had heard of his exploits and knew how Carter's wonderful power of disguise and intimate acquaintance with Indian languages had enabled him to mix unsuspected with political murderers and terrorists and learn to frustrate their criminal plans.

After dinner that night the four men discussed the situation in the district very fully. Carter was deeply interested in all that Murray and Stuart could tell him about the mysterious deaths that had occurred, as well as in the sequence of crimes attributed to Morton's gang and in the supernatural manifestations. The story of Ghost Tiger intrigued him most of all.

At the end of their recital Stuart appealed to him:

"Now, sir, you know a lot of the real India below the surface. What do you think about these queer happenings? We know that most people would laugh at us if we told them what we have told you."

Carter thought for a moment.

"Nothing that I have heard this evening astonishes me. As a child I used to dress up like a native boy, play undetected with Hindu and Mahommedan children in the streets of the bazaar—I spoke Mahratti and Hindustani better than English—and since I joined the Police I have mixed for months in disguise with Indians of all races and castes. I have seen stranger things than those you have told me of in the real India that few white men even guess at."

Simpson nodded assent.

"You have, indeed, sir," he said.

Carter went on:

"I believe that much of what is vaguely spoken of as Eastern magic and ridiculed by Europeans is actually the development of occult powers latent in Nature, in human beings, discovered and mastered in the centuries of study by adepts, philosophers, or whatever you like to call them, in the East. When you think that for hundreds, perhaps thousands of years, wise men in India, Tibet, China and Mongolia, have wrestled with problems that white men, occupied with efforts to invent death-dealing or money-making machines, have not troubled themselves to think of, it is not to be wondered at if they have arrived at applications of natural phenomena that we call magic or witchcraft or fraud—and scoff at."

"Is not mesmerism or collective hallucination suggested as the explanation of some of the supposed miracles?" asked Stuart.

"Yes, it is."

"Do you think it possible that men can take the appearance of animals—that such a creature as this Ghost Tiger can be something other than a mere beast of the jungle?" asked Murray.

"I do. Simpson here—aye, and others in the Police— could tell you of the strange killings of men by mysterious animals that might well have been humans endowed with the power of taking the semblance of brutes."

Simpson nodded.

"Yes, sir. I have seen Ghost Tiger myself. I've investigated some of his misdeeds, and I am quite prepared to say—but only here, in this company, for I don't want to be dismissed from the Service as a lunatic—that he is either a devil or a devilish human."

Carter laughed.

"Yes, it wouldn't do you any good at Headquarters, if this appeared in your 'Confidential Report'. Lots of people think I am mad; but in a way I am privileged. So I don't mind openly agreeing with you."

He turned to Alan.

"Now, Stuart, I'm going from here to Calcutta and intend to have a talk there with the Government Prosecutor about the case of the murderer Hari. Other people besides myself have been astonished at the wealth of legal talent engaged, at very great expense, to defend a poor gypsy before the High Court. We knew that there was something strange about the affair, and what you here have told me explains it. I may reveal to you in confidence that Simpson asked for one of our Intelligence men to be sent disguised as a coolie on Morton's garden. But he discovered nothing, for the gypsies keep to themselves, and he was unable to approach them. He was soon found out and had to leave. Then I sent one of our best men; but they spotted him, too, and tried to poison him."

"It's a pity that you couldn't undertake the job yourself, sir," observed Simpson. "There's no one in India who can disguise himself as a native better than you."

"It would be no good. I'd love to try it, for I enjoy diving into the criminal underworld of India—it is really awfully interesting, I assure you. But I'd be useless here. I could make myself up to look like a gypsy—which is what one would have to do to ferret out the secrets of Morton's gang. But it would not be enough; and, as I don't know their language or customs, I'd be discovered at once. And I have no one in our Department, white man or Indian, who would be any better."

He paused to light a cigarette, then went on:

"We've found that these particular gypsies are Devil Worshippers; and I have heard strange tales of demoniac possession among them. They hold some sort of equivalent of the Black Mass that followers of Satanic religion in Europe celebrate, and go in for Witches' Sabbaths, blood-offerings and human sacrifices. I wish I could learn more at first-hand of this strange sect."

Simpson then said:

"Now, Stuart, there's something that Mr. Carter and I want you to understand. We think that certain precautions should be taken with regard to the witnesses in the case against Hari. So we are going from here to Webb's estate and, by order of the higher authorities, intend to take away with us and keep in a safe place, until the trial is ended, those of his coolies who have testified to Hari's committing the murder during the raid. Your orderly was an important witness. Well, he has died mysteriously. You are another whose testimony will help to hang the gypsy. We can't hide you away for your own protection. But look out for yourself."

"He's right, Stuart," said Carter. "Be on your guard— or you'll disappear. They'll try to get you."

"I know that, sir," replied the Sapper. "But I'll take care of myself, you bet. I expect they'll set Ghost Tiger on me again. He nearly had me once. But I'd like to get another shot at the brute—beast or devil, whichever he is."

He had not long to wait.

On the following day the police officers left for Malpotha; and when, after a short visit there they quitted the district, they took with them the witnesses whose safety they wished to ensure. Their investigation into Khitab Gul's death had yielded no result.

Three nights after their departure Murray and Stuart, having finished dinner under the punkah in the hot dining-room, went out of the house to seek a little freshness in the open air. They strolled up and down, smoking, before the bungalow in the clear space between it and the serried rows of tea-bushes. The moon was nearly at the full; but its sight was frequently obscured by clouds drifting slowly across its face.

They talked in low tones of the subject ever present in their minds, the sinister menace chat brooded over the district; but at intervals silence fell on them, each man busy with his own thoughts. Stuart's ran on Margery. He had no fears for his own safety, but always dreaded danger for her and longed for the time when he could secure a hoped-for appointment in England, marry her and take her away from the peril that threatened her while she was within reach of Morton and his sinister allies.

Murray was thinking of the young man at his side, of the mysterious fate that had so suddenly struck down his two friends and his devoted follower and hung over him.

Both men were so engrossed in their meditations that they were unaware of the sinister horror creeping upon them with murderous stealth, drawing silently nearer and ever nearer. A heavy cloud drifted over the moon and blotted out the world. Darkness obscured the very ground under their feet as they were about to turn at the end of the walk.

Then with a swift, noiseless rush the horrible Thing sprang suddenly at the unconscious Stuart's back. But, checked mysteriously, it twisted in mid-air, dropped heavily to earth, striking violently against Murray, hurling him down on his face yards away, then dashed away as soundlessly as it had come. At that instant the moon shot out from the edge of the cloud—and Stuart, staggering back, saw the clumsy grey shape of an animal looming huge in the uncertain light. But he knew it.

"Ghost Tiger!" he exclaimed.

And Murray, shaken and breathless, had raised himself on his hands and stared after it, gasping:

"Man, the Devil-Beast!"

His friend sprang to him and helped him to his feet. Bruised and half-stunned, the breath knocked out of his body, the elder Scot was not seriously hurt. He grasped his companion's arm and dragged him forcibly towards the house.

"Come awa'ben! And let us thank the guid God for our lives!" he cried.

When they were safely inside the bungalow he feverishly barricaded the front door that had not been shut for years, if ever. Then with a shaking hand he poured out a glass of neat whiskey, drained it and sank exhausted in a chair; while Stuart rushed into his room and seized his rifle, loading it as he returned to the sitting-room.

"Man, that was awfu'!" exclaimed Murray. "How are we alive the noo?"

Alan, forcing himself to keep calm, answered:

"Only God knows! For He saved us this night."

Controlling his nerves with an effort he sat down, refusing the drink that his friend pressed on him.

"It was that damned beastie, wasn't it?" asked Murray.

"Yes; I'm sure of it. This is the third time that I've seen it, so I could not mistake it. The moon shone full on it. I saw the grey hide—it looked almost white. I can't understand how we escaped."

"Just as I was turning to stroll back I saw the brute out of the tail of my eye. It seemed to be leaping right on you—then somehow it swerved in the air and landed almost on top of me. Man! it was like Edinburgh Castle falling on my head."

Stuart sat down.

"I can't make it out. That's twice the beast has spared me at the last moment," he said reflexively.

The older man shook his head, and spoke in a solemn tone:

"Stuart, there's Someone in Heaven watching over you, and the de'il cannot prevail. I'm not great on releegion mysel'; but if I were an atheist before I'd believe now. I canna understan' it at a'. The demon-beast lies in

wait to attack you— and then sheers off you. It's beyond
me."

He shook himself, as if to throw off his perplexity,
and poured out another drink.

"In all the years I've lived here I've never fashed
mysel' to keep a loaded weapon in the bungalow. All I
have is that rusty old shotgun in my room, ye ken. I
havena' fired it for years. But I'm goin' to pit twa ball
cartridge in it this very moment."

He got up heavily from his chair; and Alan rose, too,
saying:

"I'll go to bed now, Murray; for I have to make an
early start in the morning. Hot as it is, I'll shut my door
on the verandah, though. There's no use taking chances.
Good night!"

"Good night, laddie!" answered the planter, as he
walked into his bedroom.

Opening his gun-case he took out the old fowling-
piece that it held and put it together, then, diving into a
dusty cupboard, found a few ball-cartridges and carried
them and the weapon into the sitting-room. He dropped
into an easy-chair, loaded the gun and, holding it
between his knees, sipped the contents of his glass,
brooding over the mysterious appearance of the devil-
tiger.

How long he sat there, whether he slept or fell into a
reverie, he never knew. He did not notice that the lamp,
the oil in it exhausted, flickered and went out. He sat
unconscious in his chair.

But suddenly he was aroused. It seemed to him that

someone or something was moving outside. He gripped the gun and listened intently. There was a shuffling noise on the verandah, as if a slippered man was creeping cautiously over its matting-covered floor. Then he distinctly heard the sound of a big animal sniffing at the barred entrance. After a few seconds it seemed to pass on to Stuart's door. For a moment a superstitious fear paralyzed the planter; but a wave of anger swept it away as the thought came to him that it was the devil-beast seeking to attack his friend again.

With no care for his own safety he tiptoed to the entrance, quietly drew back the bolts and, noiselessly opening the door, looked out cautiously.

The moon shone full on the verandah. On the windowsill of Stuart's room a huge grey-hided tiger had planted its forepaws and was raising itself on its hindlegs.

Mad with fury Murray yelled at it. The beast dropped back to the floor, swung about and rushed past him—and, as it did, he thrust his gun at it until the muzzle almost touched its ribs, and fired both barrels. But apparently unhurt it dashed by him, bounded down into the garden and disappeared, just as Alan flung open his door and sprang out on the verandah, rifle in hand.

"What is it? What is it, Murray?" he cried.

The planter was shaking with terror and rage.

"It's the de'il, Stuart! The de'il himsel'! Nae doot aboot it. My gun was touchin' its body when I fired. But it's nane the worse o' twa bullets!"

"What do you mean? What did you fire at?" asked the Sapper.

"Ghost Tiger. He was on his hindlegs at your window, going to jump in when I shouted. He ran past me, and I fired into his ribs. But look! There's nae bluid!"

The moon lit up the verandah clearly. Alan glanced at the matting. There was no stain on it.

"Come outside! There may be blood on the ground," he said.

"No, no! stay in the bungalow. I'm no' gangin' oot while that de'il's aboot."

However, Stuart went down the verandah steps, rifle at the ready. It was almost as light as day. He looked carefully around. The ground was open for a hundred yards in front of the house. Ghost Tiger had disappeared.

But twenty feet from the building the marks of the tiger's paws were deeply imprinted in the dust, showing where it had landed when it sprang off the verandah. Of blood there was no trace. Stuart retreated slowly to the bungalow, looking behind him as he went.

"Come ben! Dinna be a fule, mon!" cried Murray, in an agitated voice, pulling him into the. sitting-room and fastening the front door behind him. "Go an' shut yoursel' in. I'll not open this again before mornin'. An' I'll not go to bed tonight, either."

He lit another lamp, and in spite of Stuart's remonstrances sat up until his servant came an hour after sunrise and knocked at the barred door. The man made no allusion to the shooting in the night; and his master volunteered no explanation.

CHAPTER XV

THE THREAT OF THE
TEMPLE BELLS

DURING the weeks of waiting before the retrial of Hari, Margery lived in an agony of suspense. Like Simpson and Carter she knew that Morton would stop at nothing to prevent Stuart from appearing to give evidence; and she feared for her lover's life. She would gladly have seen the gypsy acquitted and set free, if only it meant that the cause of the enmity of his family towards Alan would be removed. To make matters worse for her just then, the Sapper was unable to visit her frequently; for work in his quarry was at full pressure and needed his constant supervision.

But in other respects life in her home was far pleasanter than it had been for a long time. Relieved of the constant fear of ruin that had weighed on him, freed from his burden of debt, and guarded by old Angus's careful management from indulging in his passion for speculation, Webb had changed completely and was the loving father and devoted husband that he had been formerly. No longer obliged to spur himself to try to force his daughter into marriage with a man whom she hated, he was always glad to welcome the one whom she loved. For he liked the young Scot for his own sake. And his wife, too, was happier than she had been for years, rejoicing in the happiness of her loved daughter, and her anxiety for her own and her husband's future relieved.

Despite Margery's distress about her betrothed, the girl was tactful enough not to worry him with her fears when he rode up to her bungalow three days after the appearance of Ghost Tiger to him and Murray. He, on his side, said nothing to her of the strange occurrence; and by tacit mutual consent they avoided all mention of Morton's machinations, and spoke only of the glowing future that lay before them. For Alan had happy tidings to bring her. His uncle, General Malcolm Stuart, had just received news of his impending appointment as Inspector-General of Fortifications in London, and had written to say that he intended to apply for his nephew as his staff Officer as soon as he took up his duties at the Horse Guards. This meant that Alan could hope to be ordered to England before long; and he was resolved to be married and take his wife with him when he sailed. He had come to Malpotha to tell Margery the good news and discuss the date of their marriage.

They were sitting on the verandah in the late afternoon, absorbed in conversation, when the girl suddenly felt that they were not alone. She rose from her long-chair and looked around. Coming towards them noiselessly on bare feet was a young gypsy woman of surprising beauty. Seeing that she was observed she stopped and drew her *sari* modestly across her face. In a low and gentle voice she said in Bengali:

"Will the Presence permit a poor girl of the Tribe of

Wanderers Without a Home, they who are gifted with the power to divine the secrets of the Future, to read in the Missie Baba's hand what of happiness Fate holds for her?"

Startled by her sudden intrusion, Stuart asked sharply in Urdu:

"How do you come here unannounced?"

Haltingly in the same language she pleaded humbly for pardon.

"Will the Protector of the Poor forgive me? I could find no servant to ask that I might be permitted to see the Missie Baba. I had heard that she is to be united soon to the man of her choice, unlike us poor women of the dark-faced races who must wed men whom we have never seen —we who are sold like beasts in the marketplace to whosoever will pay money to our fathers for us. I hoped that in her happiness she would pity me and let me earn a poor recompense for foretelling her fate."

"Oh, don't be angry with her, Alan," said Margery, in her happiness full of sympathy for all women less fortunate than herself. "She wants a chance of earning a few rupees. These gypsies are poor."

Stuart's suspicions were instantly aroused.

"Is she a gypsy, then? Where does she come from? Is she one of Morton's lot?" he demanded.

Margery questioned the woman in Bengali, in which the latter was more fluent than in the Urdu language.

"No; she says she is not. She is one of a party of a small tribe on its way from Assam to the great religious fair at Hurdwar."

The Scot still regarded the unknown with suspicion.

"I'll give her five rupees and send her away," he said.

Margery answered pityingly:

"Oh, don't do that! She would not like to be treated as a beggar. These gypsies have their pride. Let her earn the money. Besides, I'd like to have her tell my fortune. I daresay it will be all nonsense; but still it would be interesting to see if these strange folk are better at it than the usual Indian fortune-tellers who fleece the globetrotters on the hotel verandahs of Bombay and Calcutta."

"As you like, darling. I expect she will be just as much a fraud as they are. I'll go inside and get my cigarette-case while she's telling you the usual rubbish."

He rose and went into the sitting-room, while Margery turned to the gypsy and held out her hand. The woman drew near her timidly and took the girl's fingers in her left hand. Raising her eyes she glanced along the verandah. They were alone.

Suddenly the gypsy's right hand flashed out from under her sari, a short curved dagger in it, which she raised aloft. Then she struck swiftly.

But she had no soft-muscled, frightened Hindu woman to deal with. Her wrist was gripped firmly by the athletic English girl; and Alan, coming out on the verandah again, saw to his amazement his betrothed engaged in a fierce struggle with the stranger. He sprang towards them; but before he reached the pair the knife fell from the gypsy's hand and Margery held her a powerless prisoner.

A little out of breath, but quite calm, she asked her captive:

"Why did you do that?"

The woman hissed fiercely:

"I wished to kill you who try to steal my man from me."

In her surprise at the unexpected reply the English girl loosened her hold.

"Your man? Who—?"

The gypsy unexpectedly wrenched herself free from her grasp; but Alan's hands fell on the woman's shoulders, slid down her arms and held her effectually.

"No, you don't!" he cried in English. Then in Urdu, "You'll answer for this. I suppose you *are* one of Morton's murderous gang?"

"Yes, I am his woman," she replied defiantly. She nodded her head towards the English girl. "*She* wants him. She is trying to take him from me."

"I do not want him!" cried Margery emphatically. "I hate him. You are welcome to keep him." She laid her hand affectionately on the Scot's shoulder. "This is *my* man, whom I hope to marry very soon."

The gypsy looked with suspicion from her to Alan.

"Is this true talk?" she asked him sullenly.

"Yes; it is true," he answered. "So Morton sent you here to murder her?"

"No. He did not send me. He will kill me when he knows what I tried to do. But he told me that I must go away, for he means to marry her."

Again, as her hands were imprisoned, she motioned

to Margery with her head.

"He will not get an opportunity of hurting you," said Stuart. "I shall lock you up until I can hand you over to the police for what you have tried to do. Perhaps they will be able to get the truth out of you when they take you to jail."

"I shall be glad to go there. I shall be safe from him in prison. But not from the *yogi*. He can reach me anywhere."

"Not behind the walls of Alipore Jail. And that is where you shall go."

The gypsy shook her head.

"You do not know his power. Yet you have already felt it, have learned something of what he can do. You had a faithful follower—a soldier strong, brave. Neither his strength nor his courage could save him."

"What? What do you mean? The *yogi* killed Khitab Gul?" cried Alan excitedly.

"I can say no more. I dare not," said the woman.

"You shall. I will make you speak," cried Alan; and in his rage he shook her roughly.

Margery's hand arrested him.

"Don't hurt her, Alan! You cannot blame her for attacking me. I'd kill anyone who tried to take you from me," she said passionately.

The gypsy saw her action and guessed the meaning of her words.

"If you love your man, would you not slay your rival?" she asked her.

Margery answered her:

"Yes, I would. I have no blame for your aft. We shall not give you up to the police." She turned to her lover. "Alan, for my sake let her go! I would have done what she tried to do. For my sake set her free!"

Stuart could not resist her appeal.

"Well, if you want me to, I'll do it. But I think it is unwise."

He released the gypsy.

"There! You are free. You can go back to the man you love," said Margery.

"Love? I do not love him. I hate him for wanting to cast me aside. But I will let no woman take my place."

She looked incredulously at Alan and turned to Margery.

"You mean that he will let me go?" she asked.

"Yes. We shall not stop you."

In a passion of gratitude the gypsy fell at the girl's feet and kissed her hand almost fiercely.

"You are kind. You are good, Missie Baba. Ula is not ungrateful. I came to kill you—not because I love Morton, but because I would not be set aside for another woman. He told me that you were to be his wife. I was scorned, jeered at by Muda, whom I supplanted."

She rose to her feet and looked apprehensively around her. Then in a low voice, she continued:

"*Your* life is safe for the moment; for he hopes to gain you. But he"—she pointed to Alan— "he is in great danger. They will never let him live to testify against Hari again."

She turned to Stuart and addressed him in faltering

Urdu:

"You are brave, sahib; but you cannot fight the Devil. And it is the Devil himself who wages war on you—the Devil, the Evil One whom they worship. You have already seen what he can do. You beheld the mangled corpse of your servant, torn to fragments by the lesser demons that the *yogi*, his minister, can command."

Her voice sank to a whisper.

"You laugh at his power, this *yogi*. You do not know what knowledge such men as he possess. I do. He brought me, a child, to serve as a *deva dasi*, a dancer, in his temple in Benares. I was chosen by the Council out of all the young priestesses to be the bride of the Brahmatma, their Head. I was admitted to the First Degree and learned something of the magical powers of the Evocators of Spirits. I saw terrible things—things I shudder to recall."

She buried her face in her hands and shivered visibly. Then, looking up, she continued:

"To our temple came the Agora-panths, the eaters of corpses. I have witnessed their horrible orgies. I have seen the dead walk, have heard them speak. The adepts can leave their own bodies lying like corpses and project their own astral bodies across the length and breadth of Hindustan, can pass through iron doors, through stone walls, and slay those whom they have condemned to die."

Carried away by emotion she raised her voice almost to a shriek.

"Beware! This *yogi* is more powerful than all his brethren, for he serves the Evil One, the Master of Eblis. He has taught his tribe to worship Him; and in return He, the Devil Incarnate, has made him greater, stronger than all the priests of all the temples of India. He can lie buried for years, yet come to life again. He can take any shape. He has the power to make himself invisible—no bolt or bar can shut him out where he wishes to pass. I fear that, even as I speak, he may hear me. Do not laugh, sahib, it is true!"

But, indeed, her earnestness had so impressed her hearers that neither had felt any desire to laugh. The strain of superstition in the Highlander predisposed Alan to credit her words, and even the practical Margery was awed almost into belief.

"How came you back to this district?" she asked, trying to shake off the impression that the gypsy's words were making on her.

"The Brahmatma died—he was a very old man—and I was set free from temple service; so the *yogi* brought me back to the tribe. Then Morton coveted me and took me to be his mistress, putting Muda away. So she has hated me ever since; and, knowing that she is old and faded and cannot hope to win him back, she urges him to make you his wife, so that I shall be thrust aside as she was."

The woman's voice sank almost to a whisper.

"But I see that this sahib loves you and that he is precious to you. Therefore I wish to save him for you. Listen—and make him believe what I say!"

Again she looked about her nervously. But the three were alone; and, reassured, the gypsy whispered:

"Twice has he been nearly destroyed. Twice the

Devil-Tiger has all but slain him. To save him, even at the risk of my life, I will reveal the secret!"

Suddenly she stopped. Distant, yet clear, the two Europeans heard distinctly the bells of a temple ringing, heard the harsh sound of the conch-shells that the priests blow when the gods are being worshipped. Yet there was no Hindu shrine within scores of miles.

A choking sound came from the gypsy. She tore at her throat as though suffocating. Her features twisted into a look of terror, as she stared past her hearers down the verandah.

They followed her gaze. There, plainly visible although dusk was falling, Stood the *yogi*—his ash-smeared, wasted body naked but for a loincloth, his bloodshot eyes, flaming in fury, bent on the panic-stricken woman, his shriveled hand raised, and his thin forefinger pointed menacingly at her.

An agonized scream burst from her lips. She staggered, fell headlong to the ground, lay motionless.

Stuart rushed along the verandah and sprang at the priest, his hand outstretched to seize his throat.

To his amazement his fingers met *nothing*. There was no one. The *yogi* had vanished.

Margery saw her lover pass through the figure—and then Alan stood alone, bewildered. The other, apparently a solid body, had disappeared.

She turned to the fallen gypsy and knelt down beside her. Looking into the glassy eyes, still fixed in a state of terror, she laid her hand on her heart. It did not beat. The woman was dead.

CHAPTER XVI

THE HAUNTED MAN

NEXT morning Stuart was obliged to leave Malpotha, much against his will. He rode away, slowly at first, lost in thoughts of Margery, racked by concern at the unprotected state of the girl whom he loved and whom he was forced to leave. The extraordinary occurrence of the previous day, coming on top of Khitab Gul's fate and the attacks of the devil-tiger, had shaken his confidence in his ability to overcome the dangers that threatened Margery and himself. He could no longer doubt that he was faced by enemies possessed of supernatural power, or at least of a power beyond that of ordinary humans, whether of satanic origin or merely derived from the control of natural forces outside his understanding. That it was real and not merely illusion or mesmerism, was proved by the fact that it could deal death—and a horrible death at that. His one consolation was that the urgent danger was to him alone, that for the present Margery was safe. And at the thought the fighting spirit rose in him, as instinctively he urged on his pony to a faster pace.

He was well inside the forest now, moving along the path on which he had been attacked by Ghost Tiger; and the remembrance of it put him on the alert and made him

unsling and load his rifle. Suddenly as he rode on he
heard the sounds made by some large animal moving
parallel to him through the jungle near the path.
Sometimes the noise grew louder where the beast had to
force its way through patches of denser undergrowth;
sometimes it faded away where the vegetation was sparse.
For a mile it accompanied him, keeping level with him.
His pony, fortunately a steady old animal, was at first
troubled by the nearness and smell of the unseen beast;
but an encouraging word and caress from its master
reassured it.

From the first Stuart suspected that he was being
tracked by the devil-tiger. He suddenly determined to put
the matter to the proof. He had reached a spot from
which the path lay straight and wide for several hundred
yards, but the jungle undergrowth on either hand was
composed of difficult thorny bush. He touched his pony
with the spur; and it readily broke into a fast gallop. He
could hear his invisible companion striving to keep up
with him; but it fell behind, held back by the dense
vegetation. At a sudden bend of the path he pulled his
animal up sharply, sprang off and quickly looped the
reins securely over a stump, then, cocking his rifle, he
stood ready, hidden in the undergrowth.

Up the open track loped a tiger; and Alan thrilled to
recognize it. It was the devil-beast; and with fast-beating
heart he stepped out of cover to confront it and cocked
his rifle. Taken by surprise, the mysterious brute stopped
short twenty yards away from him and, standing still,
stared at him out of its fierce yellow eyes. Alan felt a stern

joy as he took a steady aim at its skull. He had the brute at his mercy. He could not miss. He fired. The animal swung about and, as it did, Stuart discharged his second barrel at its shoulder.

But, apparently unscathed, Ghost Tiger plunged out of sight into the undergrowth and forced its way noisily through the thick-bushes. The sounds of its passage died away in the distance until the normal silence of the forest closed again around the man who stood motionless, aghast, in a stupor of bewilderment.

At last he roused himself, reloaded his rifle and walked slowly down the path. He could not believe that he had not hit his mark. His aim had been carefully taken, his arms steady, when he fired. Even at that short range his weapon did not throw high. It was impossible that both shots had missed.

Nevertheless, to make sure, he searched the ground for any mark made by a bullet. There was none. But neither was there any trace of blood.

Then for the first time in his life terror over-powered him. In a panic he ran to release his frightened pony, sprang on its back and galloped madly along the winding track between the trees. Not until he reached the ferry did he regain his nerve. Ashamed of his fear he pulled himself together as he reined in his animal and slipped from the saddle, while the waiting syce came forward and took the bridle.

On the far bank Stuart mounted his second pony, and rode off at a steady pace towards Baghpota with every sense on the alert; for he could not shake off the feeling that at any moment the devil-tiger might charge out upon him. Even when he reached the bungalow at last he was obsessed by the idea that the uncanny beast had got there before him; and he would not have been astonished to find it confronting him on the verandah.

But, instead, Murray stood there awaiting him, waving an open telegram.

"Just in time, laddie. I was going to send for you. You must go to Calcutta at once. Simpson has wired to say that the date of Hari's trial has been advanced. You are— But what's wrong with yours? You're looking very queer."

Stuart brushed past him without ceremony into the sitting-room, and sank into a chair.

"A drink, for Heaven's sake!" he exclaimed. "Give me a drink, Murray. The Devil's afoot!"

"What do you mean?" asked the astonished planter, pouring out a whiskey and soda.

Stuart thirstily drained the glass.

"That's good. I needed it. I feel better. Now listen!"

He told of his encounter with Ghost Tiger, and then went on to describe the death of the gypsy and the apparition of the *yogi*. The recital was punctuated by cries of wonder from his listener.

"What's to be done, Stuart? What's to be done?" railed Murray, when the tale was ended.

"What can be done? I begin to believe all the stories we were told as children of the witches in Scotland in the old days."

"Ah, I don't doubt them now. I wish we could do as men did with them then. We'd burn that damned *yogi* at the stake—aye, and his cursed patron, too."

"If I thought that Margery was in danger from them now I'd go straight to Morton and kill him myself," said the younger man savagely. "But I'm the one they're aiming at first. I'll disappoint them; tomorrow at dawn I'll start for the railway at Jainti."

Two days later he arrived at Howrah Terminus in Calcutta, where he was met by his uncle Angus, with whom he was to stay; and as in the old man's luxurious automobile they drove through the crowded streets of the capital's European quarter with their dense traffic, palatial English hotels and luxury shops, the fantastic happenings of the past weeks seemed unreal, impossible. On the following night he dined with an old friend in a Highland regiment stationed in Fort William. At the long dinner-table of the Mess, loaded with historic silver plate, thirty officers of the corps and six or seven guests seated around the mahogany, while the strains of the band floated in through the open windows and dominated the buzz of conversation, it was difficult to realize that the far-off Terai Jungle, its dark aisles peopled with savage beasts and stranger denizens, its tragedies, witchcraft and horrors, were not all a nightmare.

Later, after the wine had circulated, the shrill strains of the pibroch skirted by the pipers marching around the table, the wail of the lament played by the Pipe Major standing behind the Colonel's chair, the familiar accents, the uniforms and badges of the Highlanders, all transported him in fancy to his native land; and he awoke with a start when his neighbour's voice broke in on his reverie and recalled him to reality. When he had taken his place at the dinner-table he had found another old friend seated beside him, a Major Barrie of the Indian Medical Service, who had been the doctor of the Sapper and Miner Battalion to which Alan was attached.

"I say, Stuart, Cameron says that you've come to Calcutta to give evidence against a convict in my charge," said Barrie. "Did I tell you that I am Governor of Alipore Jail?"

"No; you only said that you had a job in Calcutta now. So you've Hari, have you?"

"Yes. How do you come into the affair? As well as I remember the man was sentenced to death somewhere up country for a murder in a tea-garden and is being retried. How are you mixed up in it?"

Alan briefly explained and, as soon as he could, changed the subject. He said nothing whatever of the mysterious occurrences connected with the affair.

These he had fully discussed that day at lunch in his uncle's flat with Simpson and Carter, whom Angus Stuart had invited to meet him. The old man, who was hearing of them for the first time, was too true a Highlander to doubt the story, even without observing the credence given it by the two experienced Police Officers, neither of whom made any comment.

But after a pause Carter exclaimed:

"It's beyond me, Stuart! I can say nothing. Only I'd like to be able to handle that *yogi*."

"I wish I could hang him over a slow fire," cried Simpson savagely. "Then I might get the truth out of him and stop his deviltries."

Angus agreed that the sooner his nephew and Margery were married the better.

"Alan boy, you can tell your girl's mother that she and her husband will not be long after you in going to England," he said. "I'm concluding the sale of Malpotha to an English company at a good price that will clear Webb and leave him money in pocket; and the directors have agreed to make him their London manager."

Hari's trial before the High Court caused no excitement in the native population of Calcutta, as his crime had not been a political one. On the other hand, it attracted quite a large audience from the British community, including many ladies, to whom the romantic story of the dramatic rescue of the English girl by her good-looking young lover appealed. A number of Alan's friends among the garrison were present also. The case did not last long, despite the lavish expenditure of eloquence by the leading Bengali counsel engaged at great expense to defend the prisoner. And Hari for the second time heard himself condemned to die.

As the fatal words were said he turned in the dock to face Alan seated in the court, and fixed his bloodshot eyes on him in a menacing and malevolent glare before he was led away by his guards to the prison in which in due course he was to hang. Stuart watched him go with no compunction in his heart for his share in sending him to his doom. To him the gypsy was a dangerous reptile fit only to be stamped out of existence; and he wished that the rest of the poisonous brood could be brought to perish in the same manner.

He left Calcutta that night, anxious to get back to Margery again. Simpson travelled with him, as he was due to return at once to his headquarters. Angus Stuart, Major Barrie and several other friends came to Howrah Terminus to see them off; and a few minutes before the train started Carter appeared, accompanied by a police sepoy leading a large Airedale dog on a chain. He took Alan aside.

"I've got a present for you, Stuart," he said. "This animal will be a good guard for you. He's pretty fierce, I can tell you. Be on the alert day and night when you are back in the Terai! They'll redouble their efforts to be revenged on you. If they cannot get you they'll try to strike at you through Miss Webb. The police can do little to protect you; but we'll give Simpson all the help we can to stamp out this gang."

Alan looked admiringly at the dog.

"Thank you very much, sir. It's awfully kind of you. He's a beauty, this chap; and I accept him with pleasure."

"That's all right. Now I'll leave you to say goodbye to your uncle and the others, while I have a last word with Simpson. Good luck!"

But as the train slid out of the station he called out to Alan a final warning:

"Watch out, Stuart!"

Two days later, once more in Baghpota in the restful quiet of the tea-garden, with the silence of the miles of primeval forest about it, all that in the stir of Calcutta had appeared fantastic, absurd, now seemed less unreal to

Alan.

"I'll not be at ease, Stuart, until you and your wife are safely out of India," said Murray nervously, as the two sat on the verandah after dinner on the night of the younger man's return. "You're off to Malpotha tomorrow to settle the date of your marriage with her, aren't you?"

The planter had listened with interest to the account of Hari's trial.

"You don't know if they will appeal to the Privy Council, do you? Morton will leave nothing untried to save his whelp. But I suppose they would have to show good grounds before they get leave to appeal; and I don't see how those damned lawyers with all their quibbling and chicanery can do it. But you won't be safe until you are on the high seas."

His tone grew impressive and his accent stronger. "A' the wickedness o' Man an' a' the evil o' Hell will be arrayed against you, laddie! Weel, ye maun bide by Carter's advice—watch weel! Now, ye're tired. We'll say good nicht an' gang tae bed."

He rose from his chair and picked up the loaded gun that was propped against the wall beside him. He looked at it doubtfully.

"I keep this always near me," he continued. "But what guid would it be? We've baith seen that the devil-beast is proof against lead, like oor auld Scottish witches."

"Against lead?" repeated Stuart. "That gives me an idea. Maybe there's something in what you say. Well, good night!"

As he entered his room a low growl greeted him. It

was the Airedale, which was chained to a leg of the bed. Since its arrival it had proved so savage to all but its new master that Alan had been obliged to keep it fastened up. Recognizing him it wagged its tail as, having closed and fastened the door leading out on the verandah, he unchained it. It lay down on a rug near the foot of the bed.

Alan placed a loaded pistol on the table and, emptying his pockets, threw a handful of silver rupees beside it and, going to the wardrobe, took his cartridge-filling case from a box in it. From the bathroom he brought a crucible, a powerful blow-lamp and some other implements that he used for chemical experiments. Then, having taken off his coat, he worked far into the night, until at last with a sigh of satisfaction he stood up, wiped the streaming perspiration from his face, and returned all the implements and articles that he had been using. He put together his double-barreled ball-and-shot gun, and walked over to the table to take some freshly-filled cartridges from it. He stretched out his hand for them, then quickly drew it back. Beside them lay coiled a short, thick snake. Stuart recognized it at once as a Russell's Viper, one of the most venomous reptiles in India.

Stepping back he seized a riding-cane. The serpent slid off the table and fell heavily to the floor. As it glided with a rustling sound across the matting Stuart hit at it with the lithe switch. The cane struck the ground uselessly. The snake had vanished.

Alan started back. Had his eyes deceived him? It was impossible. The room was well lit by the powerful incandescent lamp. He scanned the floor. There was no snake. It had disappeared while he looked at it. It was an illusion.

Alan sat down heavily on a chair and wiped his face. Was he going mad, he wondered? Suddenly he was aroused by a noise behind him. He sprang up and looked around. The dog, a prey to terror, was cowering in a corner of the room, shivering with fear, its tail between its legs, its eyes fixed on the bed. Instinctively its master turned and followed the direction of its gaze.

On the bed, inside the mosquito net, lay the body of a man. A white man, for even through the curtain he could see the pallid face.

Stuart seized the pistol from the table and approached the bed. Its strange occupant never stirred, as the sapper lifted the netting.

It was a corpse. Livid, ghastly, the skin green and blotched as with the beginning of decay, while a foul odor of corruption filled the room. The features were horribly distorted, yet in a way strangely familiar to Alan as he stared down at them.

Suddenly the truth dawned on him. A cold sweat broke out over him. He knew the face.

It was his own. There before him lay his dead body.

CHAPTER XVII

THE CROSS

As he stood transfixed, an unearthly howl rang through the room. He started and swung round. It was the dog, mad with fright, huddling in panic in a corner. Alan turned back to the bed. The body lay there still.

A wave of fury swept over him. It was devilry, witchcraft, meant to terrify him. He raged aloud at his unseen foes; and his anger filled him with resolution. He stretched out his hand steadily and laid it on the breast of the corpse. It met nothing until it touched the counterpane. The corpse had vanished like the snake.

He looked towards the dog. It was cowering against the wall, but its abject panic had passed.

Still filled with wrath, Stuart tore off his clothes, so roughly that his fingers caught in and broke the thin gold chain that he wore around his neck, that had never been unclasped day or night for years. From it hung a small gold crucifix, the tiny figure on the cross exquisitely carved. It had been his mother's; and Alan had worn it constantly for the sake of the sainted woman who was but a shadowy memory to him. In all the vicissitudes of his life, in war and in peace, the chain had never left his neck.

He gazed at it ruefully now; and the accident seemed a disaster that made the uncanny happenings of the night appear trivial. He kissed the crucifix and laid it sorrowfully on the small table beside the bed. Then, finishing his undressing and putting on his pajamas, he lay down, leaving the lamp alight. He glanced at the dog, which had again returned to its rug and coiled itself down to sleep.

For himself the turmoil of his brain kept him awake. He tried not to think of the apparitions of the night. It was in vain. The vision of his own moldering corpse persisted before him. Was it a warning of death? But he forced himself to consider the matter calmly, dispassionately, from a scientific point of view. It was all illusion, he knew—mesmerism, perhaps; yet it seemed terrible that any human being had the power thus to influence another's brain at a distance.

But he shuddered when he thought of Margery in the power of these devils in mortal shape. He longed passionately for the time to come when he could take her away from the accursed country that harbored such demons. A madness seized him; and he revolved in his brain wild schemes for killing Morton and his uncanny accomplices.

At last exhaustion crept over him and he felt drowsy. His heavy eyes began to close. He tried to rouse himself and get off the bed to put out the lamp.

As he turned with an effort on his side he suddenly saw the door on the verandah move slowly, although he was sure that he had fastened it securely. While he stared at it, wide-awake now, it opened wide and, to his amazement and horror, through it entered the murderer Hari.

Alan tried to spring up, to cry out. Paralyzed, power-less, unable to utter a sound he watched the man, whom he had believed to be in the condemned cell of a prison three hundred miles away, step noiselessly on bare feet over the floor towards him, a fiendish smile curling his harelip, but his eyes blazing with hate. Alan's brain whirled. He tried to convince himself that what he saw was only another illusion.

But with a strong grasp the gypsy tore down the mosquito curtains and flung them on the floor. Howling fearfully the dog bolted past him out through the open door. Stuart struggled to rise, but to his horror found himself incapable of moving or of crying out.

Gloating over his helpless victim, Hari bent down and grasped his throat. Slowly the cruel grip tightened. The blood flooded Stuart's brain. He gasped, he choked, he tried to draw breath. Suffocating, strangling, he struggled desperately against his powerlessness; but his arms only moved feebly as he tried in vain to loosen the murderous grasp. In extremity he flung them out, and his hand fell helplessly on the small table beside the bed. Instinctively the fingers closed on the cross—and in a last despairing gesture Alan drew back his hand and uncon-sciously thrust the crucifix against the murderer's dark face bent over his.

A wild shriek like the awful cry of a damned soul rang through the room, through the house, echoing out into the open and awaking the trembling servants in their huts. And Murray, bursting gun in hand into the room through the inner door, saw Hari throw up his arms in a gesture of frantic despair, staggering back from the bed on which Stuart lay to all appearance dead.

With a shout of rage the planter raised his weapon and fired at the gypsy, as the man, with his hands to his face, rushed past him out to the verandah. He sprang to the open door after him to fire the second barrel; but Hari had disappeared from sight.

Then Murray ran back to the bed. Alan lay on it without sign of life; and his friend's heart sank as he looked at the rigid body. He rushed into the bathroom, seized a water-jug and dashed the contents in Stuart's face, then, hurrying into the sitting-room, he returned with a glass filled with brandy.

To his joy Alan's bare chest was beginning to heave, his lips twitched and, gasping feebly, he drew breath again. Murray forced the liquor into his mouth, and with some vague recollection of the manner of dealing with apparently drowned persons, seized the young man's arms and worked them vigorously up over his head and down again.

Before long the combined treatment proved successful and brought Stuart back to life; although his throat, bruised and torn by the gypsy's sinewy hands, pained him greatly. He could scarcely speak, but he urged Murray to pursue Hari. The planter refused firmly, barricaded the door, and gave himself up to taking care of his injured friend. Alan's strength was rapidly returning. He sat up and saw the chain still twisted round his fingers.

"I must mend this," he said. "I feel strange without it.

Do you mind passing me the pliers and that bit of wire on the table, Murray? Thank you."

Not until he had contrived to join the links together roughly was he content to lie down and rest again.

When the planter heard the full story of the night he threw up his hands.

"Stuart, ye canna fecht the de'il. Ye maun gang awa'. Awa' frae here at aince. Marry yer lassie tomorra and gang awa', baith!"

"I wish I could. How did that scoundrel Hari manage to get out of Alipore Jail? I suppose Morton bribed some of the warders heavily. In the morning I'll ride to Keighley's garden and telegraph from there to Simpson and to Barrie to tell them that the escaped convict is here."

Shortly after sunrise, in spite of his exhaustion and wounded throat, he mounted his fastest pony and galloped off to the one telegraph office of the district. He routed out the protesting Bengali postmaster from his house long before the official hour of opening, and insisted on his sending off the urgent messages.

Then he and Keighley, who was almost as excited as he, waited anxiously for hours for the replies. Murray had joined them before the first was received. It was from Simpson, and promised that all possible enquiry and search would be made at once. They sat patiently in the post-office.

"But why doesn't Barrie answer?" cried Stuart impatiently. "I'll wire him again—and Carter, too; for he'll—"

Stop! There's someone calling now," interrupted Keighley, as the machine began to tick.

"Hurry up, *babu!* Do hurry!" exclaimed Alan, as the postmaster wrote down the message with exasperating slowness.

Stuart snatched the paper from his fingers.

"What's this? Is he mad?" he cried, as he scanned the message.

Murray looked over his shoulder and read it out aloud:

> "STUART, BAGHPOTA.
> Your message not understood. Convict Hari died in condemned cell in my presence last night. BARRIE."

"What does he mean?" exclaimed Murray. "Died? Why we saw the man only a few hours ago!"

Stuart glanced suspiciously at the postmaster, and whispered to the others:

"Is this telegram a fake? Do you think it is really the message that Barrie sent? Can this *babu* be in Morton's pay and is trying to deceive us?"

"Get him to ask Calcutta to repeat the wire," suggested Keighley.

"No good. He'd do the same again," said Murray. "Hullo! there's another telegram coming through."

They listened to the ticking of the machine, and waited impatiently for the babu to transcribe the message, which he handed to Stuart. It ran:

"STUART, BAGHPOTA.

Calcutta Headquarters inform me Hari died
Alipore Jail. Must have been another gypsy
resembling him that attacked you. Am
coming—SIMPSON."

The three white men stared at each other.

Well, I'm blowed!" ejaculated Murray, "what do you
make of that?"

"If these telegrams are genuine, all I can say is that
another man has been substituted for Hari in the jail, and
probably been poisoned by whoever was in the plot. I
could not mistake anyone else for Hari. It was he, and no
one else, who nearly killed me last night."

"You're right. It was Hari sure enough," said Murray.
"I saw him plainly. Couldn't forget that harelip."

"Telegraph again to Simpson and Barrie, then come
along to my bungalow and have something to eat," suggested Keighley. "There's no use waiting here. If you go to
the quarry today I'll take you there in my car and drop
you afterwards at Baghpota. I've nothing to do; for it's a
slack time on the garden."

Over their food the three men discussed the matter
again from every side. Before they had finished their meal
Keighley's butler brought in another telegram for Stuart.

"Who is this from now, I wonder?" remarked the latter, tearing open the envelope.

He read the message and shouted for joy.

"What luck! It's a cablegram from my uncle, General
Malcolm Stuart. He's taking up his appointment at the

Horse Guards, and I'm to start for England as soon as my orders arrive. The official letters are coming to India by Air Mail."

He looked at the date of the cablegram. "By Jove! they will be here in a week. Tomorrow I'll tell Margery that we must be married at once and start for Bombay to catch the first steamer for England, as soon as someone from the regiment arrives to replace me here. I must wire Uncle Angus."

In the excitement of his news they forgot for the moment the mystery of Hari's reported death. But very soon they began to speculate fruitlessly about it again, until it was time for Keighley and Stuart to start for the quarry, while Murray drove back to Baghpota.

At sunrise next day Alan started for Malpotha. Instead of his rifle he carried the ball-and-shot gun loaded with cartridges that he had filled two nights before. With every sense on the alert he rode through the forest, expecting each moment to see Ghost Tiger appear. But nothing happened; and he reached the Webbs' bungalow safely.

It was hard to say which of the three there was most overjoyed at the news that he brought. His appointment and approaching departure, which made immediate marriage necessary, and the welcome prospect of the sale of the estate, which meant a future in England for Mr. and Mrs. Webb, provided subjects for endless discussion; so that the result of Hari's trial was scarcely spoken of. To the ladies Stuart carefully avoided all mention of the gypsy's reappearance; but when he had an opportunity of taking his future father-in-law aside, he told him the whole story and warned him to be on his guard against any attempt on Margery.

Alone with his betrothed Alan forgot everything but the golden future that stretched before them. The girl was as impatient as he was to leave the Terai and get away from the dangers that threatened their happiness. There was much to arrange, as their marriage must take place in a few days. The old missionary, Mr. Saunders, who would have to perform the ceremony, had to be notified and messages sent to all their friends on the widely-scattered tea-estates around; for every planter in the Duars—with one grim exception— would expect an invitation.

Suddenly Margery gasped:

"Oh, but, Alan, I can't be married so soon!"

"Can't? But we must! I've got to sail as soon as I receive my orders," he exclaimed, in surprise.

"No; I can't!"

"Why, what's the difficulty?"

"Don't you see it's impossible, darling? I haven't got my trousseau!" cried the girl.

Stuart burst into a roar of laughter.

"Good Lord! is that all? You really alarmed me. I thought it was something serious. Sweetheart, you are a true woman. But—I'm very sorry—we cannot wait for your *trousseau*. You'll have to buy clothes in Bombay before we sail."

"But it is serious, Alan. Whoever heard of a girl buying a *trousseau* after her marriage?"

"Well, you must set the fashion, my darling," he said,

laughing. "As there is not a shop or a dressmaker nearer than Calcutta—and that's three hundred miles away—I'm afraid you must wait until we get to Bombay."

Two days later Alan reached Baghpota again after another journey through the forest without incident. In the bungalow he found Simpson awaiting him. The District Superintendent had already heard Murray's story and was frankly bewildered.

"I can't make out what's happened, Stuart," he said, after they had greeted each other. "I wired again to Calcutta, and got the reply that Hari had undoubtedly died in Alipore Jail, apparently on the very night that you were attacked. Are you both sure that it was not someone else you saw? These gypsies are as alike as peas."

"Sure. Of course we're sure," answered Alan impatiently.

He related in detail all the events of the fateful night. Just as he ended his story Murray's butler entered with a bundle of letters. The daily post had arrived.

Stuart took his mail.

"Perhaps Barrie has written too—yes, by Jove! he has. Here's a letter from him. Maybe this will explain."

He tore the envelope open, while the others gazed at him expectantly.

"Well, I'll be! Listen!" he exclaimed.

"This is what he says."

He read out the letter slowly . . .

"MY DEAR STUART,

I cannot understand your telegrams at all. The first arrived just as I was about to write and give you the news of Hari's extraordinary death. He was in the condemned cell, always closely watched by two warders, who were frequently relieved. Well, after midnight, in the early hours of the very morning you wired to me, I was awakened by a message from the jail that there was something wrong with him. I dressed and went to his cell. I found the two warders standing by his cot on which he lay unconscious, rigid, apparently lifeless. He was not breathing. His heart had stopped beating. I thought at first that he was dead. But I was puzzled; for other signs of death were absent. It suddenly occurred to me that he was in a state of catalepsy. As I looked at him he suddenly showed signs of returning consciousness. He breathed; his chest heaved. Then he shrieked—it was the most horrible sound I have ever heard. He foamed at the mouth, he tossed his arms about; and the warders were just in time to grab hold of him as he tried to spring up. He struggled wildly with them; and a third jailer and I had to help them. It was as much as all four of us could do to hold him down. Then he gave another awful shriek, a convulsive movement shook him violently from head to foot, and he fell back on the cot. Dead, really dead this time. And now to my amazement I saw on his cheek a mark that had not been on it a moment before. It was a burn, freshly made. It was shaped like a cross."

Stuart stopped and stared at his companions. Then he said slowly:

"Murray, do you remember I told you that in my last desperate struggle I shoved my hand against Hari's face?"

"Yes, yes. What of it?"

Stuart answered slowly:

"That hand held the chain—and the cross. I pressed the crucifix against Hari's cheek!"

The three men looked at each other in silence. Like a flash of revelation the truth came to them. At last Simpson said in an awed voice:

"It was Hari, then! His astral body, or whatever they call it."

Murray said solemnly:

"And the sacred Sign of Man's Redemption prevailed over the power of the Devil—and destroyed his disciple!"

Then he gasped and cried excitedly:

"Stuart! Don't you see? That's what preserved you when Ghost Tiger attacked you. The cross! Each time you were wearing it. And that night you had taken it off when you broke the chain—and you were unprotected against the demon of Hell sent by that arch-fiend the *yogi*, until by God's mercy your hand fell on the crucifix and you were saved."

Again silence fell on them. After a while Stuart resumed the reading of the letter; but it had little more to tell them. Barrie and another surgeon had performed an autopsy on Hari's corpse, but failed to find any cause of death. They were forced to put it down as due to heart failure.

CHAPTER XVIII

THE SILVER BULLET

A WEEK later under a starry sky in the warm tropic night, dinner-tables, lighted by oil-lamps of all kinds, were set out in the flower-garden and by the side of the tennis-court in front of Lane's bungalow. And at them sat every European—manager, assistant or engineer—from the tea estates in the Terai for many miles around.

Alan Stuart's orders for England had arrived. On the morrow he and Margery were to be married and to start for Bombay. So on this last night before the wedding the planters of the district were giving a farewell dinner to them and to the bride's parents, who were soon to follow her to London. Lane's bungalow had been chosen, for it was the nearest to the Webbs'. In every spare room, on the verandahs in both houses and in tents outside them, camp-beds were crowded together to accommodate the few ladies and the many men who, in motor-cars, in bamboo carts or on horseback, had come thirty or forty miles to take part in a festive gathering such as the Terai had never known.

Each one had made his or her contribution to the feast in food and drink, and had lent furniture, crockery, plate, linen, cutlery and glassware, as well as servants to wait, in the usual generous spirit of British hospitality in India.

At the head-table Lane and his wife, Murray, Keighley, Cartwright and Carey were acting as chief hosts to the four guests; and with them sat the old clergyman, Mr. Saunders, who was to officiate at the marriage, and Langley, the Deputy Commissioner, who, as head executive officer representing the Government of India, ruled like a king this district which was larger than an English county. At the next tables with others of the hosts were placed Simpson, Dr. Venner—who was the medical officer of all the tea-gardens—Hawley the Forest Officer, Hardy the Sub-divisional Officer from Alipur Duar, and Captain Brady, the Royal Engineer who had come to replace Stuart.

The dinner was over, the wine had gone round, and the toast of the King-Emperor duly honoured. So now the serious business of the evening, the speech-making, was to begin. Murray, as the oldest planter in the little community and the 'best man' in the morrow's ceremony, had been chosen to propose the health of the young couple. But unfortunately at the last moment his courage, in spite of being stimulated by copious libations—or perhaps, by reason of them—failed; and he refused pointblank to rise and speak. Entreaties and abuse were equally useless; so Lane leapt into the breach and made an excellent impromptu speech. He expressed the universal regret at parting with the girl whom everyone loved and, from his safe position as a married man, voiced the despair of the bachelors at losing their one spinster, and declared amid cheers that their only consoling thought was that she had been won by a thoroughly good fellow who had made himself universally popular and whose sole drawback was that he was not a planter. He wound up by calling on all to drink the health of the happy pair with Highland honours; which was done at imminent risk to some of the lent tables and chairs.

Margery, seated beside her lover, was touched to tears by the thunderous response and the hearty good wishes from her friends; and Alan could hardly trust himself to speak when he rose to return thanks. Other toasts followed—the bride's parents, the Deputy Commisioner, the old clergyman and the rest of the guests, all of whom responded. Then songs were called for; Mrs. Lane's piano was carried out on the verandah for its fair owner to play the singers' accompaniments, and over the acres of tea-bushes and into the dark forest beyond rang choruses from musical comedies long forgotten in England, but still new to these exiles.

The groups about the tables broke up, their members changed places; and friends from the farther ends of the district who had not met for many months pulled up their chairs beside each other to talk of old times. Carey, who was a good pianist, found some ancient volumes of dance music; and lancers, quadrilles, polkas and Roger de Coverleys were rioted through by joyous couples on Lane's lawn tennis-court, as its surface was impossible for fox-trots and waltzes.

At the head-table a group gathered around Murray. It consisted of Keighley, Simpson, Langley, Saunders and

Dr. Venner, all of whom had been a long time in the district. None of them were ignorant of the sinister menace that hung over it and the dangers that threatened the lovers who were to leave it on the morrow. The Deputy Commissioner in particular was well acquainted with every phase of Morton's evil activities, thanks to Simpson.

To him, Saunders and Venner, as Simpson and Keighley already knew of them, the old Scot now revealed the extraordinary events that had recently taken place, the gypsy girl's death, and the apparition of the yogi, the attacks on Stuart by the Ghost Tiger, and the mystery of the murderous assault on him by Hari at the very hour at which the condemned man was declared by Barrie to have died in his presence.

His hearers stared at Murray and at each other in awed wonder. At last the Deputy Commissioner asked him:

"You saw the man yourself? You recognized him?"

"I saw him as clearly as I see you now, sir. It was Hari, and no other. Remember, I kept guard over him day and night when he was first captured."

"It was a real man and no ghost?"

Simpson broke in. "I saw the scratches and bruises on Stuart's throat when I arrived two days later. They had not been made by ghostly fingers or astral bodies."

"The scratches have not all disappeared," remarked the doctor. "I noticed them myself when I greeted Stuart tonight."

"I thought that it must have been some other gypsy

resembling Hari," said Simpson. "But in face of Stuart's and Murray's insistence that it was he and no one else, I could not go searching among the men of Morton's tribe for such a one."

"What do you think of it all, padre?" asked Langley, turning to the missionary. "You know the natives better than we do."

"When in the Divinity School we read of the Witch of Endor and the magicians who competed against Moses before Pharaoh, we were told that such things were not articles of faith," he replied. "But in my forty years here I have had proof of supernatural happenings that leave me unable to assert positively that there are no wizards, no witchcraft."

"You know of this *yogi*?"

"Indeed I do. Children have disappeared from my Mission, stolen by the gypsies, so their parents believed. Several distracted fathers have followed their traces. Some of these were never seen again; but one or two returned with incredible tales of this *yogi* and the devil-worship of which he is high-priest. They said that a monstrous demon actually appears at their Black Masses and is adored and propitiated by human sacrifices and the blood of young maidens murdered to provide it."

"And this question of astral bodies?"

"Who shall answer it? Can we confidently assert that we of Europe and America possess all the scientific knowledge in the world? Do the sages of the East know nothing? We can transmit thought, light, heat, power, the spoken word, the penciled picture, to immense distances.

Why should it be impossible to project solid objects, such as human bodies, in a like manner?"

"He is no faker, this *yogi!*" exclaimed Simpson. "I'd like to clap handcuffs on him. I wonder how long they'd hold him, though. He does Morton's evil work for him." He stopped and pointed to Alan and Margery, who were laughingly dancing through a Sir Roger de Coverley. "I shall not be happy until I know that those two young people have sailed out of Bombay harbour. The devils of India have no power over blue water."

"Has anyone news of what Morton is doing?" asked the Deputy Commissioner.

Keighley shook his head.

"No one's seen or heard of him since Hari's first trial," he replied. "But rumors filter through the coolies, tales of wild orgies, debauches, horrible doings. It is whispered that he is mad."

"He is all the more dangerous for *them,*" said Simpson, nodding towards the lovers.

"You have taken precautions?" asked Langley, lowering his voice.

"Yes, sir, I have men watching the road out of Morton's garden, to tell me who leaves it. Not that it's much use against people who can project their bodies through space. But, as it would be easy in the darkness around us to shoot anyone sitting at these tables or dancing on the tennis court in this light, I have others hidden in the tea-bushes here."

The Deputy Commissioner nodded approval.

"Good. When we go back to Webb's bungalow tonight

I am driving Stuart and Miss Webb in my car. I'll put the
hood up so that no one can get a shot at them from the
jungle as we pass through it. I want you to sit beside me,
Simpson. You are armed?"

"Yes, sir. I am sending a constable with a rifle in
Keighley's car with him and Murray."

"I have an automatic in my pocket," interjected
Keighley.

"As there will be other cars and pony-carts and
several fellows riding I think we need not fear an attack in
the forest," said Langley. "But we must all keep together."

"Tonight is Morton's last chance, and he is desperate," Simpson went on. "I'll have men around Webb's
house until daylight. And when after the marriage you
drive Stuart and his bride to the railway, I'm coming with
you, sir. I shall put armed constables on the train as far as
Gitaldaha, which is the limit of my district."

"Excellent. I think they'll be safe after that," said the
Deputy Commissioner with satisfaction. He looked at his
watch. "How late it is! It will be daylight in another
couple of hours. Ought we not make a move, Murray?"

"Oh, not yet, sir, please!" pleaded the Scot. "They're
all enjoying themselves. We've never had a night like this
in the district."

Certainly, no one else showed any desire to break up
the party. Another hour passed before the end came, and
the contingent of planters who were bound for Webb's
house had finished their goodnights to those who were to
sleep at Lane's. They set off in a body, the automobiles
moving at a slow speed over the rough, unlighted track

through the forest, so as not to outpace the riders and the drivers of the horse-drawn traps.

In the back seat of Langley's car Margery nestled in her lover's arms, while he kissed her rapturously and murmured that in a very few hours they would be joined together, never to part while life lasted. All too soon for them, slow as the pace of the convoy had been, the drive ended and they had to separate—"for the last time!" whispered Alan.

Room had been found for Mr. Saunders and the married couples in the house. Mr. Langley, Stuart, Simpson, Murray and the other men were to sleep in tents pitched in front of the building. After the former had retired and Webb, in compliance with Simpson's warning, had locked and barred all the doors, Alan and the Police Officer, pistol in hand, went carefully round the outside of the bungalow to make sure that no one was lurking near it.

"It was a good idea of yours, Stuart, to have those iron bars fixed on the windows."

"Yes; they'll keep out dacoits, but there are worse things than robbers," replied the young Scot doubtfully. "I am not going to bed tonight—or this morning, I should say; for it's nearly dawn."

"Oh, come, you must lie down. Remember you're being married today. You'll look an awful worm if you don't have at least an hour's sleep. Turn in! I'll keep guard."

"Thanks very much, old fellow. But I'm too anxious. I couldn't sleep."

"Well, come into Murray's tent and have a nightcap.

It may make you sleep. I see his lamp is alight. I hope he will not funk his duties as 'best man', like he did his speech tonight."

They found the planter sitting on his bed in pajamas, a full glass in one hand, a prayer-book in the other.

"Good heavens! What are you doing? Praying?" cried Simpson in surprise.

Murray answered solemnly:

"Hush! Don't interrupt! I am reading the drill-book. I mean, I am studying the Marriage Service to see what I've got to do. Mrs. Burton lent me the prayer-book."

Simpson laughed. "As you are holding it upside down I don't think you'll learn much from it. I know you've a bottle of whiskey somewhere. Trot it out!"

"It's on the dressing-table," replied Murray, indicating a tray with a bottle and glasses.

"Thanks! Here, Stuart; have a *doch-an-dorris* or whatever is Scotch for 'nightcap' and go to bed! We'll take our drinks to your tent, so you'll have no excuse."

Simpson filled their glasses; and they sat down in Alan's tent. The hearts of the three men were full, for they knew this to be their last night together—for a long time, at least. They had been good friends, they had passed through much side by side, and tomorrow two of them would say goodbye to the third and might never see him again. They sat talking longer than they realized. In their absorption they forgot for the time the danger they feared outside.

Suddenly piercing shrieks rang out from the house, a gunshot, a fierce roar, loud shouts! Then followed a babel of strange snarling, screeching sounds, the curses of men and the shrill screams of women.

The three men sprang up and rushed out of the tent, Alan seizing his gun as he went. The day had dawned. By its light they saw a terrible sight.

On the verandah a huge black-shaped, grey-hided beast, reared on its hind-legs against Margery's window, was biting, worrying with its white fangs at the iron bars, trying with powerful paws to tear them out of their sockets or force them apart. From inside the room came piercing screams and loud shouts.

"The Ghost Tiger!" cried Simpson and, pulling out his pistol, fired at it.

From the other tents suddenly-awakened men ran out in their pajamas, two or three with rifles. And they, too, fired at the animal. But, apparently unscathed, it tore frenziedly at the bars, snarling, roaring with anger at being baulked by the unexpected obstacle.

From inside the room Webb fired at it point-blank. But the great brute seemed proof against bullets.

Stuart ran forward. "Stop firing! Leave it to me!" he cried. To the men behind him he shouted, "Keep back, for God's sake! Leave it to me, I tell you! Keep them back, Simpson!"

He sprang towards the house, stopped, and raising his gun, fired at the devil-beast. In his haste he missed his mark. The bullet stuck the wall a foot from the tiger's head, knocking out flakes of plaster, and fell flattened to the floor.

"Margery! Keep clear of the window!" he shouted,

trying to make himself heard above the wild roaring of the maddened brute.

He steadied himself, drew a deep breath and lifted the gun to his shoulder again. Then he fired the second barrel.

Loud above the cries of the women in the house, the shouts of the men held back by Simpson, rang an awful scream of agony, as the grey tiger dropped back, swung round, leapt clean over the verandah rail and twenty feet beyond it and, pursued by a ragged volley from the planters, bounded away among the tea-bushes and disappeared from sight.

Alan sprang up the verandah steps and ran to Margery's window. As he reached it he trod on the flattened bullet and, even in his haste, stooped and picked it up. Then he thrust his face to the bars, and cried:

"Are you safe, darling? Are you hurt?"

Margery came to the window. She was trembling but calm.

"Oh, Alan, is it *you?* How are you? Are you safe? Are *you* hurt? I am all right."

"Oh, thank God!" he cried fervently. "Is everyone all right inside?"

"Yes. We were very frightened; and Mother nearly fainted. But she is recovering. Has that awful beast gone?"

"Yes. It is wounded and has bolted. Simpson and the others are chasing it."

Through the window he could see Mrs. Webb lying on the bed, while her husband and Mrs. Burton, another planter's wife, bent over her.

"Tell your father he can open the front door. It is quite safe now. I want to come in to you."

In another minute he held her in his arms and rained kisses on her upturned face, while she clung to him desperately.

"Oh, Alan, I was so afraid for you. I knew you would come to help me; and I feared the brute would kill you. What is that? They are calling for you outside! Oh, don't go, beloved! Don't go into danger again! It was the Ghost Tiger, was it not?"

"Yes, sweetheart. But it has gone. There's no risk now. I must go, Margery. Be brave, my darling!"

He put her gently from him and went out on the verandah, where Mr. Langley, Saunders, Simpson and the other men were gathered.

"The brute is wounded, Stuart. Look at the blood on the matting!" said the Deputy Commissioner.

"There's blood on the track through the bushes. It is splashed everywhere," added Simpson. "The beast must be badly hit. It is bleeding profusely and can't go far. If we follow it up at once we may overtake it and finish it off. Stay here, Stuart, and look after Miss Webb. We'll go!"

Alan shook his head.

"No; I must go myself." He turned to the others. "There is no need for all to come. Will you please let me take charge? I have a reason. I know what I'm doing. I have met this brute before!"

The rest hesitated. But he took their consent for granted, and went on:

"Will you come with me, Mr. Langley, please? And you, doctor? Mr. Saunders, I'd like you, too. And, Simpson, Murray, Keighley! That's enough. Will the rest please stay here and guard the ladies?"

The others gave way reluctantly.

Alan, gun in hand, led his party off, following the clearly marked track through the crushed and broken tea-plants, which showed where the brute had passed. The leaves were splashed with its blood. Behind Stuart came Langley, Simpson and Keighley with loaded rifles; while Venner, Murray and the old missionary brought up the rear.

And on the verandah Margery, clinging to the railing, followed her lover with anxious eyes; while her father and the other men strove to reassure her.

The blood-marked trail led the little party out of the tea-bushes and along a track through the forest leading towards the mountains. Alan soon recognized it. It was the path up which Margery and he had gone on the day when she had been attacked by the bear. He was not surprised. For he remembered that she had told him it was a short cut to Morton's garden.

It soon drew clear of the jungle and began to climb the foothills until it reached the spot where the track up the mountains branched off from it. But it continued along the brink of a steep precipice. And everywhere the leaves of the bushes bordering it and the ground underfoot were splashed with blood.

"Look out, Stuart! We must be near it," whispered Keighley, as he and Simpson closed up on him to protect him against a sudden charge of the wounded beast.

Alan silently pointed to the path ahead of them. In the dust the heavy footprints of a tiger were plainly visible. They were irregular, as if the brute was staggering from side to side, exhausted by the loss of the blood that now lay in patches. The armed men brought their guns to the ready and moved slowly forward.

Suddenly Alan stopped.

"Do you see that?" he cried.

On the crumbling edge of the precipice lay a huddled mass.

Simpson stared.

"It's a man! A dead man! He must have met the brute face to face; and it killed him," he said in a low tone.

The others looked over his shoulder.

"He was a jungle coolie," said the Deputy Commissioner. "The corpse is naked."

Alan's eyes shone with a strange light. He stepped forward.

"Look! See who it is" he cried.

Before them in a pool of blood lay the naked man, a wound plainly visible in the left breast. They knew him.

It was Morton. Dead!

Venner pushed through the others and dropped on his knees beside the corpse.

"No tiger killed him. He was shot!" he exclaimed. "That hole was made by a bullet. It has gone through him. See! It has nearly come out at the other side. I can feel it—here, lying flattened just under the skin."

He laid his hand on the breast.

"Why, he has not been dead five minutes! The body is still warm. The blood has barely stopped flowing. It is not dry yet. But who has stripped his body?"

He clapped his hand to his pocket.

"I've got a scalpel here. I'll have that bullet out in a jiffy."

He bared the blade. As he stooped over the body Alan touched his shoulder.

"One moment, doctor!" he said, in a strange tone. "Before you cut out that bullet look at this one."

He opened his hand. On the palm lay a mushroomed bullet. On its still intact base a deep cross was cut.

"Now go on!" he said.

Venner looked at him in surprise. Then he bent over the corpse and made an incision where a lump showed under the skin.

"Here it is!" he cried, and held up a flattened bullet. Then he wiped it clean of blood and stared at it.

"Good heavens! What—what is this?" he gasped.

On the base the others saw that a cross was cut.

"It's—it's the mate of the one you showed me, Stuart," he said.

The Deputy Commissioner took both and examined them.

"Yes; they're the same. What does it mean, Stuart?" he asked.

Alan looked at Simpson.

"You saw me fire at the Ghost Tiger over Barter's body—and miss." He turned to Murray. "And you fired two shots into it pointblank. I gave it two bullets at a few yards' range. It was not hurt."

"Yes, yes. That's so. Go on!" cried the planter excitedly.

"You reminded me in the bungalow that in Scotland in the old days it was believed that a leaden bullet could not wound a wizard. Only a silver one would do that."

"Yes. Go on!"

"That night I melted several coins and made them into bullets for cartridges that I filled. I cut a cross on the base of each one. Just now I fired two of them at the tiger on the verandah. My first missed and struck the wall. I picked it up on the verandah floor. That is the one I showed you, doctor. With the second bullet I mortally wounded the Ghost Tiger at last. There he lies—dead!"

"What? Morton?"

"Morton was Ghost Tiger?"

"Impossible! Yet—"

"Did you guess who it was, Stuart?"

All had spoken except the missionary. Langley turned to him and said:

"What do you say, *padre?*"

The old man had taken off his sun-helmet and was praying silently.

He looked down at the corpse with a shudder.

"I suspected it. I knew that the natives here firmly believe that the three generations of the Mortons—this man, his father, his grandfather—possessed the power to transform themselves into tigers to procure blood for the infamous rites of their devil-worship. Look!" He pointed to the dusty track. "You see the imprints of the tiger's paws end at the corpse. Beyond it there are no tracks visible of man or animal."

The others stared at the ground.

Past the body the thick dust lay undisturbed.

Simpson gasped:

"Of course. He could change the substance of his body. But not his clothes. Therefore he is naked."

There was an awed silence. Then Langley spoke:

"Gentlemen, this is incredible, impossible. It could not have happened. Yet it has. I trust to your discretion to be silent."

He turned to the Police Officer.

"You and I represent Law and Order, Simpson. Therefore you and I shall commit a crime—if crime it is. Help me to push this body over the edge of the precipice. It will fall a thousand feet sheer down, and will be smashed beyond recognition on the rocks of the ravine below."

Solemnly the two men stepped forward and rolled the corpse over the overhanging brink. None heard it strike the bottom.

The Deputy Commissioner stood up.

"Gentlemen, Mr. Morton, on his way to be present at the marriage, met with an unfortunate accident, fell from this dangerous path and was killed. I rely on your honour to stick to that story."

They all looked into his eyes and nodded.

There was a portentous silence. Then the Deputy Commissioner straightened himself and said in a different tone:

"Mr. Stuart is to be married this morning. Let us return for the wedding!"

L'ENVOI

THE deep notes of Big Ben striking ten o'clock floated in through the open window of Captain and Mrs. Stuart's Westminster flat; and Murray stopped speaking to listen to the sound.

"Man! It's grand to hear that again after five years. How long since you did, Simpson?" he asked.

"Four years. These are fine flats in this big new building, Mrs. Stuart," said the Deputy Superintendent, turning to their hostess.

"Yes, we were lucky in getting one," replied Margery, who sat on the arm of her husband's chair. "We are so near Alan's office in the Horse Guards and not far from my parents."

"The rooms are so large and lofty; and your son and heir's nursery is just fine—he's a great lad, that boy," remarked the planter. "It seems only the other day that we were looking at you two getting married."

"Yet it's two years, to the day," said Margery.

"We were so glad that your steamer arrived yesterday, just in time for you fellows to dine here tonight and help us to celebrate the anniversary," said her husband.

"Here in the heart of London it's hard to believe that all those terrible happenings before your marriage were really true," remarked Simpson.

"It's different out there in the Terai. When the night hush of the jungle surrounds you and the strange creatures it holds are afoot, you can credit anything."

Margery shuddered. Alan Stuart withdrew his arm from her waist and rose. Going to the desk he took out a small box.

"If ever I'm tempted to think that it was all a nightmare," he said solemnly, "I look at this!"

He took a small object from the box and held it up. It was a flattened piece of discolored metal that had once been a silver bullet.

TIGER GIRL Apendix
Excerpt from *OCCULT SCIENCE IN INDIA*
By
Louis Jacolliot
1884

Chief Justice of Chanenagur (French East Indies) and of Tahiti (Oceanica)

CHAPTER XIII.

FORMULAS OF MAGICAL INCANTATION—*VULGAR MAGIC.*

The formulas of magical incantation, addressed to evil spirits, are kept as secret as those used in the evocation of superior spirits. They even form a part of a special book of the Agronchada called the Agrou-chada-Parikeliai, treating of magicians.

They are also written, as well as read, in a manner similar to that we have just described, in order to hide from the profane their real meaning. We pass them over, however, and turn our attention to the external manifestations, exorcisms, and cases of demoniacal possession which are so frequent in India.

We propose to give an impartial account of the numerous facts that have fallen under our own observation, some of which are so extraordinary from a physiological, as well as from a purely spiritual point of view, that we hardly know what to say of them.

We merely allude to the chapter of the Agrouehada treating of formulas of incantation and are unable to give any further information as to the magical words, to which the priests attribute so much virtue in exorcising Rakchasas, Pisatchas, Nagas, Souparnas, and other evil spirits that frequent funeral ceremonies, take possession of men's bodies, and disturb the sacrifices.

We have already, in another work*, discussed that portion of the Book of the Pitris, notwithstanding its vulgarity, and we see no reason to change the opinion therein expressed, which it may not be amiss to call to the reader's mind. He will excuse us for quoting ourselves:

Magic seems to have established itself in India, as in some highly favored spot. In that country nothing is attributed to ordinary causes, and there is no act of malignancy or of wickedness of which the Hindus deem their magicians incapable.

Disappointments, obstacles, accidents, diseases, untimely deaths, the barrenness of women, miscarriages, epizootics, in short, all the ills that humanity is heir to, are attributed to the occult and diabolical practices of some wicked magician, in the pay of an enemy.

If an Indian, when he meets with a misfortune, happens to be on bad terms with anybody, his suspicions are immediately directed in that quarter, and he accuses his enemy of resorting to magic in order to injure him.

The latter, however, resents the imputation. Their feelings become embittered against each other, the disagreement soon extends to their relatives and friends, and the consequences often become serious.

As malign spirits are exorcised, pursued, and hunted by the followers of the Pitris, it is the vulgar belief that they enter the service of vagabonds and miscreants, and teach them special magical formulas, by which they seek together to do all possible harm to others.

Several thousand years of sacerdotal despotism, during which every means have been employed to keep the people in ignorance and superstition, have carried popular credulity to its highest pitch.

In the South of India particularly we constantly moot with crowds of soothsayers, and sorcerers, vending their oracles to anyone who would purchase them, and spreading before rich and poor alike for a consideration the pretended mystery of human destiny.

These people are not much dreaded.

**History of the Virgins*

But there are others, whose diabolical art is thought to be un-limited, and who are supposed to possess all the secrets of magic.

To inspire love or hatred, to introduce the devil into any one's body, or to drive him away, to cause sudden death or an incurable disease, to produce contagious maladies in cattle, or to protect them therefrom, to discover the most secret things, and to find lost or stolen articles—all this is but child's play for them.

The mere sight of one who is supposed to be endowed with such vast power inspires the Hindu with the deepest terror.

These doctors of magic are often consulted by persons who have enemies, of whom they desire to be revenged, by means of sorcery. On the other hand, when any one who suffers from disease attributes it to a cause of this kind, he calls in their aid, that they may deliver him by a counter-charm, or transfer the disease to those who have so maliciously caused it in his case.

The supplementary volume of the Agrouchada-Parikchai, treating of the practices of vulgar magic, does not seem to question them in any respect; it merely attributes them to the influence of evil spirits.

In its view, the magician's power is immense, but he only uses it for evil purposes.

Nothing is easier than for him to afflict any one whom he may meet with fever, dropsy, epilepsy, insanity, a constant nervous trembling, or any other disease, in short. But that is nothing. By his art he can even cause the entire destruction of an army besieging a city, or the sudden death of the commander of a besieged city and of all its inhabitants.

But while magic teaches how to do harm, it also shows us how to prevent it. There is no magician so shrewd that there is not another who can more than match him in ability, or destroy the effect of his charms, and make them rebound upon himself or his patrons.

Independent of their direct intervention, the magicians have a large assortment of amulets, talismans, and powerful and efficient preservatives against sorcery and enchantments, in which they do a large business and make a great deal of money.

They consist of glass beads, enchanted by mentrams, of dried and aromatic roots and herbs, of sheets of copper upon which cabalistic characters, uncouth figures, and fantastical words are engraved.

The Hindus of the lower castes always wear them upon their persons, thinking that a supply of these relics will protect them from all harm.

Secret preparations to inspire love, to kindle anew an expiring passion, to restore vigor to the weak and infirm, come also within the province of the magicians, and are by no means the least unproductive source of their income.

It is to them a woman always applies first when she wishes to reclaim a faithless husband, or prevent his becoming such.

It is by the aid of the philters they concoct that a young libertine or a sweetheart usually tries to beguile or captivate the object of his passion.

The Agrouchada also discusses the subject of incubi. "These demons in India," says Dubois, "are much worse and more diabolical, than those spoken of by Delrio the Jesuit, in his 'Disquisitiones Magicse.' By their violent and long-continued embraces they so weary the women whom they visit in the form of a dog, a tiger, or some other animal, that the poor creatures often die of fatigue and exhaustion."

It then speaks at some length of the means by which weapons may be enchanted or bewitched.

These arms upon which magical mentrams have been pronounced, have the virtue of producing effects which will compare in every respect with those caused by the celebrated sword of Durandal, or the lance of Argail, by which so many were disabled.

The Hindu gods and giants, in their frequent wars with each other, always made use of enchanted arms.

Nothing could withstand, for instance, the arrow of Brahma, which was never unsheathed without destroying an entire army; or the arrow of the serpent Capel, which, whenever it was cast among his enemies, had the property of throwing them into a state of lethargy which, as may well be imagined, put them at a great disadvantage and contributed largely to their defeat.

There is no secret that magic does not teach. There are magical secrets how to acquire wealth and honors; to render sterile women prolific by rubbing the hands and feet with certain enchanted compounds; to discover treasures buried in the earth, or concealed in some secret place, no matter where; and to make the bearer invulnerable, or even invincible, in battle.

The only thing they are not so clear about is the subject of ever-lasting life; and yet who can tell how many alchemists have grown white in the crypts of the pagodas, and how many strange philters have been there concocted in order to learn the secret of immortality?

To become expert in magic the pupil must learn from a magician himself, whom the sorcerers call their Guru, like the believers in the philosophical doctrine of the Pitris, the formulas of evocation, by means of which the malign spirits are brought into complete subjection.

Some of these spirits the magician evokes in preference to others, probably on account of their willingness to do anything that may be required of them.

In the first rank are the spirits of certain planets. The name, Grahas, which is used to designate them, means the act of seizing or taking possession of those whom they are commanded, by a magical incantation, to torment.

In the next rank come the boutams, or demons, from the lower regions, representing each a principle of destruction, the pisatchas, rakchasas, nagas, and other evil spirits.

The chaktys are female genii, who force men whom they meet at night.

The malign spirits are Kali, the Goddess of Blood, Marana-Devy, the Goddess of Death, and the others whom we have enumerated.

In order to set them in motion the magician has recourse to various mysterious operations, such as mentrams, sacrifices, and other different formulas. He should be nude when he addresses himself to goddesses, and modestly clothed when he addresses himself to male spirits.

The flowers that he offers to the spirits evoked by him should all be red, and the boiled rice should be colored with the blood of a young virgin, or a child, in ease he proposes to cause death.

The mentrams, or prayers, which have such efficacy in all magical matters, exercise such an ascendancy upon the superior spirits themselves that the latter are powerless to refuse to do whatever the magician may order, in heaven, in the air, or upon the earth.

But those which are most certain and irresistible its their effects are what are called the fundamental mentrams. and consist of various fantastical monosyllables, of uncouth sound and difficult pronunciation, after the manner of those which we have already given while speaking of the formulas used by the priests.

Sometimes the magician repeats his men trams in a respectful tone, ending all his evocations with the word *Namaha*, meaning respectful greeting, and loading the spirit that he has evoked with praises. At other times he speaks to them in an imperious and dictatorial tone, exclaiming in angry accents:

"If you are willing to do what I ask you, that is enough; if not, I command you in the name of such and such a god,"

Thereupon the spirit had to submit.

It would be impossible to enumerate the different drugs, ingredients, and implements that compose the stock-in-trade of a magician.

There are some spells in which it is necessary to use the bones of sixty-four different kinds of animals, neither more nor less, and among them are included those of a man born on the first day of the new moon, or of a woman, or a virgin, or a child, or a pariah.

When all these bones, being mingled together, are enchanted by mentrams and consecrated by sacrifices, and are buried in an enemy's house or at his door, upon a night ascertained to.be propitious, after an inspection of the stars for that purpose, his death will infallibly follow.

In like manner, if the magician, in the silence of night, should bury the bones in question in an enemy's camp at the four cardinal points of the compass, and then, retiring to a distance, should pronounce the mentram of defeat, all the troops there encamped would utterly perish, or else would scatter to the four winds of heaven, of their own accord, before seven days had elapsed.

Thirty-two enchanted arms thrown among a besieging army would cause such a fright that a hundred men would seem like a thousand.

Of a mixture of earth taken from sixty-four most disgusting places —we refrain from accompanying the Hindu author in his enumeration of the places in question—mingled with his enemy's hair and nail-clippings, small figures are made, upon whose bosom the name of the person upon whom it is desired to take revenge is inscribed. Magical words and mentrams are then pronounced over them, and they are consecrated by sacrifices. As soon as this is done, the grahas, or evil genii of the planets, take possession of the person who is the subject of animosity, and he is subjected to all sorts of evil treatment.

Sometimes these figures are transfixed with an awl, or are injured in various ways, with the object of really killing or disabling him who is the object of vengeance.

Sixty-four roots of various kinds of the most noxious plants are known to the magicians, which in their hands become the most powerful weapons for the secret infliction of the deadliest blows upon those at whom they are aimed.

Notwithstanding, the occupation of a magician is not without danger by any means. The gods and evil genii are very vindictive and never obey the injunctions of a miserable mortal very good-humoredly. It often happens that they punish him very severely for the brutal way in which he orders them about.

Woe to him if he makes the slightest mistake, if he is guilty of the most insignificant omission of the innumerable ceremonies which are obligatory upon him in the performance of an evocation. All the ills that were intended for others are incontinently showered down upon his own head.

He is constantly in fear, it seems, lest some other member of the same confraternity, of greater ability than himself, may succeed in making his own imprecations rebound upon himself or his patrons.

All these superstitious doctrines still exist in India, and most of the pagodas belonging to the vulgar cult possess, apart from the higher priests whom they are compelled to lodge and feed, a body of magicians whose services are let out to the lower castes, in precisely the same way as those of the Fakirs.

Now they undertake to rid a woman from the nocturnal embraces of an incubus: at another time they undertake to restore the virile power of a man where it has been lost in consequence of a spell cast by some opposing magician.

At other times, they are called upon to protect flocks, that have been decimated through the enchantments of others, against all noxious influences.

From time to time, in order to keep alive in the public mind the belief in these sacred doctrines, these jugglers send out challenges to other pagodas, and publicly engage in contests, in the presence of witnesses and arbitrators, who are called in to decide which of the two champions is the more accomplished in his art.

The object of the contest is to obtain possession of an enchanted bit of straw, a small stick, or a piece of money.

The antagonists are both placed at the same distance from the object, whatever it may be, and they both make believe to approach it, but the mentrams they utter, the evocations they perform, the enchanted powders which they reciprocally throw at each other, possess a virtue which repels them : an invincible and overpowering force seems to stand in the way; they make fresh attempts to advance but they are forced back; they redouble their efforts; they fall into spasms and convulsions, they perspire profusely and 6pit blood. Ultimately one of them obtains possession of the enchanted object and is declared the victor.

It sometimes happens that one of the combatants is overthrown by the power of his adversary's mentrams. In that case he rolls on the ground as though he were possessed by a demon, and remains there motionless for some time, appearing to have lost his mind.

At last he recovers the use of his senses, arises in an apparent state of fatigue and exhaustion, and seems to retire covered with shame and confusion. He returns to the pagoda and does not make his appearance again for some time. A serious sickness is supposed to have ensued in consequence of the incredible, though ineffectual, efforts he has made.

There is no doubt that these pitiable farces, with which those who have been honestly initiated into the genuine worship of the Pitris are in no way connected whatever, are all concerted in advance, between the priests belonging to the vulgar cult of the rival pagodas and the charlatans by whom they are performed, and the victory is ascribed to each in turn. But the multitude who witness these spectacles, and who pay generously for them, are filled with fear and admiration of the sorcerers themselves, and are firmly persuaded that their contortions are due to supernatural causes.

There is one fact of which there can be no doubt, and that is, that these men perform their part with extraordinary truthfulness and expression, and that within the domain of pure magnetism they are really able to produce phenomena of which we have no idea in Europe. They are, however, inferior in ability to the Fakirs, belonging to the first class of initiates.

When, however, we come to consider the external manifestations by means of which the believers in the Pitris display their power, we shall look upon the performances of the magicians as trifling in comparison and unworthy of further consideration. They are obviously due to trickery and deception; we have already devoted quite enough space to them to give the reader an idea of what they can do.

There also exists in India another kind of enchantment, which is called *drichty-dotcha*, or a spell cast by the eyes. All animated beings, all plants, all fruits are subject to it. In order to remove it, it is customary to erect a pole in all gardens or cultivated fields, at the top of which is attached a large earthen vessel, the inside of which is whitened with whitewash: it is placed there, being a conspicuous and noticeable object, in order to attract the attention of any passing enemy, and thus prevent his looking at the crops, which would certainly be thereby injured.

We have rarely seen a rice-field in Ceylon or India that was not provided with one or more of these counter-charms.

The Hindus are so credulous upon this point that they are continually fancying that they cannot perform a single act of their lives, or take a single step, however insignificant it may be, without danger of receiving from a neighbor, or a mere passerby, or even a relative, the *drichty-dotcha*. There is nothing in the appearance of those who possess this fatal gift to indicate that they are so endowed Those who have it are often unconscious of it themselves. For this reason every Hindu, several times a day, causes to be performed in the case of himself, his family, his fields, and his house, the ceremony of the *arratty*, the design of which is to counteract any harm that might otherwise befall him from spells cast by the eyes.

The *arratty* is one of their commonest practices, whether public or private. It may almost be elevated to the height of a national custom, so general is it in every province. It is always performed by women, and any woman is qualified to perform it except widows, who are never admitted to any domestic ceremony, their more presence alone being unlucky.

The ceremony is performed as follows:

A lamp full of oil, perfumed with sandal-wood, is placed on a metal plate. It is then lighted, and one of the women of the household when her father, or husband, or any other member of the family, comes in from outdoors, takes the plate in her hand, and raises it as high as the head of the person upon whom the ceremony is to be performed, and describes therewith either three or seven circles according to his or her age or rank.

Instead of a lighted lamp, a vase is often used containing water perfumed with sandal-wood and saffron, reddened by vermilion, and consecrated by the immersion of a few stalks of the divine cousa grass.

The *arratty* is publicly performed several times a day upon persons of distinction, such as rajahs, provincial governors, army generals, or others of elevated rank. It is a ceremony to which courtiers are bidden, as formerly with us to the king's *levée*. One practice is quite as ridiculous to ns as the other, and judging from what we have ourselves seen, in certain provinces in the Deccan, where the English have allowed a few phantoms of rajahs still to remain, the courtiers in this country are quite as degraded and servile a class as with us. They pay for the crumbs they receive and the favors they enjoy by the sacrifice of every feeling of conscience or dignity. It is the same everywhere. We must say, however, to the credit of the Hindu courtiers, that they never made their wives or daughters the mistresses of their rajahs.

As a general thing, a Hindu of any caste would blush to owe his own preferment to the dishonor of his wife.

Whenever persons belonging to a princely rank have been obliged to appear in public, or to speak to strangers, they never fail, upon returning to their palaces, to summon their wives or send for their devadassis from the neighboring temple to perform this ceremony upon them, and thus prevent the serious consequences that might otherwise result from any baleful glances to which they may have been exposed. They often have in their pay girls specially employed for that purpose.

Whenever you enter a Hindu house, if you are regarded as a person of distinction, the head of the family directs the young women to perform the ceremony of *arratty*. It is also performed for the statues of the gods.

When the dancing-girls at the temples have finished their other ceremonies, they never fail to perform the *arratty* two or three times over the gods to whose service they are attached.

This is also practiced with still more solemnity when their 6tatues are carried in procession through the streets. Its object is to avert any bad consequences resulting from glances which it is as difficult for the gods to avoid as simple mortals. Finally, the *arratty* is generally performed upon elephants, horses, domestic animals, and particularly upon the sacred bullocks, and even sometimes upon growing fields of rice.

Beside the more elevated doctrines taught by those who believe in the Pitris, vulgar magic in India takes its place as a degenerate descendant. It was the work of the lower priesthood and intended to keep the people in a constant state of apprehendsion. In all times, and in all places, by the side of the most elevated philosophical speculations, we always find the religion of the people.

We have dwelt at some length upon the practice of magic and sorcery in India, though they have nothing whatever to do with the higher worship which initiated Brahmins pay to the shades of their ancestors and the superior spirits, for the reason that nothing was better calculated to prove the Asiatic origin of most of the nations of Europe than a detailed description of these strange customs, which are identical with many that we meet with upon our own soil, and of which our historical traditions furnished us no explanation until we made the discovery that we were related to the Hindus by descent.

People in the middle ages believed implicitly in succubi and incubi, in the efficacy of magical formulas, in sorcery and the evil eye. Coming down to a period nearer our own times, we have not forgotten those fanatical *leaguers*, who carried their superstition to such a pitch that they used to make little images of wax representing Henry HI. and the King of Navarre. They were accustomed to transfix these images in different places and keep them so for a period of forty days. On the fortieth day they stabbed them to the heart, fully persuaded that they would thus cause the death of the princes they were designed to represent Practices of this kind were so common that, in 1571, a pretended sorcerer named Trois-Echelles, who was executed on the *Place de Gréve*, declared in his examination that there were more than three thousand persons engaged in the same business, and that there was not a woman at court, or belonging to the middle or lower class, who did not patronize the magicians, particularly in love matters.

The execution of Gauffredy, the *curé*, and of Urbain Grandier, by Richelieu's orders, sufficiently demonstrate that the greatest minds of the time were not able to withstand the influence of these superstitions.

We read in Saint Augustine's Book, called "The City of God," that disbelief in the power of evil spirits was equivalent to a refusal to believe in the Holy Scriptures themselves.

The Bible, which is taken from the sacred books of antiquity, believed in sorcery, and the sorcerer must stand or fall with the authority of the Bible.

It is scarcely a century since persons convicted of magic were burnt at the stake, and we are struck with amazement by some of the sentences rendered by magistrates, still highly esteemed by their countrymen, according to which, upon the mere charge of sorcery, poor people suffered death by fire as charlatans, who, at the most, were only guilty of having cheated their neighbors out of a few sols by contrivances which were rather calculated to excite mirth than to do any serious injury.

It is difficult to understand these sentences, except by supposing that the magistrates themselves were in the occult power of the sorcerers.

In 1750, a Jesuit named Girard had a narrow escape from being burnt alive by a decree of the parliament of Provence, for having cast a spell upon the fair Cadière. He was saved by the disagreement of his judges, who were equally divided in opinion as to his guilt. He was given the benefit of the doubt.

A nun of the noble Chapter of Wurtzburg was burnt at the stake in the same year for being guilty of magical practices.

Since that time, fortunately, we have made some progress.

When we threw off the yoke of the Romish priest, from that day common sense, conscience, and reason resumed their sway, and while our Hindu ancestors, who are yet under the dominion of their Brahmins and Necromancers, still slumber on in the last stages of decrepitude and decay, we have made great strides in the path of scientific progress and intellectual liberty.

We always meet the priest and sorcerer upon the same plane of social charlatanism. They are both products of superstition and grow out of the same causes.

From an ethnographic point of view, it is interesting to observe that the Romans also inherited similar opinions from their Hindu ancestors.

We remember what Ovid said of Medea, the magician:

> *Per tmnulos erat passis discincta capillis,*
> *Certaque de tepidis colligit ossa rogis,*
> *Devovet absentes, simulaoraque cerea fingit*
> *Et miscrum tenues in jecur urget aous.*

Horace also speaks of two magicians, named Canidia and Sagana, whose apparatus contained two figures, one of wool and the other of wax.

. . . . *Major*
Lanea, quae pcenis oompesceret inferiorem:
Cerea suppliciter stabat: servilibus utque
Jam peritura, modis.

We must confess, however, that the Lydian singer was not very much in earnest in speaking of them, when we consider the noise—*Proh pudor!*—by whose aid he caused them to be put to flight by the god of gardens, who was annoyed by their enchantments.

Horace would certainly not have sent his two witches to the stake.

The same ideas with regard to visual influences also existed among the Romans, as shown, among other things, by the following line from Virgil:

Nescao quis teneros oculus ruihi fascia at agnoa.

They had their god Fascinus and their amulets of that name, which were designed to protect children from injury from that source. The statue of the same god, suspended from the triumphal car, was a protection to its occupants from any harm that might otherwise befall them from the *evil eye* of envy.

The object of the present work is not so much the study of magic in ancient times, as that of the more elevated religious beliefs, under whose guidance the vital atom successively progressed from one transformation to another, until it was absorbed in the Great All; which look upon the world of souls as being nothing but a succession of off-spring and ancestors, who never forget each other: beliefs which indeed we may not entertain, but which are embalmed in a most mysterious and consolatory creed and are entitled to our respect.

The present chapter with regard to Hindu magic is merely an episode which we do not propose to extend further; otherwise we might show that the popular traditions with regard to sorcery in India found their way also into Greece, Home, and ancient Chaldea.

One word however about this latter country, which, as claimed by Berosus, Æschylus, and Herodotus, was colonized by a multitude of unknown people and mixed tribes, speaking different languages.

India, with its hundred and twenty-five dialects and its various castes, so different from each other, was the only country, at that time, from which emigration was constantly going on, in order to avoid sacerdotal persecution, and from which, consequently, the countries bordering upon the Tigris and the Euphrates could possibly have been colonized.

To all the ethnographic facts, which go to show that the assertion here made is historically correct, may be further added the great similarity existing between the magical practices and beliefs of the Hindus and Chaldeans.

The following are some of the Assyrian inscriptions relating to magical enchantments, taken from a recent publication by Messrs. Rawlinson & Norris, which show how largely Chaldea was indebted to India.

"The form of the Chaldean conjurations against evil spirits," says the eminent Assyriologist, "is very monotonous. They are all cast in the same mould. They begin with a list of the demons to be overcome by the conjuration, together with a description of the character and effects of their power. This is followed by the expression of a desire to see them driven away, or of being protected from them, which is often presented in an affirmative form. The formula finally concludes with a mysterious invocation, from which it derives all its efficacy. 'Spirit of Heaven, remember; Spirit of Earth, remember.' That alone is necessary and never fails; but sometimes similar invocations to other divine spirits are also added.

"I will give as an example, one of these conjurations to be used against different bad demons, maladies, or acts, such as the *evil eye.*

—The pestilence, or fever, that lays waste the country. The plague that devastates the land, bad for the body, and injurious to the bowels.

—The bad demon, the bad Alai, the bad Gigim.

—The evil man, the evil eye, the evil mouth, the evil tongue, may they come out of the body, may they come out of the bowels of the man, son of his God.

—They shall never enter into possession of my body.

—They shall never do any harm before me. They shall never walk after me.

—They shall never enter into my house.

—They shall never cross my frame.
—They shall never enter the house of my habitation.
—Spirit of Heaven, remember! Spirit of Earth, remember!
—Spirit of Moul-ge, lord of countries, remember!
—Spirit of Nin-gelal, lady of countries, remember!
—Spirit of Nin-dar, powerful warrior of Moul-ge, remember!
—Spirit of Pa-kou, sublime intelligence of Moul-ge, remember!
—Spirit of En-zouna, eldest son of Moul-ge, remember!
—Spirit of Tiskou, lady of armies, remember!
—Spirit of Im, king whose impetuosity is beneficent, remember!
—Spirit of Oud, king of justice, remember!

"The following is another, where the final enumeration is not so long:

—The evening of evil omen, the region of heaven that produces misfortune,
—The fatal day, the region of the sky bad for observation,
—The fatal day, the bad region of the sky, that advances,
—Messengers of the plague,
—Ravagers of Nin-ki-gal,
—The thunder that rages throughout the country,
—The seven gods of the vast heavens,
—The seven gods of the vast earth,
—The seven gods of the fiery spheres,
—The seven malicious gods,
—The seven bad phantoms,
—The seven malicious phantoms of flames,
—The seven gods of heaven,
—The seven gods of the earth,
—The bad demon,
—The bad alal,
—The bad gigim,
—The bad tilol,
—The bad god, the bad maskim,
—Spirit of Heaven, remember!
—Spirit of Earth, remember!

—Sprit of Moul-ge, king of countries, remember!
—Spirit of Ningelal, lady of countries, remember?
—Spirit of Nin-dar, son of Zenith, remember!
—Spirit of Tishkou, lady of countries, who shines in the night, remember!

"More commonly, however, there are no such mythological enumerations at the end. As an example of the more simple kind of formulas, I may mention a conjuration against the seven subterranean demons, called maskim, who were reckoned among the most formidable of any.

—The seven! the seven!
—At the lowest bottom of the abyss, the seven!
—Abomination of heaven! the seven!
—Hiding themselves in the lowest depths of heaven and earth,
—Neither male nor female,
—Water, stretched out captives,
—Having no wives and producing no children,
—Knowing neither order nor good,
—Hearing no prayer,
—Vermin, that hidest in the mountain,
—Enemies of the god Ea,
—Ravagors of the gods,
—Abettors of trouble,
—All-powerful by violence,
—Agents of enmity,
—Spirit of Heaven, remember!
—Spirit of Earth, remember!"

We shall dwell no further upon this point, however. The above inscriptions are superabundant proof that the practice of magic, as handed down to the ancient Chaldeans from their ancestors, the Hindu emigrants of the lower castes or mixed classes, as Berosus calls them, was the utmost limit of their attainments in that direction.

The pure doctrines, which formed the subject of initiation, the worship of the Pitris and the superior spirits, awoke no echo upon the banks of the Euphrates. The nomads and brick moulders of the Sennar country lived in constant apprehension of the sorcerers and magicians, with no idea even of the existence of the sublime conceptions of Brahminism.

Inscriptions recorded upon granite, marble, stone, or baked earth, invariably contain everything that is most elevated in the popular belief. We do not select the superstitious ideas of the multitude to bequeath to future ages, and, as it were, to immortalize them.

> *I am all and in all!*

says the Trinitarian inscription at Elephanta, in India.

> *I home begotten the world!*

says the record upon the statue of Isis, which was the emblem of mother Nature in Egypt.

> *Know thyself!*

such was the inscription that appeared in front of the temple at Delphi.

And the column erected in the Agora at Athens was inscribed:

> *To the unknown God!*

Mingling in their inscriptions their gods and evil spirits, such as the gigim, the maskim, and other demons, trembling with constant fear in the presence of sexless, wifeless, and childless monsters, before these telals, these ravagers of heaven, these enemies of Ea, the King of the Gods, who also seemed to tremble in their presence, the Chaldeans engraved upon their burnt bricks nothing but expressions of the grossest superstition, for the simple reason that they had nothing else to put there. If there is any one thing at which we have a right to express our surprise, it is that some Assyriologists have taken these ridiculous conceptions as a text from which to prove that the ancient Hindus got their first ideas from the primitive Chaldeans.

The Agrouchada-Parikchai, in a fourth book, which we have already alluded to, in which it gives an account of the magic practices, whereby bad spirits are set in motion, but which is entirely ineffectual as far as the Pitris, or the superior spirits, or

Swayambhouva, the Supreme Being, are concerned, and which fourth book is entirely disconnected from the other three, which are wholly devoted to the pure doctrine of the Pitris, makes no secret of the fact that magic and sorcery were the only things that had any influence upon the impure Soudras, or the common people and Tchandalas, or mixed classes.

Before passing on to the subject of the phenomena and external manifestations produced by those who had gone through the various degrees of initiation in India, it may not be amiss to compare the doctrine of the Pitris, as we have sot it forth, with the beliefs of the Jewish cabalists and of several other philosophers of ancient times, who seem to us to have drank from the same fountain.

Bruin Asylum

Make Your Reservations Today!

BRUIN CRIMEWORKS
Visit the scene of the crime

David Dodge
-*DEATH AND TAXES*
-*TO CATCH A THIEF*
-*THE LONG ESCAPE*
-*CARAMBOLA*

Fredric Brown
-*KNOCK THREE-ONE-TWO*
-*MISS DARKNESS*
New **Fredric Brown**
   Double Novels:
-*Vol. I: THE FAR CRY &*
THE SCREAMING MIMI
-*Vol. II: NIGHT OF THE*
JABBERWOCK &
THE DEEP END

Wadsworth Camp
-*HOUSE OF FEAR*

James Hadley Chase
-*NO ORCHIDS FOR MISS BLANDISH*
-*FLESH OF THE ORCHID*

Bruno Fischer
-*HOUSE OF FLESH*

Edward Anderson
-*FEELS LIKE RAIN*

C. St. John Sprigg
-*PASS THE BODY*
- *THE CORPSE WITH THE*
SUNBURNED FACE

Elliott Chaze
-*BLACK WINGS HAS MY ANGEL*

Paul Bailey
-*DELIVER ME FROM EVA*

Made in the USA
San Bernardino, CA
15 February 2020

64521904R00163